THE IMPOR... OF
BEING U... ST

THE IMPORTANCE OF BEING URNEST

Sandra Balzo

This first world edition published 2017
in Great Britain and the USA by
SEVERN HOUSE PUBLISHERS LTD of
Eardley House, 4 Uxbridge Street, London W8 7SY.
Trade paperback edition first published
in Great Britain and the USA 2018 by
SEVERN HOUSE PUBLISHERS LTD

British Library Cataloguing in Publication Data
A CIP catalogue record for this title is available from the British Library.

ISBN-13: 978-0-7278-8737-5 (cased)
ISBN-13: 978-1-84751-850-7 (trade paper)
ISBN-13: 978-1-78010-910-7 (e-book)

Typeset by Palimpsest Book Production Ltd.,
Falkirk, Stirlingshire, Scotland.

To Jim and Shilow,
for welcoming me home.

ONE

'You can't keep a man dangling – and I do mean dangling,' Sarah Kingston crooked her little finger and then let it go limp, 'forever. What are you so afraid of?'

My partner and I were alone on the front porch of our coffee-house, or so I'd presumed until a nice-looking older gentleman rounded the corner and hesitated. He was holding a to-go cup and must have exited through the trackside door of the historic Brookhills Junction train station that housed Uncommon Grounds.

And, judging by the red tinge of his unlined face, had been just in time to witness both Sarah's dangling pinkie and preposition.

'I'm sorry,' I said. 'My partner meant—'

'I'm sure whatever it is, it's none of my business.' With a grin, he hurried past us and down the porch steps, keys jingling in his pocket.

'Please watch what you say,' I said, watching him continue down the sidewalk. 'You're chasing away customers.'

'Chasing away, how? He'd already bought the coffee.'

'And probably will never buy another.'

'Not everybody is as touchy as you are, you little weenie.' She waggled the finger at me.

'Enough.' I nodded toward a well-coiffed blonde woman approaching from the other direction with a young boy in tow.

'Morning, Monica,' Sarah called, apparently deciding to censor herself for the kid's sake, at least.

'Good morning.' Holding up a hand, the woman took the steps up toward our coffeehouse two at a time, the kid flapping behind her like a kite that couldn't quite get airborne.

'She's in a hurry,' I said as the door closed behind her. 'Regular customer?'

In the early days of owning Uncommon Grounds, I'd beaten myself up for not remembering names and faces. Then Sarah pointed out that it wasn't so much that my memory was failing me as I just didn't give a shit. A fact that would have bothered me, if . . . well, I gave a shit.

'You know Monica,' Sarah said. 'Always in a hurry, comes in about this time and orders "just my black coffee, please" and a juice for her son.'

'Oh, yeah.' It was all coming back. 'If the kid looks at a cookie or something else in the pastry case, she says, "No, darling. You know we don't eat sweets," in the same tone people use when they say they don't watch TV. Or read fiction.'

Sarah was nodding. 'Plays holier than the rest of us but never leaves without a sticky bun.'

That, in itself, wasn't unusual. Chef and baker Tien Romano was gaining an almost cult-like following for her gooey pecan breakfast rolls, produced hot out of the oven early each morning.

But while I hadn't recognized this bun-lover's face, her shtick was coming back to me. 'She remembers the bun just as you're ringing up, right? Always an apparent after-thought.'

'More *trans*parent than apparent,' Sarah said. 'Sends the kid off to the condiment cart to get a straw for his juice, then buys the bun and stashes it in her purse. Probably stashes herself in the bathroom later while she gags it back up.'

'She does look trim,' I admitted.

'Too trim for a sticky-bun-a-day habit, in my opinion.'

Mainlining breakfast pastry.

'Not sure there's a bun left for her to slurp and urp today, though,' Sarah continued. 'The gang from Goddard's has pretty much cleaned us out of pastry this morning.'

Until last year, Goddard's Pharmacy anchored the opposite end of the strip mall that had also housed the original Uncommon Grounds. We all were sad the pharmacy was gone, and not just because the same freak snowstorm that took down Goddard's had also leveled the rest of the mall, including Uncommon Grounds. Goddard's Pharmacy had been a slice of Brookhills history. A reminder of when drug stores had lunch counters and comic-book stands instead of grocery sections and computer supplies. The old pharmacy was sorely missed.

As had been its owner, until this morning. Gloria Goddard had suffered a stroke in January and been confined first to the hospital and then the rehabilitation facility at Brookhills Manor senior home. 'It's good to see Mrs G.'

'Ornery though she might be. Oliver has his hands full.'

For years, Gloria Goddard had been a sort of surrogate mom to Oliver Benson, whose father had owned the strip mall. When both Oliver's mom and dad were killed, the two had formed an impromptu family. Oliver went to school at the University of Wisconsin-LaCrosse but was home for semester break.

'I don't think she likes Oliver seeing her like this.'

'Or the gang seeing it, either,' Sarah said. 'She's known some of these people for a long time.'

It was true that the group had frequented the pharmacy on Sunday mornings for the better part of the last two decades. The lunch counter had featured good diner-type food and bottomless cups of coffee, meaning free refills for as long as people stayed. We had a one-refill policy, but bent that rule to breaking each Sunday morning for what had become known as the Goddard Gang.

The front door flew open with a jangle of bells and a woman – maybe forty – with long brown hair just starting to streak with gray burst out with two older women. One had a fresh-scrubbed face and was wearing a long, bohemian-style skirt and loose cotton jacket. The other was in full-on Sunday finery – silk dress, hat and heels – all topped by blonde hair, a more than generous spackling of makeup and a dousing of flowery perfume.

'I'm so sorry,' the brunette said when she saw us.

'Sorry for what?' My hand had flown reflexively to cover my nose and mouth against the assault of the perfume and I forced myself to bring it down.

'I'm afraid Nancy,' she nodded toward the woman in the skirt, 'had a bit of an accident.'

Sarah sneezed from the perfume.

'Bless you,' I said, then tried again. 'What kind of accident?'

'I just couldn't control it,' the old woman said hoarsely.

That gave me a hint of what we were talking about, at least. We'd pretty much had every type of accident in the shop, including a car landing on the porch where we were now standing. 'Don't worry about a thing. We'll take care of it.' Or, with luck, our barista, Amy, would have by the time we got inside.

'Thank you,' the younger woman said, helping the ladies down the steps and toward a Porsche Cayenne parked on the street. 'I'll settle them at home and then come back and pay the bill. And any damages, of course.'

'No need to—'

Sarah elbowed me in the ribs. 'You don't know there's no need,' she hissed. 'Maybe the old coot flooded the place.'

Happily, the threesome was out of ear range of the coot comment, though a couple coming up the steps didn't miss it. Not being coots they didn't seem offended, though they did open the door and peer in cautiously before stepping through it.

So far as I could see, there was no common denominator among the Goddard Gang members other than a love of coffee and the fact they'd all shown up on Sunday mornings long enough to form a bond. Gloria told me that one of the things she found most interesting was that she'd never heard anybody ask what somebody did for a living, a normal conversational starting point. Instead, they talked about whatever was the news of the day and then parted to go about their business. People came. People went. And came again. There were marriages and divorces. And remarriages – sometimes to the same person.

With Goddard's no more, the group had been like bees without a Sunday-morning hive. Buzzing from place to place, they'd finally alighted on our new location in the train station.

One of the challenges for the gang had been finding a restaurant or coffee shop with enough space so they didn't have to fight for tables every Sunday morning and enough tolerance to let them hang out for hours. The chosen venue's parallel challenge was not ticking off their regular customers when the gang descended on the shop en masse.

No problem on either front for Uncommon Grounds.

Riders of the new commuter train in and out of Milwaukee were our bread and butter – or coffee and cream – during the week, with seniors, soccer moms, students and the occasional business meeting filling in the middle hours. Saturday mornings were also busy, with people heading to the shops or the farmers' market or whatever organized sport they were ferrying their kids to.

But Sundays?

Let's just say coffee can't compete with God. Or Green Bay Packer football.

We'd considered closing on Sundays, but the arrival of the Goddard Gang had made it profitable enough for us to open from eight to three. And now even some of our weekday regulars had started to pop in to join them.

'I suppose we should go in and see what the "accident" was,' Sarah said, glancing at the door with trepidation.

'We have to finish this.' My hair-trigger gag reflex had barely made it through Eric's childhood.

A BMW convertible – top down – pulled up in front as I turned the key in the padlock and slipped the chain from around the leg of a wrought-iron patio table. The temperature the last few days had been so unseasonably mild for March in Wisconsin that iced-drink sales had picked up and the occasional customer even asked to sit outside on the wrap-around porch.

Sarah stopped folding the tarp we'd used to cover the tables and chairs to look up as the driver of the BMW hopped out of the car. 'Morning, Mort.'

Now this one I knew. Mort was the unofficial ringleader of the Goddard Gang. Late fifties, he had a thick head of springy white hair you wanted to tug on to see if it was real.

'Morning, Mort,' I parroted as he mounted the steps toward us. When I actually tipped to a name, I tried to use it. Supposedly the repetition helped you to remember the person. The jury was still out on that one, at least for me.

'Good morning. Spring has sprung early, hasn't it?'

'It certainly has,' I agreed.

'May I hope the gang's all here?' Mort smiled at the small joke, which he made – and smiled at – every Sunday.

'Sophie and Henry are inside, along with six or seven of your regular group,' whose names, of course, I didn't know. 'Oh, and Gloria, of course!'

'Oliver did convince Gloria, after all?' Mort asked, pausing at the door. 'She seemed to think it would be too much trouble leaving the manor just for coffee.'

After being released from the hospital, Gloria had gone to

the manor for rehabilitation and physical therapy and hadn't left since, as far as I knew. Until now.

'The kid seems to be managing fine,' Sarah said. 'His SUV was too high, so they're using Gloria's Chrysler. I guess somebody in the manor parking lot helped him with the transfer into the car, but he managed to get her out and into wheelchair here by himself. I just helped guide them up the ramp to the train platform door and into the shop.'

'I'm sure Gloria was grateful.'

'Actually, she told me I stank,' Sarah said.

Mort cracked a small smile. 'Language confusion, or so we might hope.'

'Language confusion from the stroke?' I asked.

'Yes, I noticed it when I visited. She seems to swap words. For example, Gloria might very well have meant to say "thank you" but it came out "you stank."'

'How frustrating for her,' I said.

Sarah was looking sheepish. 'I answered her, "You're welcome," though I wish now that I'd taken some of the attitude out of it.' The attitude most likely being sarcasm. It was Sarah's thing and she did it well.

'It was probably a safe answer, since Gloria could just as easily have meant the insult.' Mort grinned full-on now. 'I'm certain she's frustrated. The woman is not one to sit still, especially in a wheelchair.'

'No, she's not.' I returned the smile. 'Why don't you go in and say hi. Amy is behind the counter.'

'Ah, our multihued barista.' Mort pulled open the door. 'Wonderful.'

As the door closed behind him, I got a whiff of coconut butter. 'Sixty degrees and Mort's pulling out the sunscreen. And this is just March. You'd think people would remember what happened on May first last year.'

Over a foot of snow was what happened. Not to mention a death or two.

'That freakishly long winter is exactly why everybody's enjoying the warmth.' Sarah took the end of the chain from me to unwrap it from around the next chair's legs. 'You know, *carpe diem* or . . . what's that other expression?'

'Make hay while the sun shines?'

'I was thinking more "eat, drink and be merry, for tomorrow we die." Which brings me back to Pavlik. Aren't you afraid that if you wait too long to answer him he'll change his mind?' She straightened with a handful of chain and a smirk. 'Again?'

I ignored the smirk and took the chain from her to unwrap the next chair in the rotation. It was kind of like taking the lights off the Christmas tree.

And about as festive, given the company.

But Sarah was right that Brookhills County Sheriff Jake Pavlik had broken up with me shortly before he'd reversed course and unexpectedly asked me to marry him. Taken by surprise, I'd yet to give him an answer. 'Better that he changes his mind now, I guess.'

'Rather than after you're married, you mean?' My partner cocked her head, studying me. 'If you're having flashbacks of your cheating ex-husband, don't. I have a feeling that Dr T would never have strayed if he hadn't hired that bimbo Rachel as his hygienist.'

'That's kind of the definition of cheating, isn't it? Having somebody to cheat with?' A link snagged on the foot of the chair and I yanked.

The chain caught and then swung up, but Sarah one-handed it neatly before it could take out her eye. 'I was trying to be nice, Maggy. Supportive, even, of both you and Ted. And you wonder why I don't do it more often.'

I felt ashamed, which was exactly Sarah's aim. Now she could put 'nice' on the backburner for another year. 'I do appreciate the support. And I truly don't worry about Pavlik being another Ted. I just don't know if I . . .' I let it drift off.

'Want to marry Pavlik? You're crazy about him. Do you remember what kind of hell you put us through when he broke it off? The whining, the sniffling, the howling?'

'The howling was Frank.' My sheepdog was also quite fond of the sheriff. 'And, yes, I'm crazy about Pavlik, and, no, I don't want to lose him.' Before she could do it, I added, 'Yes, I know. Lose him *again*. I just don't know if I want be married right now. To anybody.'

With our son Eric having just left for college, my stunned reaction to Ted's announcement that he was leaving had been anger followed by terror and then loneliness. For the first time in my life, I was truly on my own.

Over the last two years, I'd adjusted to single life and even come to value my independence. I'd taken Eric's dog to live with me when Ted and I split and, though Frank might not be much of a conversationalist, I was grateful to have him overstuffing my tiny post-divorce house.

And . . . while I cared about Pavlik and certainly had fantasized about a future with him, suddenly the thought of starting life all over again was throwing me into a panic. 'I don't know why we can't just leave things as they are.'

'Maybe Pavlik figures if he's going to put up with your stumbling over bodies every few months, he'd like to know it's for more than the occasional booty call.'

'Isn't that supposed to be every guy's fantasy?' I snapped. 'No-strings-attached booty calls?'

'There are always strings.' Sarah's expression changed. 'But then maybe, flip side, he imagines that once you're married you'll stop the cavalcade of hot- and cold-running corpses.'

My head jerked up. 'You make it sound like I generate them. Or go out looking. They find me. Besides, Pavlik knows me better than to think he can control that. Hell, *I* can't con—'

'Morning, ladies.' Another cheery greeting, this time from a female voice and accompanied by a yellow-gloved wave from across the street.

'Morning, Christy,' I called back to our neighbor, just as happy to put the discussion with Sarah on the backburner for now. 'We haven't seen you for a while. Have you been out of town?'

'No, I've been here.' Piano teacher Christy Wrigley had crossed from her driveway to our side of the street, stripping off the rubber gloves as she came. 'I've been working a lot lately, though. And, before that, I was at Ronny's house, first getting it spic and span and then putting it on the market. So much so that I'm afraid I've neglected my own house.'

Fat chance of that. Christy made Mr Clean look like a slacker. Once I'd caught her scrubbing the wheels of our condiment cart with a toothbrush. And, no, she wasn't an employee. Just one crazy-ass customer.

As for Ronny, that was Ronny Eisvogel, Sarah's cousin by marriage and Christy's new boyfriend, at least on visitors' days. Currently, Ronny's room and board was provided by the state prison system.

'Ronny's selling his place?' Sarah asked before I could.

'Why not? He won't be home for years, thanks to you two.' Christy said it without malice.

Ronny was an incarcerated nutcase and Christy a naive germaphobe. I figured it had worked because visits at the jail were conducted by video feed and, as far as I knew, the two lovebirds had never so much as touched. But the thought of them living together? Well, the gloves would be off. Or maybe not, in Christy's case.

'You've already listed the house?' Sarah's Kingston Realty had taken a back seat to the coffeehouse in the months since she'd partnered with me in Uncommon Grounds, but she still seemed miffed she'd missed a new listing.

'We had an offer within the week and closed less than a month later.'

I noticed Christie hadn't said who the listing agent was. Probably didn't have the nerve.

'When was this?' Sarah asked, probing further.

She reminded me of a dentist making chit-chat so you don't notice he's drilling into the nerve. But then maybe I just had my dentist ex on my mind. Could Sarah be right and my failed marriage had more to do with my non-answer to Pavlik than I wanted to admit?

'I must have missed the listing on MLS,' my partner was saying casually.

'We closed mid-December, but—'

'December.' My partner's eyes flickered in what might have been reluctant admiration. 'The holidays are a tough time to sell a house. Your agent was either lucky or good.'

'Well, thank you,' Christy said, pink tinging her face. 'I used Craigslist.'

Sarah's own face darkened at the mention of the ad website that allows sellers to bypass the traditional real estate agent and the multiple-listing service databank. And the associated fees, as well. 'I hope you had a good lawyer do the closing, because—'

I cut in before we could be treated to a Real Estate 101 lecture. 'So the new buyer has already moved in, then?'

Christy glanced uncertainly at Sarah's face before pivoting to answer my question.

'Yes. In fact, she's meeting me here. Hannah has been a bit housebound since she cares for both her mother and another elderly woman. I'm trying to get her out and meeting new people.'

'Not only a broker, but you're a regular Welcome Wagon, aren't you?' Sarah sniffed, her nose apparently still out of joint.

'I think it's nice of you to take an interest, Christy,' I said to counter my partner's snit.

'Hannah is a lovely woman. Besides,' Christy dipped her head, 'I kind of owe her my job. Along with Vickie, of course.'

I was confused. 'So, you knew her?'

'Of course. Vickie was one of my students when I taught piano.'

I wasn't sure what Vickie she was talking about, but, 'I meant your buyer. The person who moved into Ronny's house.'

'Oh, no. Like I told you, Hannah just moved here in December.' Our neighbor was squinting at me like she thought I was losing it.

'But you also said you owed her your job. I thought—' I stopped.

Christy had a habit of sprinkling a conversation with names and facts, as if you should know these things. I, for one, did not. Not about Hannah, nor about the other factoid I realized she'd just dropped.

So I switched on the back-up beepers and rewound the conversation. 'Wait. You said when you *taught* piano, past tense?' I went to gesture at the piano lessons placard in the window across the street and realized it was missing. 'What happened to your sign?'

'Heavens, that sign's been down since January. You really should pay more attention to your surroundings, Maggy.'

'*Yeah*, Maggy,' Sarah said, spirits apparently on the rise.

I ignored her. 'But I thought you loved teaching piano, Christy. Was it not going well?'

'Oh, it was going fine, money-wise.' She looked first to the right and then to the left and lowered her voice. 'Though seeing some of Ronny's prison mates did give me pause.'

'Because . . .' I would have continued, but I didn't have the faintest idea where she was going.

'Convicts hate piano music?' Sarah guessed. 'Did they threaten you with a beat-down? Or Ronny with a shiv?'

'Of course not,' Christy said. 'In fact, I've been asked to play at the prison and received a standing ovation each time.'

'As the convicts got up to shuffle off in their leg-irons?' Sarah again, naturally.

Christy wrinkled her nose. 'Oh, they don't wear leg irons inside. Besides, there are white-collar criminals, too – fraud and such. Some are quite refined.'

As they're stealing your money.

Sarah raised her eyebrows. 'My dear cousin is a killer. What's he doing in with white-collar criminals?'

Christy's chin went up to match. 'Ronny is not your normal killer and you know it, Sarah Kingston. There were mitigating circumstances.'

'I'll give you he's not normal,' Sarah said. 'And the mitigating circumstances are he's bat-shit nuts.'

Christy's mouth dropped open.

Before she could retaliate, which would only egg Sarah on, I asked, 'You said seeing some of these prisoners gave you pause?' I couldn't paraphrase because I didn't have the faintest idea what she meant.

'Yes, about the cash.'

'Cash.' I was giving parroting, a technique Pavlik used when interviewing witnesses, a try.

It worked. To an extent. 'Yes, I certainly didn't want to end up like them.'

'In prison?'

She nodded and I put together the pieces of the puzzle. Prison, white-collar crime, cash. 'You weren't paying taxes on your income?'

'Yes, I was.' Christy's bottom lip went out. 'Most of it, at least. Or maybe some.'

'Lay off, Maggy,' Sarah said. 'Piano teaching is probably a cash business. Who'd know?'

'The coffeehouse is a cash business, too, at least partly.'
I felt my own eyes widen. 'Please tell me you haven't been
skimming—'

'Of course not,' Sarah said, looking hurt. 'How can you
ask me that?'

'Perhaps because you don't seem to think tax evasion is a
crime,' I said. 'Did you know that's how they finally convicted
Al Capone? The guy ordered the St Valentine's Day massacre
and it was tax evasion that finally brought him down.'

'Isn't that what bit the bad guy in *The Firm* in the butt, too?'
Sarah asked.

'Among other things,' I said. 'I was reading an article the
other day that claimed the Cayman Islands bankers still can't
forgive John Grisham for bringing attention to them as a tax
haven.'

'It was a good book,' Sarah said. 'And movie, too.'

'Which isn't always the case.'

Christy cleared her throat.

'I'm sorry.' I decided to leave movies, books and tax evasion
behind. What Christy did was her business and Sarah's views
on what was OK in a cash business was going to be a private
conversation between the two of us. 'You were saying you're
not teaching piano anymore.'

Christy nodded. 'Happily, I've found where my real passion
lies, and it doesn't require having grubby little fingers all over
my piano keys every day.'

Passion wasn't something I associated with Christy.

'Thoooough . . .' Christy seemed to be giving it some further
thought, too. 'Maybe passion doesn't quite capture this feeling.
It's almost more a higher calling.'

'You're becoming a nun.' Sarah was coiling the chain.

'Heavens, no, although I did consider joining Angel of Mercy
a couple years back. Did I tell you that?'

Angel of Mercy Catholic Church was one of two churches
in Brookhills, the other being Christ Christian just down the
street from me. 'I didn't know you're Catholic.'

'I'm not. But Father Jim was looking for an office adminis-
trator who could also serve as an organist on Sundays. If I'd
taken the job, I thought it only right that I join.'

I frowned, trying to remember. 'Aren't you musical director at Christ Christian?'

'Not any more. Not only did Pastor Shepherd not want to pay me, but every time I introduced myself as "Christy from Christ Christian," I cringed.'

'Too matchy-matchy?' I asked the woman whose yellow rubber gloves matched . . . well, nothing.

'Definitely. Besides, it turns out I'm an omnist. Who knew?'

Not me. 'Is that like an atheist?'

'Heavens, no,' Christy said again. 'An omnist respects all religions.'

Sarah frowned. 'You made that up.'

'Did not,' Christy said, settling into her subject. 'It's a real word that goes all the way back to 1839. Ronny says it fits me perfectly because I'm so open.'

Sarah started to say something but I shot her a warning look. 'Be nice.'

She raised her eyebrows. 'If you'll recall, I told you I was done with being nice.'

'To me, fine. But the rest of the world deserves better.'

'I'm not sure what your problem with Ronny is, Sarah.' Christy's eyes were scrunched in what she probably imagined was a glare but she looked more like a near-sighted squirrel.

Sarah sighed, apparently deciding it wasn't sporting to take aim. 'You know me, Christy. I just like to kid around. I think Ronny is just . . . fine.'

'Well, that's good,' Christy said, unscrunching her eyes. 'Because he has only the nicest things to say about you.'

'I bet,' Sarah said under her breath. And then added, more audibly and with a different inflection, 'I bet! We were always like this as kids.' She held up crossed fingers.

Knowing Sarah, I assumed the gesture was to ward off a lie, not to show the two cousins-by-marriage were peas in a pod. Sarah and Ronny hadn't even known each other as kids, her aunt and Ronny's father having married later in life.

Still, Sarah had made an effort and she deserved props for that. 'That's so sweet.'

My partner threw me a look and I held up my hand, fingers crossed to match hers.

'It *is* sweet,' Christy echoed.

'Thanks,' Sarah said. 'Ronny's right. You *are* very accepting and open.'

If Sarah meant 'gullible,' I had to disagree. Our neighbor might be quirky and sometimes downright peculiar but she wasn't dumb. And she had me curious about this non-religion. Or maybe it was an ultra-religion. All things to all people. 'So, do omnists have churches? Is it like being a Unitarian or something?'

Christy tilted her head to think. 'I'm not sure, really. I just officially became one in January.'

'Did you take an oath of omniscience?' Sarah couldn't restrain herself.

'If I had, I would have known you were going to ask that,' Christy pointed out primly.

Point to Christy.

'I guess what I mean,' she continued, 'is that I may have been an omnist all my life but it's only recently that I realized the belief has a name.'

'Found it on Google?' Sarah asked.

'No, Brookhills Mortuary and Cremation. It's how we describe our chapel in the brochure. So much more positive and inclusive than nondenominational, don't you think?'

'I suppose so.' Assuming anybody knew what omnist meant. But she'd dropped another tidbit. 'You said "our chapel." Are you—?'

'Working at the mortuary, of course!'

TWO

'I've been with Brookhills Mortuary and Cremation for nearly three months now,' our neighbor told us proudly. 'I'm surprised you haven't heard.'

I was too, quite honestly. Brookhills was a small town and Christy – even without the yellow rubber gloves – one of its most colorful characters.

'What are *you*, of all people, doing at a mortuary?' Sarah tossed the rolled chain toward the corrugated cardboard box already containing the tarps that we'd pulled off the furniture. The chain uncoiled mid-flight and landed at my feet.

'I'm doing what I do best.' Christy stuck out her chin, which wasn't much chin at all. 'Cleaning. It was Ronny's idea.'

I'd leaned down to gather up the chain and now I swiveled my head toward our neighbor. 'I'm confused. Didn't you say a Vickie and this woman who bought the house—'

'Hannah Bouchard,' Christy supplied. 'She's wonderful. And you know Vickie. She's Sophie's friend?'

'Oh, Botox Vickie.' A fan of 'looking your best at any age,' Vickie LaTour was in her seventies, a member of the Red Hat Society and hosted Botox and collagen parties the way my mom did Tupperware parties in our neighborhood.

'But it was Ronny who inspired me, yet again,' Christy explained. 'He said I needed to play to my strength.'

'Which means cleaning a funeral home.' I still couldn't quite believe it.

'Oh, he wasn't as specific as that,' Christy said, her pale skin taking on a pink tinge again. 'Ronny was speaking more big picture.'

'From his small cell,' Sarah muttered.

Christy shook a finger at her. 'You can laugh, Sarah, but give your cousin credit. He sounds just like one of those motivational speakers when he waxes philosophical.'

Ronny was waxing philosophically while sitting on his butt in prison, while Christy would be waxing literally. And dusting. And vacuuming. 'But a funeral home?'

Christy frowned. 'Ronny says it's important to recognize what makes us different.'

'However does one choose?' I heard Sarah mutter.

'Cleanliness,' Christy continued, 'is obviously something I value. And I'm extraordinarily good at achieving it. The question that Ronny posed was how I could best use my talent. Find my niche, so to speak.'

'And you believe your niche is at the funeral home?' Between regular visits to prison and a job among the dead and the mourning, our neighbor seemed to be veering off her neatly cultivated garden path to take a walk on the dark side.

'As it turns out, yes. When both Hannah and Vickie mentioned – the same day, mind you – that the mortuary was looking for somebody to clean, I realized it was a sign.'

'Prescient *and* omniscient,' Sarah said. 'Too bad you didn't know you were going to get the job *before* you sold the house. Short commute.'

'Why? Where's Ronny's house?' The funeral home was just a few blocks north of me on Poplar Creek Road. Given that Ronny kind of tried to kill me, it might have been nice to know he had been a neighbor.

'Right next door to the funeral home,' Sarah said and then sneezed again.

'Bless you.' I wrinkled my own nose as I thought. 'But Christ Christian is on one side of the funeral home and there's nothing but a rutted dirt path leading to the Poplar Creek woods on the other.'

'Thank you.' Sarah swiped at her nose with an Uncommon Grounds napkin. 'And that rutted dirt path is what the Eisvogel clan calls a driveway. The house itself is set back behind the funeral home.'

Christy held out a tissue to Sarah, dangling it between thumb and index finger so as not to accidentally touch Sarah's fingers. 'You're not technically incorrect in calling BM&C a "funeral home" but it's really much more than that. It's a full-service mortuary and crematorium.'

I had a feeling that Christy was quoting the aforementioned brochure. But yet another fact had been dropped, this one something that I probably should have known. 'It's a crematorium? Do you—'

Christy raised her hand to stop me. 'I know what you're going to say, Maggy. That for somebody like me, a crematorium would be . . .' She was searching for a term.

'Icky?' I supplied. 'Horrific' and 'morbidly depressing' came to mind as well. But that wasn't what I'd been about to ask. 'They don't actually do the cremations there, do they?'

'Of course. What did you think?'

'I guess I assumed that sort of thing was . . . outsourced.' Preferably to some big anonymous building far, far away from my house. 'And the funeral home – or mortuary – got the ashes back and maybe packaged them for the family to pick up.'

I saw Sarah grin, and God forbid she should keep her mouth shut.

'Oh, I get it. You thought it was like my dry cleaner.' She turned to Christy. 'All this time I thought they were cleaning the stuff right there but turns out they ship it out and then just put it in plastic bags for me to pick up.'

'Exactly,' Christy said. 'That's how things get lost, you know.'

I wasn't sure if we were talking about corpses or clothes now. 'But at Brookhills Mortuary and Cremation you do it all right there?'

'One hundred percent in-house,' Christy said proudly. 'Our pledge is that we will walk your loved ones through every step of the journey to their final resting place, whether that be a dignified casket or lovely – and life-appropriate – urn. Mort,' she nodded to the convertible, 'is quite inspiring. Did you see the article about him in last week's *Observer*?'

'Mort of the Goddard Gang?' I asked.

'Yes,' Christy said. 'He's my new boss.'

'Wait,' Sarah said. '*Mort* is a mortician?'

'Yes,' Christy said. 'Mortician, funeral director and owner of Brookhills Mortuary and Cremation. You didn't know that?'

Again, I probably should have. But I didn't. 'Mort is a nickname, then?'

'I'd assume so.' With her green eyes wide in the heart-shaped face, now Christy resembled an owl. 'Why?'

'I don't know – it just seems a little flippant,' I said, and then shrugged. 'Though I suppose it's one of those fields where black humor is necessary to survive. Like being a cop or a coroner.'

'Humor?' Christy seemed completely lost. 'I don't understand what you mean. Mort is short for Morton. Morton Ashbury.'

'Wait, wait.' I thought Sarah was going to wet herself. 'Mort Ashbury owns Brookhills Mortuary?'

'And Cremation. Yes, I—'

But my partner had turned to me. 'You have the marketing background. He has to have made that up, don't you think?'

I shrugged. 'I suppose it could be a matter of what came first, the name or the profession. Maybe Mort went into the business because of his name.'

'Then why not take full advantage of it? If I were Mort, I'd make hay where the sun *don't* shine, in this case.'

'Where's that?' Christy asked before I could shake my head in warning not to encourage Sarah.

Who was breaking herself up, at least. 'In the grave, of course. Remember the song "Ain't no sunshine when she's gone"? Which would be a great theme for Mr Mort Ash & Bury, come to think of it.'

'Bill Withers might disagree,' I said as evenly as I could. 'Are you off your meds?'

My partner was bipolar, and I had a hunch which of the two caps we were visiting today.

But Sarah just looked offended. 'I'm not manic, if that's what you're insinuating.'

'I'm not insinuating anything,' I said.

'Which is your passive-aggressive way of saying you're coming right out and saying it.'

'I am not passive-aggressive,' I snapped.

'And I'm not manic. Just—'

'High on life?' I suggested.

'I was going to say "clever." Not that you would know anything about that.'

I felt my eyes narrow. 'I'm clever, too. Just not—'

As the door into Uncommon Grounds opened behind me, I heard a loud *snap* and something sailed over my head. Monica Goodwin, busy stashing a napkin-wrapped sticky bun in her purse, didn't notice as a yellow rubber glove splatted on the floor in front of her.

Her son looked down at the glove. 'Can I have it?'

Monica glanced up from her purse guiltily. 'No, dear. It's for Grandma. You know how she likes pastry.'

I had a hunch the boy, who appeared to be six or seven, sensed there was a sweeter score to be had than a rubber glove. 'I like it, too.'

'But you know we don't eat sweets, Timmy. Grandma—'

'Is old enough to decide what she wants to eat.' He seemed

to be parroting what he'd been told. 'Is that because she's old and going to die soon anyway?'

'Heavens, no.' Monica zipped up her purse, bun safely stowed. 'At least I hope Grandma's not going to die soon. Whatever gave you that idea?'

'Because Daddy says Grandma's a diabetic and sweet stuff will *kill* her.' The kid was transforming into a devil child before my eyes. Apparently the cumulative result of systematically being denied pastry. 'You're not trying to kill Grandma, are you, Mommy?'

'Mommy' was appropriately mortified that we were watching. And listening. 'No, of course not, Timmy. I wouldn't—'

'So why are you giving her sticky buns then?' The kid's eyes were an innocent blue, but I wouldn't have been surprised if pea soup had started spurting out of the mouth of his rotating head. In fact, I'd have applauded it. Who needed television when you had this kind of reality playing out on your front porch?

Mom was trying to pull Timmy toward the sidewalk but his feet were planted wide on the bottom step. 'Daddy says you never liked his mother.' He cocked his head and looked at her cherubically. 'That's Grandma, right?'

'Well, I . . . She . . .' She was looking wildly around, as if for help.

So Sarah gave it to her. 'Maybe, kid. Or she could be your mom's mom.'

'Nope.' Timmy shook his head decisively. 'She's dead already.'

'Well, then, yeah. The grandma that Mommy is feeding sticky buns to is probably your dad's mom.'

'I'm not feeding her sticky buns!' Monica exploded. 'I'm eating them myself, all right? Are you satisfied?'

The surprise admission must have startled Timmy because his mother was able to pull him away down the sidewalk.

The last words we heard were, 'But Mommy, you know we don't eat sweeeee—'

'Perfect imitation,' Sarah said. 'The kid has a gift.'

I shivered. 'Kind of spooky the way he handled her. It was like he was a six-year-old adult.'

'A malevolent six-year-old adult.'

'His father is a lawyer,' Christy offered.

'Oh,' Sarah said, like that explained everything.

And speaking of explanations . . . 'Christy, what in the world made you snap your rubber glove like that and send it flying?'

'I was just trying to get your attention,' Christy said, crossing her arms in front of her.

'You could have hurt somebody,' I said.

But Christy was the one who looked hurt. 'One minute we were talking about my job and the next you were arguing about something. I'm not sure even sure about what.'

Bill Withers' song, Sarah's sense of humor, my passive-aggressiveness – take your pick. So I just settled for, 'I'm sorry, Christy. You know we couldn't be happier that you've found something that you love to do.'

She didn't look so sure. 'Then what was all that about Mr Ashbury's name and marketing and songs and such?'

'Sarah was just,' I glanced at my partner, 'brainstorming.'

In truth, I was feeling ashamed I'd brought up Sarah's bi-polarity in front of Christy. Not that my partner made any secret of it. But still, it wasn't my place to talk about it.

Sarah seemed grateful to drop the quarrel as well. 'It's what we do to come up with new ways of marketing the store.'

'Well, then,' Christy said, cocking her head. 'Tell me again. Maybe it's something I could suggest to Mort and impress him.'

Or tick him off. Sarah wouldn't be the first to find the convergence of name and occupation hilarious. 'When you brainstorm, you throw out all sorts of ideas, good and bad. I barely remember what we said, do you, Sarah?'

Sarah hesitated and then mumbled, 'Barely.' Breaking up with a good theme song is hard to do.

I turned back to our neighbor. 'But tell us more about this new job. You were saying cremations are done right there at the funeral home? I had no idea.' An understatement.

'Oh, you wouldn't notice anything,' Christy assured me. 'Perhaps a little puff of smoke when the cremator starts up. But there's no smell or black smoke, unless there's some problem with the cremator or the person is . . .' She let it drift off.

But now that I realized the so-called cremator was in my neighborhood, I had to know more. 'Or what?'

Christy squirmed. 'Well, I heard that if the load is very large,' she spread her hands wide, 'it can cause more smoke momentarily—'

'Wait a minute,' Sarah interrupted. 'Load? You mean the body?'

'Yes,' Christy said. 'Apparently if there's a very high percentage of body fat it can cause problems.'

'Oh.' I wasn't sure what else to say.

'That's assuming the retort – that's the chamber inside the cremator – is large enough. At our mortuary, we have—'

I waved surrender. 'No more. But are you sure the mortuary is your' – ugh – 'niche, Christy? You've been amazing, visiting Ronny in jail, which is enough of a challenge. Don't you think you might be pushing your cleanliness boundaries a little too—'

'Oh, heavens, Maggy. A crematorium is a picnic,' she seemed to brush an imaginary ant off her arm, 'compared to either county jail or state prison. And cremains – or cremated remains, as Mort prefers we call them – are totally sanitary.'

'Not surprising, after toasting in a thousand-degree furnace,' Sarah said.

'Cremator,' Christy corrected. 'And they get much hotter than that – even twice as hot.'

'So you see my point.' Sarah reached for the chain we'd all but forgotten during our wide-ranging exchange.

I nudged it nearer to her with my foot. 'But surely you're not cleaning out the actual cremator, are you?'

Christy looked pleased at my retention. Me, I was afraid I'd never forget.

'Not yet,' Christy said, putting her hand over her heart. 'I'll consider the process a sacred trust when Mort decides I'm finally ready. It's not just sweeping out the ash and bone fragments for packaging, you know. You have to go over them with a magnet to remove metals like surgical screws and such, so the rest can be pulverized, bagged, tagged and given to the family.'

Bagged and tagged. Better and better. 'I'm sure the families are grateful for the attention to . . . detail.'

'What happens to things like gold fillings?' Sarah asked curiously. 'I've always wondered.'

'Gold isn't magnetic, so I think anything left after the cremation would have to be sifted out. The dental gold used for fillings now doesn't have much value, though. Especially after . . . well, you know.'

Now she chooses to mince words?

'The family can also request the teeth be pulled prior to cremation.'

I must have made a noise because Christy turned to me. 'Removing teeth is optional, of course. But things like pacemakers *have* to be removed because they can blow up in the chamber. And I understand silicone implants,' she shivered, 'make a terrible mess.'

I wasn't sure if the shiver was for the implants or the mess. I was betting the latter.

'But the point is,' Christy continued, 'that it's essential the retort be spic and span for the next person.'

Having coiled the chain, Sarah aimed for the box again and this time made it. 'Assuming they're deader than the not-quite-dead guy in Monty Python, why would they care? It's not like they're going to catch something.'

I restrained a grin. The 'bring out your dead' scene from *Monty Python and the Holy Grail* was one of my favorites.

But our Christy seemed less amused. 'It's for the families. The cremated remains mustn't be blended.'

'Like frozen custard,' Sarah said.

First the dry cleaner, now this, God help us.

Visit a 'custard stand' in southeastern Wisconsin and you'll be treated to one of the flavors of the day, scooped just as the rich, egg-based ice cream worms its way out of the machine that churns and freezes it.

'Making frozen custard is about as far removed as you can get from cremating bodies, I would think.' Ugh. Double ugh.

'I didn't mean the process itself,' Sarah said. 'Just the idea of cleaning out the chamber for the next person.'

'Or flavor, in keeping with your analogy.' Christy was nodding. 'I worked at a stand and we had to thoroughly flush the frozen custard maker before the next flavor was put in to freeze. After all, who wants leftover Death by Chocolate mixed with their Peach Melba?'

'Or George down the street mixed with Aunt Edith?' Sarah was nodding back.

Before they could descend further into the dead rabbit hole – not to mention ruin the remainder of the flavor of the day list for me forever – I cleared my throat. 'So, Christy, any idea how Clare's Antiques and Floral next door is doing?'

The building was owned by Ronny and had been sitting empty. Now, with Christy in charge, the place had been speedily rehabbed and then leased to Clare Twohig. Probably also through Craigslist.

'The shop is doing well, I think,' Christy said. 'And Clare is ever so clever. Have you seen how she's displayed the coffee and tea services?'

'I have,' I said, hefting the box. 'Using the steps of that wrought-iron staircase is genius. Made me wonder if we shouldn't do some kind of history of coffee with—'

'We're already surrounded by history,' Sarah interrupted. 'The depot dates back to the 1880s, which means nothing to me except that not a day goes by when we don't have to fix something. And now you want to add more old crap?'

The depot with its graceful wraparound deck and vintage ticket windows – now used for serving coffee – was gorgeous and Sarah knew it. She also owned it. In fact, she had been the one who'd suggested re-opening Uncommon Grounds in the depot with herself as my new partner.

It was a package deal and had worked out amazingly well to date. Like any relationship, of course, it required acceptance and respect. I accepted that Sarah was going to be her smart-ass self and she respected my ability to ignore ninety percent of what she said.

Now, balancing the heavy box of tarps on my hip, I opened the shop door. 'There's a difference between old crap and antiques.'

'Yeah, if crap is old enough, it becomes antique. Still old, though, and still—'

The door, blessedly, closed behind me.

THREE

Unfortunately, moments later Sarah and Christy opened it again and followed me into Uncommon Grounds.

'Everything all right?' I asked Amy as I set down the box. 'I heard there was an accident.'

'Just a wet chair. All taken care of.' Only Amy could be so perky about a piddle puddle, especially one she'd had to clean up. But that's why we loved her.

She went where neither Sarah nor I dared to go. Consider her our Starship Enterprise.

As the door closed again behind Sarah and Christy, a manicured hand caught it. The tall woman who'd gone running out with the two elderly ladies poked her head in.

Christy clapped her hands. 'Hannah! I was afraid you weren't going to make it.'

The Goddard Gangers, who took up four of our six tables, turned en masse to look as the brown-haired woman stepped in.

'Who's rat?' Gloria Goddard demanded from her wheelchair.

'Rat?' Already seeming on edge from earlier events, Hannah glanced around nervously as the door closed behind her.

Oliver grinned and shook his head. 'Sometimes Mrs G's words don't come out quite right. But you're getting better at the manor, right, Mrs G?'

'Better? Better to die.'

Oliver's face dropped.

'I'm sure she didn't mean that either,' I said.

'My mother gets confused sometimes, too,' Hannah added gently.

He tried to smile and I patted his shoulder. 'Wow, Oliver, you've got guns!'

Now the young man blushed with pleasure while still managing to flex his new bicep muscles. He was wearing a T-shirt on this March day and I had a feeling it was more to show off his arms than beat the heat. 'Can't major in Exercise and Sports Science without looking the part. Who'd listen to me?'

'Practice what you eat,' Gloria said, patting his cheek.

'You tell him, Gloria,' I said and turned to Hannah. 'You must be Hannah Bouchard. I didn't get a chance to introduce myself earlier. I'm Maggy Thorsen.'

'Oh, Maggy. I'm sorry about what happened. I think Nancy must be getting the flu or something. She was complaining of a headache last night and now it's aches and pains and a scratchy throat. But incontinence has never been a problem before. I suppose a cough or a sneeze might cause her to . . .' Her face was bright red as she trailed off.

I thought we should change the subject. 'I understand you just moved to Brookhills.'

'Yes, with Nancy and my mother, Celeste.'

'Your mother cut quite the figure in that hat.' I skipped past the makeup and suffocating perfume.

A wan smile. 'Mother won't leave the house without being fully decked out and with "her face on."'

'Celeste owned a string of boutiques out east,' Christy told me and then turned to Hannah. 'I'm so sorry I didn't get to meet her today.'

'With Nancy feeling ill, I thought it best to take them both home to rest. It's such an effort to get everybody up and out – I'm afraid we don't do it as much as we should.'

'That's certainly not your fault,' Christy said. 'Taking care of both your mother and her friend – you're a saint in my book.'

'What book would that be?' Sarah asked, joining us. 'You're an unbeliever.'

Christy's bottom lip jutted out again. 'I told you, I believe *everything*.'

'And that *I* believe.'

'This is my partner, Sarah Kingston,' I told Hannah.

She smiled a greeting. 'Christy exaggerates. I'm just doing what anybody of good conscience would.'

'Well, aren't we holier than—' Sarah stopped as I elbowed her in the ribs.

'Not at all, I'm afraid,' Hannah said with a patient smile. 'My mother doesn't have anybody else and Nancy is my mother's longtime companion. Almost a second mother to me.'

'Companion? You mean—'

I elbowed Sarah in the ribs a second time. 'Can we make you a drink, Hannah?'

Sarah threw me a dirty look, but the newcomer didn't seem at all put out at my partner's cross-examination. 'I would love a non-fat latte. I didn't get to drink mine earlier.'

'One non-fat latte coming up,' Amy called from behind the counter. 'And it's our treat.'

I sensed Sarah's scowl.

And ignored it. Giving away a drink or two wouldn't kill us. 'Hannah, have you met Amy Caprese?'

'Not formally. Good to meet you, Amy.'

'Hannah bought the house next to Christ Christian.'

'Oh, up that little lane,' Amy said, confirming my hunch that I was the only one who didn't know there was a house there. 'Welcome. Have you met Langdon Shepherd, the pastor of Christ Christian yet? He should be here this morning.'

'He stopped by the house to say hello just after we moved in,' Hannah said. 'Such a nice man. I was sorry to have to tell him I'm Catholic.'

'Not to worry.' Amy twisted the portafilter onto the espresso machine as the sleigh bells on the front door jangled, signaling a new customer. 'Father Jim will be here today, too.'

Langdon was the kind of guy who loved to say that recruiting members was his 'soul mission.' And then spell out s-o-u-l. Father Jim thought that was corny but wouldn't hurt Langdon's feelings by telling him that. The two facts pretty much summed up the respective pitchers in this friendly theological rivalry.

'Oh, good. I have a message for him from Nancy. She— Vickie!'

Vickie LaTour had come in and was looking around expectantly. Her bright burgundy hair was a color that did not appear in nature but she looked remarkably good for her seventy-seven years. It might be worth asking about those 'treatments' she was always talking about.

'Well, look who's here!' Vickie said, giving the younger woman a quick hug. 'Maggy, I assume you've met Hannah?

We're so happy to have her – and her ladies, of course – at Angel of Mercy.'

Christy joined us. 'I didn't finish telling you, Maggy. Vickie took that job I was considering at Angel of Mercy.'

Vickie grinned, though nothing on her face budged but her lips. 'I'm Catholic – we decided it was a better fit.'

I said, 'Christy says you were a student of hers. I had no idea you played the piano.'

'There are many things people don't know,' Vickie said, waving her hand. 'Some of which I'm just fine about keeping hidden. For example, I played the accordion when I was young. But an accordion is just a keyboard attached to a big bag of air, when you think of it. Christy helped me brush up to move on to the piano and organ.'

Sarah, who'd been listening to the goings-on in silence, raised her eyebrows. 'And now, in Christy's new job, she'll be helping even more people move on.' Whistling the *X-Files* theme, Sarah slipped away into the back of the store.

'. . . Think Father Jim will be here,' Vickie was saying to Hannah. 'Do you know if there's anything else I can help with? We were trying to balance the church books but she said trying to find the discrepancy was giving her a headache so we decided to call it a night.'

'Oh, dear. When Nancy sets aside a balance sheet you know she's not feeling well. In fact, she's come down with the flu. I hope you don't get sick.'

'Oh, heavens, don't worry about that,' Vickie said. 'With the people I come into contact with at the manor and the church, I'm constantly being sneezed or coughed on. I have the constitution of a horse.'

I thought I heard a whinny from in the back. Sarah might have snuck away, but not far enough.

'. . . Didn't mention anything,' Hannah said. 'Though she did say I should tell Father Jim in no uncertain terms that he needs to check his messages.'

Vickie laughed. 'I've been telling the man the same thing ever since I took over the office job. After meeting Nancy, I have a feeling she could shape him up in no time if she was able to get out of that house and into the office.'

'She is a force to be reckoned with – or was, when she was managing my mother's chain of boutiques.' Hannah laid her hand on Vickie's shoulder. 'And thank you for coming to the house last night. It's been months since I've been able to go out on a Saturday night. Especially without worrying.' She glanced my way. 'I run errands for an hour or two during the day. But late afternoon into evening are difficult for both my mom and Nancy, so I don't like to leave them alone if I can help it. And since we're new to town . . .' She shrugged.

'Well, I was just happy to help,' Vickie said. 'And even happier to have her help with the books and the committee reports. The least I could do was drive over with what she'd asked for and try to answer any questions she might have.'

'It's good that she has something to occupy her mind,' Hannah said. 'Nancy's as sharp as a tack. Sharper, even, with a tongue to match sometimes. She ran my mother's company *and* my mother, most days.'

Vickie chuckled. 'I saw your mother in the living room last night as I was waiting. I think she was dozing so I didn't say hello, but what a beautiful woman.'

'Even now,' Hannah said a little wistfully.

'And quite the fashionista, too, in her silk evening pajamas. Not a blonde hair out of place.'

'Wigs. She has a half-dozen that she rotates and she'd have more if I let her. They are easy, I must say.'

Vickie patted her own perhaps too thick and certainly too red hair. 'Nothing wrong with wigs or anything else we do to keep ourselves looking good.'

'You know, you should throw one of your make-over parties at our house,' Hannah said. 'Nancy would make fun but Mother would love it.'

Vickie pulled out her cell phone, likely to send out the invitations on the spot. 'Collagen, Botox and maybe makeup?'

'What, no boob jobs?' I was kidding.

'My mother already has better boobs than I have,' Hannah said with a grin. 'Or, at least, newer ones.'

Amy laughed as she set Hannah's latte on the counter. 'Brew of the day, Vickie?'

'Please.'

Hannah moved on to the condiment cart as Amy poured Vickie's coffee and Christy sidled in next to me. 'I can only imagine how tough it is on Hannah. Her mom is failing a bit and Nancy had a stroke last year that limited her mobility. Neither has anybody else to take care of them.'

'Wah, wah, wah. People have strokes or heart attacks every day,' a voice declared from behind Christy. 'Or so it seems at the manor. Last night it was Matilda. Or was it Berte? They all look alike.' Sophie Daystrom blew a curl of gray off her forehead and held out her cup for a refill.

Sophie had moved into Brookhills Manor to be with her paramour, Henry Wested, who already lived there.

'I guess you have to expect that,' Christy said. 'It *is* a senior home.'

'Do you know there's a panic button in each room for emergencies? Even the residential apartments like ours have them, even though we're far from the "Help! I've fallen and I can't get up!" stage of life.'

'Until you do take a fall or something,' Christy reasoned. 'It's not like you have to use the button. It's just there if you need it.'

'They do force some people,' Sophie said. 'They have to flip a switch every morning so the desk knows they aren't dead. Can you believe it?'

'Again, it is a senior—' Christy started.

But Sophie wasn't through grousing. 'God's waiting room is what I call the place.'

Christy tilted her head to one side. 'I thought that was Florida.'

'Old is a state of mind, not a state of the union, is what I tell Henry,' Sophie said, nodding across the room. 'Especially these days when he's going on about his heart.'

I turned to see Henry Wested moving his signature fedora from the next chair to make room for Vickie with her cup of coffee and cell phone. 'I didn't know Henry was having heart problems.'

'Oh, don't you start fussing now,' Sophie said. 'He's doing enough of that for all of us.'

'That's men,' Christy said. 'Ronny had a cold last month and you should have heard him complaining about the quality of the tissues in prison.'

My heart went out to the lunatic. But I was still thinking about Henry. 'What exactly is Henry's heart problem?'

'Oh, just a little angina.'

At least Henry still had a heart. I wasn't so sure about Sophie, given how she was talking. 'Are you and Henry doing OK?'

'*We're* fine. I'm just sick to death of living at the manor. Though I don't say that out loud there in case somebody hears me out of context and delivers it from my lips to God's ears.'

As she said it, the sleigh bells on the door rang and in came Brookhills' pipeline to God, Langdon Shepherd, pastor of Christ Christian Church.

'Over here, Pastor Shepherd,' Vickie trilled, setting down her phone. Langdon was tall, thin and a little stooped – think Ichabod Crane in a church collar. He lifted his hand in greeting to us as he passed on his way to the table.

Sophie signaled with a chin-cock that we should come closer. 'I'm starting to think that there's a wormhole between Brookhills Manor and Langdon's stomping grounds.'

'Christ Christian?' Christy asked.

'Not the church. Heaven and hell, depending on which direction one is heading.' Sophie shrugged. 'I like to think I'd be going up, of course, but let's face it: nobody really knows until it's too late.'

'As in dead.' At least that part I was fairly sure I understood. 'By a wormhole, do you mean like in sci-fi movies? Shortcuts between space and time?'

'Or in this case, between Brookhills Manor and the after-life.'

'You yourself called the manor "God's waiting room,"' I told her.

'True, but it's getting creepy. Somebody falls and breaks a hip or gets a cough and, whoosh, off they go.' She scuttled her fingers across the countertop. 'Hurried off into the light like in that movie.'

'*Ghost Story*?' I guessed.

'That's the one, I—'

'Martha,' Christy interrupted.

We both looked at her.

The former piano teacher's bottom lip was trembling. 'The

woman who had the heart attack last night and died – her name was Martha. Not Matilda. And not Berte.'

'And she was a friend of yours?' I asked, concerned.

'No, but people treat the elderly like they're invisible. We're handling the arrangements for Martha Anne Severson. She was ninety-three years old, had three children, ten grandchildren and two great-grandchildren. She deserves to have her name remembered.'

'I didn't mean any disrespect,' Sophie said in her own defense, 'but I can't tell one of the old biddies from another. They all have gray hair, wrinkled skin and flirt with Henry.'

What was this all of a sudden? 'Flirting with Henry? Is that what this is about?'

'You mean am I jealous?'

'Well, yeah.'

Sophie didn't answer the question, at least not directly. 'If we'd moved into my house, instead of Henry convincing me to move in with him, it wouldn't be an issue. Thank God we're in the residential section facing the Poplar Creek woods, which is nice and private.'

'Is that a separate entrance from the nursing home and assisted living?' Christy asked.

Sophie ducked her head. 'Yes, though the new rehab wing shares our entrance. At least people like Gloria are mostly too impaired to go after my Henry.'

Sheesh.

'Are the residential units subsidized by the county?' Christy asked.

'Some of them,' Sophie confirmed. 'Which is one of the reasons why Henry was so adamant about staying there. It's cheap, though there's also the downside.'

'The women?' I asked.

'No. Well, yes,' Sophie said, 'that does bug me. There must be a dozen females for every male there. Feels more like a harem than a home, with Henry one of the only sheiks still standing. And technically he's single, so they figure he's fair game.'

'Have you ever discussed getting married?' Why was I, of all people, asking? I was having enough trouble sorting out my own affairs.

'I have.' A flush crept up her cheeks.

'But Henry . . .?'

'Thinks things are just fine the way they are, thank you very much,' Sophie finished for me.

I felt my own face get warm. 'Just because he doesn't want to get married doesn't mean he doesn't love you.'

'You wouldn't know it by the way he preens under a little female attention.' She was trying to get Amy's attention.

An ill-timed laugh from Henry in response to something Vickie had said punctuated the point.

'But you were saying the downside of the residential facility isn't the male-to-female ratio?' I asked.

'Probably more the junkie-to-senior ratio,' Christy said.

While I appreciated the former piano teacher abetting my attempted change of subject to get poor Henry off the hook, once again I wasn't sure what she was talking about. 'Junkie?'

'"Recovering."' Sophie made air quotes. 'They have to let them in because, like I said, the county provides subsidies for the manor's residential units and finding housing for the addicts in the rehabilitation program is part of their mission. But before long, recovering turns into relapsed and they have to be evicted. And don't get me started on the outright criminals like the guy next door to us.'

'How do you know he's a criminal?' I asked.

'Because he freely admits serving time like it's some kind of badge of honor that he's come out the other side.'

'It is, in a way,' Christy said. 'Assuming he's now leading a productive life.'

'More reproductive, if you ask me.' Sophie was building a low burn. 'The man is nothing special but can certainly turn on the charm when he wants to. Has women over there practically every night. And don't think we can't hear every moan, groan and butt slap through the cardboard they call walls there.'

Lovely.

'No doubt those prison groupies,' Sophie continued. 'Never understood why women fixate on those lowlifes. Write them letters in prison, visit—' She broke off as she seemed to realize there was a groupie in our very midst.

But Christy was rocking forward on the balls of her feet. 'Oh, Sophie, you're so right. Like when I visit Ronny.'

Sophie and I glanced at each other. 'Oh?'

It seemed a safe response given that we didn't know where Christy was going to take this.

'Oh, yes. Ronny's cellmate is a serial killer and you wouldn't believe how much mail he gets. And the visits.'

Ronny was no angel, but, 'A serial killer? Last time I heard, his roomie was a drug dealer or something.'

'That one got shivved,' Christy said, waving it off. 'This one's a much better fit.'

'Like, how?' I couldn't help myself.

'Well, you know how creative Ronny is. Remember how when we met him he was dressing to celebrate a different era each day of the week? Greaser Tuesdays, Disco Wednesdays?'

How could I forget? Earlier this year, Ronny's Elvis Sunday had nearly put a permanent end to my week.

'He does that in prison, too?' Sophie seemed fascinated now, too.

'Not quite to that extent. Prisoners have to wear their jump-suits, you know, so creativity is limited. But Ronny likes to do small things that signal the era. Like wearing his jumpsuit collar up for the nineties or wearing a work glove on one hand for the Michael Jackson look. Other inmates get a kick out of it and have started helping. Especially Lionel, the serial killer. He loves to sew, believe it or not.'

'All that practice making lampshades,' I said without thinking.

'Lampshades?' Christy asked. 'Isn't that what Jeffrey Dahmer did?'

'No, he ate people,' Sophie said. 'Maggy is talking about Ed Gein, a Wisconsin serial killer back in the fifties. He—'

'But please,' I interrupted politely. 'Tell us more about your serial killer, Christy.'

Pink rose in Christy's cheeks. 'He's not mine. Or Ronny's. And I probably shouldn't call him a serial killer. They've only found two bodies so far.'

I cleared my throat. 'How does a guy like this get hold of needles?'

Christy looked blank.

'For sewing,' I explained, since needles might have other connotations, especially in prison. 'Needles and thread for alterations?'

'Honestly, I don't know,' Christy said, eyes wide. 'But the prison population is amazingly creative. Ronny says—'

Time to turn the conversation away from Ronny & Company and back to semi-sanity.

'Interesting,' I said in response to whatever Christy had just finished saying. 'Speaking of prisoners, Sophie, your neighbor – the one with the noisy sex. Is he older?'

'Older than who exactly?' Sophie seemed offended. Or prepared to be offended. 'Are you insinuating people our age don't have noisy sex?'

'I was just asking if the guy next door is a senior.' I could dodge a question, too. 'He's living in a senior facility, after all.'

'So what? You think crooks just stop being crooks when they get old?'

I guess I kind of did. Or maybe that they were in jail or dead by the time they reached their golden years. Hard to live to a ripe old age when you're addicted to cocaine or robbing banks, I would think. But then, what did I know?

'. . . In his seventies, though I'm betting he's had work,' Sophie was saying.

'Ooooh,' Christy squealed. 'Maybe to hide his identity, like in *Face/Off*.'

'Wasn't that a whole face transplant?' Sophie said.

'To change John Travolta into Nicholas Cage and vice versa?' I said. 'It would have to be.'

'I assume this was a little tucking and lifting,' Sophie said. 'But who knows what the guy is into?'

'So exciting.' Christy was fanning herself with her hand, like she was going to pass out.

'Hopefully not for long,' Sophie said dryly. 'There have been strange men hanging around. Henry thinks they're cops but I'm betting it's mobsters out to whack him. If they do it next Tuesday, I'll win the pool.'

Wait. 'You have a betting pool on the date your neighbor dies? Like people do on the score of a football game?'

'Of course not.'

A relief.

Until Sophie opened her mouth again. 'We're not singling him out. We have pools for everybody. It's the only group activity I participate in at the manor. Sure beats trips to the Mitchell Park Domes like today's big adventure.'

For my part, I thought the horticultural center was charming. And 'sure beat' placing bets on when people are going to die.

'Don't be looking at me like that,' Sophie said. 'Everybody who bets knows that they're also being bet *upon*.'

I was having a 'soylent green is people' moment.

'It's the only fun we have in that place,' Sophie grumbled. 'And now you're making it sound dirty.'

Excuse me for not being a ghoul.

FOUR

Speaking of ghouls, Brookhills' aspiring ash-sweeper seemed to be on a conversational trajectory of her own.

'. . . Right to prohibit discrimination against somebody like your neighbor, Sophie,' Christy was saying. 'There are very strict guidelines so long as he meets the age requirement.'

Understandable, given the public funding. Still, it was worrisome to think of grandma and grandpa living out their golden years next to Larry the Torch or Danny the Corner Drug Dealer.

'I had no idea such a thing was possible when I moved in,' Sophie said. 'And Henry didn't think it was a big enough deal to tell me. Everybody deserves a second chance, according to him.'

'Amen to that,' Christy said fervently. 'Wouldn't it be awful if, when Ronny gets out, there was no place for him to go?'

Sophie raised her eyebrows. 'I assumed he'll be living at your house. I mean, you did sell his, after all.'

Christy flushed. 'Well, of course. I was speaking hypothetically, of course.'

From the look on Christy's face, I had a feeling that, as romantic as she imagined her relationship with Ronny was while he was in the slammer, she hadn't given much thought to his appearing at her tidy little doorstep in ten to twenty.

But Sophie was still grousing about *her* love. 'Go-along to get-along – that's what Henry does. We had a meeting the other day about the rates on the assisted living and nursing home wings of Brookhills Manor, and you think he'd speak up about the increases? By the time we need care we won't be able to afford it, and it'll serve him right.'

'What *does it* cost?' Christy asked. 'If you don't mind my asking.'

I wasn't sure it was a deliberate change of subject, but I was grateful. It's hard when mom and dad fight. Even if they're not *your* mom and dad.

'Nearly five grand a month,' Sophie said. 'And that's assisted living, not full nursing care. The new memory unit for Alzheimer's and dementia is going to be seven thousand a month, I hear.'

Christy glanced toward the table where Hannah had joined Langdon, Henry and Vickie. 'I suggested that Hannah consider the manor should the time come when she can't take care of the ladies anymore.'

'A retirement fund or savings would go fast at that rate,' I said. 'Are the fees covered by insurance?'

'Or the government?' Christy added.

'Government?' Sophie snorted. 'Not for what they call long-term care. That kicks in right around the time you're knock, knock, knocking on heaven's door.'

Christy cocked her head like a puppy. 'Isn't that a song?'

'Bob Dylan,' I said.

'You *are* an old soul, Maggy.' Sophie was nodding her approval. 'The man is in his seventies now – more my generation than yours.'

She had a point, though I couldn't think of Dylan that way. 'He's an icon, and icons are ageless.'

'Unlike the people at the manor.' Sophie wasn't going to let it go.

'Baggy?'

The word – though semi-recognizable as my name – was slurred. Gloria was holding up her cup shakily, Oliver grinning proudly next to her.

I went over and took the cup. 'The same, Mrs G?'

A head waggle, with an emphatic, 'Unleaded.'

I laughed. This wasn't a slip of the stroke-impaired tongue – unleaded had been Mrs G's term for decaf at the lunch counter. 'One unleaded coming right up.'

One half of her mouth curved into a smile as she turned back to Oliver and Mort.

'So, tell me who this woman is,' Sophie said as I handed the cup to Amy to fill.

'You don't know Gloria Goddard?'

'No, I've been living in a hole the last fifty-some years,' the octogenarian said testily. 'Of course I know Gloria. I mean the woman you two were talking to when I came in. She's sitting at the table with Henry and Vickie now.'

'That's the Hannah I was talking about,' Christy answered. 'Hannah Bouchard. She bought Ronny's house.'

'I saw you had it listed on Craigslist,' Sophie said. 'Too big and too expensive for the likes of us.'

'You're really serious about moving?' I asked.

'Hell, yes. If Vickie's smart she'll start looking for a place, too, before the manor finishes sucking her dry. The woman has an efficiency apartment the size of a postage stamp two doors down from us and even that is costing her a fortune. If I'd thought more, maybe we could have bought the Eisvogel place together.'

I hadn't realized that Vickie lived at Brookhills Manor. Somehow she seemed too young, in spite of her seventy-seven years, but maybe that was the Botox and collagen doing their jobs. Or their purported jobs. 'You trust Vickie around Henry?' I asked.

'Hell, yeah. They've known each other for years and Henry's not remotely interested. Says Vickie's way too high maintenance.' She nodded toward the table where Langdon Shepherd was now laughing at something Vickie had said. 'Besides, she's had something going on with somebody for the last few months. I'm just not sure who.'

Which was likely killing her, if I knew Sophie. 'Are you thinking she and Langdon might be involved?'

'It has crossed my mind,' Sophie admitted. 'For some reason, she's being very closemouthed about it.'

'Vickie is working at Angel of Mercy now, you know.' I took Gloria's now-full cup carefully from Amy.

'This I do know,' Sophie said. 'I assume you have a point?'

I wondered if Sophie was getting sarcasm lessons from Sarah. Or vice versa. 'Just that if Vickie is dating Langdon while she's working at Angel of Mercy it could be awkward. Maybe that's why she's keeping it quiet.'

'I doubt that Father Jim would care,' Christy said. 'It's not like she's dating a priest or a married man or something.'

Like a convicted killer, for example. But I kept my mouth shut and went to deliver Gloria's refill.

'. . . By a difference in religion in this day and age,' Sophie was saying when I came back.

'It could be Langdon who doesn't want it made public,' Christy said. 'The ladies in the altar guild are wild about him. I wouldn't put it past half of them to quit if he started seeing somebody romantically. And then who would do the work?'

'The men, maybe?' Sophie suggested. 'But getting back to Vickie, she went off on a cruise two weeks ago and I'm certain it was with him, whoever it is.'

'I wouldn't be caught dead on a cruise. All those people and germs in a combined space.' Christy brightened. 'Though they do have those hand-sanitizer dispensers everywhere.'

Always an antibacterial lining somewhere for our little germaphobe.

'Cruises aren't my cup of tea either,' Sophie admitted. 'But Vickie came back glowing. Spouting all this nonsense about retiring on a cruise ship and seeing the world.'

'You mean living on a ship year-round?' I asked. 'Wouldn't that be awfully expensive? I thought you said the manor was already bleeding her dry.'

'You know, I've heard of this,' Christy said. 'Supposedly it's not that much more than the cost of assisted living. There are things to do, a doctor onboard if you get sick and your food is free – all you can eat, twenty-four hours a day.'

'Yeah, and who pays for the crane that has to lift you out of the room once you hit 400 pounds?' Sophie asked.

'But think of it,' Christy persisted. 'It would be like a floating senior home.'

Sophie snorted. 'Bad enough living in one on dry land. At least I can jump ship when I need a break away from all the old coots. And what happens when somebody dies? They throw them overboard?' Her eyes brightened at the thought.

'You're living among a different demographic than you were before – an older demographic,' I pointed out. 'And let's face it. Eventually we all die.'

'Spoken like somebody who *thinks* she's decades away from death,' Sophie said. 'And can I please get a refill here?'

She shoved her still-empty cup across the counter and Amy just about caught it with a bemused grin.

'Temper, temper,' a voice behind me said. 'Anybody need absolution? We have a Sunday special.'

I turned and saw Father Jim, whose entrance must have been covered by Sophie's whining. 'Sunday services are over already?'

'Father George took the ten o'clock,' Jim said, moving up the counter. 'Which any of you sinners would know if you came to church.'

'Ahem.' Mort was raising his hand. 'You'll recall I was at the eight.'

'Indeed you were, Morton, and a fine tenor you were in the choir as well.'

Christy giggled. 'I love it when you speak Irish priest.'

'Don't encourage the faker,' I said. Jim and I had dated in high school, way back when. We'd been better friends than sweethearts, and I'd never had the nerve to ask him if the lack of electricity in our relationship had anything to do with him going priest.

'Ah, but the parish expects a Father Jim to be Irish, don't you know.' He wasn't going to stop.

'Despite the fact your family came from Eastern Europe. Romania, right?'

'Hungary, and thank you for remembering.' Jim was about six inches shorter than Langdon but had twice the energy and probably ten times the sense of humor. I was surprised people weren't converting in droves. 'How's the family back in Switzerland?'

'Norway.' Which he knew, of course.

'Oh, Father Jim,' Christy was digging in her purse and came up with a stack of leaflets. 'Vickie said to ask you if it's OK to put these in the bulletin.'

Jim took one. 'Buy-one-get-one-free cremations?'

Christy giggled again. 'No, it's just a reprint of the story on Mort that the *Observer* wrote.'

'I do appreciate the soft sell,' Jim said. 'Tell you what, it wouldn't be appropriate to go in the church bulletin but I'll put it on the bulletin board.'

'That would be wonderful,' Christy chirped breathlessly. Maybe the omnist would be one of the converted. If you were in the market for an untouchable man, a priest was even better than a prisoner.

'Done,' Jim said, slipping the paper into his inside jacket pocket. 'Now, I didn't mean to interrupt. Sophie, you were threatening Maggy with death, I believe?'

Having gotten her coffee, Sophie seemed to have settled down. 'No, just telling her she had no idea what it is like to be surrounded by people who have one foot in the grave.'

'Or the cremation urn, should you choose that option. Would you like some of the leaflets to take back to the manor?' Christy was a dog who wasn't going to drop this stick. 'Or some of my business cards?'

I held up my hand as she slipped her purse off her shoulder again.

She stopped, hand in the bag, and looked up at me. 'Bad form, you think?'

'I think.'

She straightened up. 'Thank you. Sometimes I get carried away with my own enthusiasm.'

'Entirely understandable,' Sophie said, throwing me an 'is she crazy or what' look as she went to join Henry and company. Christy followed.

'Hello, Father Jim.'

'Good morning, Hannah,' Jim said, turning to greet our new neighbor. 'And how are you this fine morning? And you brought the lovely Celeste and Nancy, I understand?'

He just wasn't going to give up the brogue.

'That was the plan, but I'm afraid I had to take them home,' she said. 'Nancy's not feeling well today – coming down with the flu, she thinks. But the truth is that both she and my mother would rather stay at home with a good book or TV show anyway.'

'It's good of you to try to get them out. But I'm sorry to hear Nancy is under the weather. Would you like me stop in?'

'I'm afraid a visit from the priest would mean one thing to them.'

'Last rites,' I said, a shiver going up my spine. 'My grandmother was the same way.'

'I know it's silly,' Hannah said, nodding. 'But Mother was never a churchgoer, which is perhaps why I am.'

'We do sometimes go the opposite way of our parents,' Jim said, 'but whether we see them in church or not, we'll say a prayer. Nancy has been a godsend, virtually taking over as finance chair when Fred was taken.' He crossed himself.

'Wait. Fred Lopez died?' I didn't think I'd heard right. The man couldn't be more than fifty and he was a pillar of our banking community.

'Deported.' Vickie had an empty cup in her hand. 'And an awful shame, if you ask—'

Father Jim held up his own hand. 'A battle we've already fought and lost, sadly. I'm just glad that Nancy was willing to fill his shoes.'

'Did Hannah tell you that Nancy asked that you check your email?' Vickie said in an I-told-you-so tone.

'Shame on me,' Hannah said. 'I came up to give you that message and it just went out of my head.'

'She's likely sent the report for this afternoon's meeting,' Jim said, pulling out his phone. 'It amazes me how technologically savvy Nancy is. Although that's true of a lot of our older parishioners these days.'

'I think Nancy prefers computers to people. She says she's sat through enough meetings for one lifetime.'

Jim was scrolling through his mail. 'I don't see anything new here. 'Do you know when she sent it?'

'I don't, but I can call the house. I wanted to check on them anyway.'

As Hannah turned away, Vickie put her cup in the dirty dish

bin. 'If you forward the report to me as soon as you have it, Father, I can print and copy it for the members.'

'Hopefully you'll have time,' Jim said, and then broke off. 'Hannah, are you leaving?'

Our new neighbor turned, one hand on the door and a puzzled look on her face. 'Yes. Nancy's not answering the phone.'

'Maybe they're both lying down,' Vickie said. 'Or in the bathroom.'

'I'm sure it's fine, but . . .'

The door closed behind her.

FIVE

Uncommon Grounds closed at three on Sundays, so I'd invited Pavlik over for a late afternoon barbecue. When I got home a little before four, he was sitting on my porch steps, throwing the tennis ball for Frank.

Or faux throwing it. One of the sheriff's greatest joys was duping my poor sheepdog by sending him out for a long one: 'Are you ready? Are you ready? Huh? Huh?' And then palming the ball even as he pretended to toss it.

Frank, impeded by both the hair in his face and the trust in his heart, bounded blithely away and turned for the pass. Another arm chug from Pavlik would send the sheepdog first this way and then that, before the human – if not the adult – finally let the ball fly for real.

'Torturing my dog again?' I asked as Frank dove under the bushes for the ball.

Pavlik laughed and stood up, wiping his hands on his jeans. 'Frank loves it. Besides, he's a big dog living in a small house. He can use the exercise.'

'And you can use the laughs.' As Frank came running back to his tormenter, I intercepted him and grabbed the ball, intending to toss it properly for him. Instead, I dropped it. Predictably already slimy with dog drool, the trip under the bushes had added mud to the mix. 'Ugh.'

'You're right that I can always use a laugh, and I want to thank you for that one.' The sheriff leaned down to kiss me.

Pavlik has dark hair he wears just a little long so it curls over his collar. Today he was wearing a blue dress shirt, sleeves rolled up, and jeans. A soft brown leather jacket was draped over a Schultz's Market bag on the top porch step.

Despite my non-answer to the sheriff's marriage proposal, things hadn't cooled down on either side. In fact, if anything they were hotter. As if we were clinging to each other on a cliff, not knowing quite where our next move might take us.

'Did you bring the steaks?' I asked a little breathlessly as I slid my hand down to his very nice butt.

'I did,' he said into my ear. 'And don't think I'm unaware of the fact you're surreptitiously rubbing Frank slime onto my jeans.'

Hearing his name, Frank looked up from where he'd been nuzzling the dirt ball on the sidewalk. Even he seemed loath to pick it up, though given his hand was his mouth, that was doubly understandable.

'Blame him,' I said, indicating Pavlik. 'He's the one who threw it under the bush.'

Frank's tail waved.

'He loves me,' Pavlik said. 'I can do no wrong in his eyes.'

I lifted the jacket and moved the bag aside before settling down next to him, jacket over my lap. 'Nor mine. What a beautiful day.' I ran my hand over the buttery leather of the jacket and sighed.

Pavlik took the thing away from me and hung it over the porch railing. 'If you're going to fondle anything, fondle me.'

'Gladly.' I slid closer to him, laying my head on his shoulder and my hand on his thigh. 'I do love your jacket, but I love you . . .' I stopped.

'More?' Pavlik cranked his head around and down so he could see may face. 'Why are you afraid to say it?'

'I'm not.' I sat up and met his eyes. 'But it's kind of a . . . door.' I'd almost said Pandora's box. 'Once it's opened it leads to a whole lot of other doors.'

'Like marriage?'

'For one.' I laid my hand on his cheek. 'I do love you. I think you know that.'

He put his hand over mine. 'But?'

'But I feel like I've just now gotten my feet under me after the divorce. You know, so I can stand up on my own.'

'And you don't want to give up your independence.' Pavlik's eyes were a cloudy gray as they bored into mine. If he was trying to figure me out, good luck. I was as confused as he was.

'I don't know if that's it. I don't think so. But I do know I don't want to lose you.' I kissed his lips lightly.

After a moment, they responded and then got more forceful.

I was pressed back onto the steps and Pavlik's hand was up under my shirt when the sound of toenails up the steps was followed by a *bounce/plotch, bounce/plotch.*

A muddy tennis ball landed on my bare belly where the shirt was hiked up.

I jumped up. 'Oh, God, Frank. You have the worst timing.'

Pavlik was laughing as he stood. 'They do have a way of worming their way in, don't they? Muffin's the same.'

The sheriff had adopted a toothless pit bull rescued from a dog-fighting ring they'd raided when he was on the job in Chicago. Not fit for fighting, the pit pup was kept for breeding purposes. It was probably the only reason she was alive. That and Pavlik.

'How's Muffin doing?' I was holding up my shirt so it wouldn't touch the muddy sludge on my stomach.

'Not good,' Pavlik said, his eyes darkening. 'She's fourteen and feeling her age. Sleeps a lot and when she's awake she's not herself. I've taken her to the vet but he says it's just age. And what she went through before I got her. He doesn't think it'll be long.'

I let my shirt fall. Much as I complained sometimes about Frank, he had been a lifeline after the divorce and, from what little Pavlik had said about his own split, I knew it had been the same for him. 'You gave Muffin thirteen happy years – time she'd never have had if you hadn't taken her home that day.'

'I know.' There was a trace of moisture in his eyes, something I'd never seen before. 'It's just hard saying goodbye. Or maybe knowing when to say goodbye.'

'Is she in pain?'

'Not that I can tell, which is why I haven't wanted to . . .' He let it trail off.

I laid my hand on his arm. 'Is she all right by herself? We could go get her and she could have steak with us.'

'That's nice.' Pavlik kissed me on the forehead. 'But Tracey insisted on taking her home this past weekend. Susan's not working, so there'll be somebody at home if something happens.'

Tracey was Pavlik's twelve-year-old daughter with his ex-wife, Susan. After the divorce in Chicago, Susan had moved to Southeastern Wisconsin for a job opportunity and Pavlik had followed, wanting to stay close to his daughter. As luck would have it, Susan's job hadn't panned out and she'd moved them back to Chicago. Pavlik, already in his own newly elected role as Brookhills County Sheriff, had stayed.

I hoped I'd been at least partly responsible for that decision. 'Muffin was well enough for the drive down to Chicago?'

Pavlik looked surprised. 'They're back in Milwaukee – I didn't tell you that?'

Not likely I'd forget, especially since Pavlik and I had just gone through a traumatic – if short-lived – break-up. My suspicious nature would have glommed on to Susan's return as the possible cause. Not that I'd so much as met the woman to assess the threat level. I kept my voice casual. 'No, when did that happen?'

'I found out just before we left for Florida, though at the time I didn't know why. I was too ticked at Susan for bouncing Tracey back and forth like this to ask. The one saving grace is at least now they'll have to stay put.'

'Susan's taken a job here?' For the life of me, I couldn't remember what the woman did.

'More like taken a husband with a job here.' Pavlik snagged his jacket and flipped it up over his shoulder before picking up the grocery bag.

Now I was certain Pavlik hadn't told me any of this. 'Susan's getting re-married. Are you all right with that?'

'Sure, why wouldn't I be?' He'd pulled open the screen door to the house and now he turned back. 'I'm happy for her.'

That's what all we divorced folk say. Well, except for me,

who'd been slightly less accepting when my dentist husband had announced he'd been drilling his hygienist and was leaving me to marry her. All pretty much in the same breath.

But it had been a lot to digest in a short amount of time.

Kind of like when Pavlik did a 180 – or a full 360, really – first dumping me and then asking me to marry him all within forty-eight hours, which made me wonder if there was a connection. 'So, Susan moved back and then broke the news?'

'What news?' He continued into the house.

'That she's getting' – I caught the screen door just before it could slap me in the face – 'married.'

'Oh, that. The wedding invitation with a plus-one was in the mail when I got back.' He slipped the jacket over the door knob of the front closet.

'Ouch, that's cold.'

He shrugged. 'Like I said, I didn't give her much of a chance when she called to say they were back. I was on the way to pick you up for the airport.'

'What about Tracey?' I asked, following him and the groceries into the kitchen.

'I think Susan wanted to tell me herself.'

By way of an impersonal wedding invitation. 'I mean, how does she feel about the guy her mother is marrying?'

I hadn't told Eric about Pavlik's proposal, not because he'd object but because he'd push me to accept. I mean, the kid loved his dad but Pavlik treated Eric like an equal and an adult. Plus, he had a gun and a badge. How do you say no to that? And yet . . .

'. . . Says he's nice enough,' Pavlik was saying.

'Sounds like what Eric said about Rachel.'

'He was wrong on that score.' Pavlik should know, since he'd put Rachel away.

'Yes, as it turns out.' I got a bottle of red wine out of the cupboard, along with two wine glasses.

Pavlik was unloading a butcher-wrapped packet of meat and a bakery box that had a smudge of chocolate on the side.

The perfect man. Why was I even hesitating?

A buzz, and the sheriff reached into his jeans pocket for his phone. He read the message and slipped it back. 'I'm sorry.'

'You have to go?' Log that under 'dumb question.'

'A guy we've been looking for just turned up at his brother's place. Time to go smoke him out, much as I'd rather spend the afternoon with you looking smoking hot.' He pulled me toward him and kissed the top of my head before letting go to retrieve his jacket.

'Be careful,' I said as he slipped it on.

He raised his eyebrows. 'Don't want me to rip the jacket?'

In truth, I wasn't sure why I said it. 'You got it.'

'I know that I have,' he said, taking me in my arms. 'But it's you that I want.'

With that, the sheriff let me go and bounded down the porch steps.

SIX

'Here is ex-wife moves back to get married and his dog is dying,' I told Sarah as we cleaned up from the next morning's commuter rush. 'I think there's a connection.'

Sarah scooped beans from the container labeled Kenyan AA into the grinder, spun the dial to 'drip' and pushed the 'on' button. 'Please don't tell me you think the ex-wife is poisoning the dog.'

'Why would I think that?' I shoved a plastic bucket under the chute just as the freshly ground coffee started to spill out.

'You said they're connected,' she said, repositioning it.

With effort, I ignored the grounds now glancing off the edge of the container and onto the counter. 'I didn't mean that Muffin's failing health and Susan's marriage are connected. Though her moving back here and the wedding certainly are. I was talking about Pavlik's proposal.'

'You can grind coffee yet you can't form a coherent sentence.'

'You're grinding the coffee,' I pointed out. 'And making a mess of it, I might add.'

'Done,' she said, turning off the grinder. 'Now explain yourself.'

'It's not hard to understand,' I said. 'Pavlik's feeling alone. Besides needing a plus-one for the wedding.'

'He doesn't have to marry you to take you to a wedding unless it's his,' Sarah said. 'I assume you're going to watch the ex get safely hitched?'

'Wouldn't miss it. I've only met his daughter Tracey once and never even laid eyes on Susan.'

'Time to meet the family, huh? Wonder how he'll introduce you. I'm betting it won't be as his plus-one.'

I thought about that as I swept the remaining spilled coffee grounds from the counter and into my hand. 'Good point.'

'If you're nice, you'll let him say "fiancée,"' Sarah said, holding out the waste basket.

I deposited the grounds and clapped my hands above it. 'I'm not sure that's being nice. I don't want to mislead anybody, especially Pavlik.'

'What is *wrong* with you?' She returned the basket to its place under the sink.

'I ask myself pretty much every day. But in this case, I assume you mean why won't I marry Pavlik?'

'You care about him, right?'

'Of course I do. I even told him I loved him yesterday.'

Sarah turned, astonishment on her face. But not for the reason I'd expected. 'You've been together for what – two years? That's the first time you've used the "L" word?'

'In my defense, he only said it for the first time in November. And that was when he was breaking up with me. And then, again, when he asked me to marry him.'

Sarah didn't seem to think it was important. 'So you said you loved him and . . .?'

'No "and." More of a "but."'

'Figures. "But" what?'

'But I still wasn't sure about marriage. That I'd just gotten—'

The sound of sleigh bells interrupted both my lame explanation and whatever Sarah would have said to counter it. Christy burst in. 'Did you hear? Hannah's mother died.'

'Oh, no,' I said. 'I'm so sorry. When?'

'Yesterday morning, after Hannah brought them both home. I guess Celeste was watching television on the couch and fell asleep. Or at least that's what Nancy thought until she tried to rouse her and couldn't.'

'Is that why nobody picked up when Hannah called home?'

'I guess Nancy was so shook up that she couldn't find the phone to call for help. The poor woman was nearly hysterical by the time Hannah walked in the door.'

'Are – or were – Nancy and Celeste a couple?' Sarah asked. 'I started to ask but Maggy thought it was rude.'

As if that ever stopped her. An elbow to the ribs had been effective, though, as I recalled. 'I just don't think it's anybody's business, one way or the other.'

'You *know* I'm not judging, Maggy,' Sarah said. 'I was just curious.'

It was true. Both that Sarah wouldn't judge and that she was curious – aka nosy.

'Hannah refers to them as "partners,"' Christy said, 'though whether she means partners in the boutiques or domestic partners, I don't know. I believe they kept separate finances, in any case.'

'However would you know that?' And I thought Sarah was up in everybody's business.

'The purchase of the house was in just Celeste's name, for one thing. And when Hannah and I were talking about what she'd do if she couldn't care for Celeste or Nancy anymore, she said her mother has plenty of money but that Nancy's social security wouldn't go very far.'

'You'd think if they were life partners it would have been share and share alike.' By which I meant Celeste wouldn't let Nancy die destitute while she had private care or checked into the country club of nursing homes. Or maybe a cruise ship, a la Vickie.

'Exactly. But whatever the relationship, it was deep. Hannah says Nancy is absolutely devastated. That's what happens to committed partners, you know – one dies and the other's life light is dimmed. I know that's the way it would be for Ronny and me.' She put her hand over where her life light presumably was.

'Sounds to me like Hannah is the one whose light should be dimmed,' Sarah said. 'She should have never come back here after the old lady got sick.'

'Nancy told Hannah she was fine, just coming down with the flu, and encouraged her to come back,' Christy said. 'And, besides, Nancy's not the one who died.'

'Give the woman a break, Sarah,' I said. 'She couldn't have known.'

'Hannah doesn't like to talk about it,' Christy said, 'but I understand it's been a long haul since her mother started failing.'

'She did tell Oliver that Celeste got confused sometimes,' I said, 'like Gloria.'

'She wasn't even at the closing – the attorney had to sign the documents for her.'

At the mention of the closing she hadn't taken part in, Sarah's expression darkened further. 'Even more reason her daughter should have stayed home with her.'

Empathy is not one of my partner's strong points.

'That's not fair,' Christy said indignantly. 'Hannah takes – took – care of her mother and Nancy all day, every day. One time she runs out to get a cup of coffee—'

'And an old lady dies,' Sarah said.

'Get up on the wrong side of the bed this morning?' I asked.

'At least I got up,' Sarah said, turning. 'Which is more than I can say for Hannah's mother.'

'My goodness,' Christy said as she watched Sarah disappear into the back room. 'What does Sarah have against Hannah?'

'She's nice and people like her?' Not to mention she didn't need a real-estate agent for a house sale and purchase. Which meant Christy should watch out, too.

'You mean Sarah's jealous? But she certainly shouldn't be. People like her, too.' She thought for a second before adding, 'Mostly.'

Not being able to add to that, I just shrugged.

'It's true, though, that the people who bluster the most are the ones who are insecure. I'll have to keep that in mind when I'm dealing with Sarah, poor thing.'

Christy would be the 'poor thing' if Sarah got a whiff of pity off her. Compassion and understanding ticked my partner off, too.

'Can I get you something?' I asked Christy.

'The brew of the day would be lovely but I'll take it in

a to-go cup,' Christy said. 'I want to be at the mortuary for Celeste.'

'That's kind of you,' I said, lifting a pot to pour her coffee.

'Well, to be fair, it's my job.' Christy was slipping bills out of her wallet. 'But if I can help, I'd like to do that. Now that Hannah and Mort are dating—'

'They are? I don't remember them so much as speaking to each other yesterday.' Not to mention that Mort had to be nearly twenty years older than Hannah.

'It's new, so I think they're keeping it on the cutie.'

Cutie. 'The QT, you mean?'

Christy frowned. 'It's not cutie? Like isn't that cute?'

'No, just the initials Q and T. Short for "quiet."'

'Really?' Christy's face was puzzled. 'Why not just Q? I mean, if you're going to use the first and the last letter, why skip the three in the middle? Besides, QT is two syllables, so it's just as easy to say "quiet." That's two syllables, too.'

'I . . . well, I don't know.'

'No matter.' Christy seemed satisfied she'd stymied me. 'I introduced Hannah to Mort the day she moved in and thank the Lord. Not only did she tell me the position was open at the mortuary, but he was the first person she called when she found Celeste dead.'

I had no idea what you do if somebody just ups and dies a natural death. Most of my bodies met an untimely – and *un*natural – end.

'Mort notified the doctor,' Christy continued, 'and then arranged to move Celeste to the mortuary, before Nancy could get even more upset.'

'I'm not sure how I'd feel about dating a mortician.' I hadn't really meant to say it aloud, but there it was.

Christy cocked her head, not so much in the 'I don't understand' way, as the 'I'm ready for a fight and waiting for you to make the first move' way. 'What do you mean?'

Trying to suppress the 'yuck' factor, I said, 'I know that Pavlik deals with death on a daily basis, too. And you can add violence and criminals to that as well. It's just that I hope Celeste's death won't . . . shadow their relationship.' Lame, but heartfelt. Kind of.

Christy was shaking her head. 'Oh, no, I think trying times make couples stronger. Look at Ronny and me.'

Brrr. Nope, not going there. 'Well, I'm glad Hannah has Mort to lean on and help her through.'

'Even if she didn't, we have trained counselors on our staff.' Christy had her business hat on again. It was black and somber. 'Both for the emotional and business sides of death.'

'Business?' I repeated, handing her the change from her coffee.

'Of course,' Christy said solemnly. 'It's bad enough to lose somebody, but then there are all the notifications that have to be made. Not just to friends and family but to government agencies, utilities, charge card companies, credit agencies and the like. And then there's the estate and trusts and taxes. We provide checklists for the bereaved, detailing each step from death notices to estate settlement, complete with a directory of professionals who can help.'

And likely are paid for the privilege of being listed in that directory. Funeral homes were businesses, too, despite what Christy might like to think. And I was willing to bet that a mortuary business had a whole lot healthier profit margin than a coffeehouse did.

Though we arguably had more repeat business.

'Oh, dear,' Christy said, glancing up at the clock. 'I've been jabbering here and now I'm going to be late for our ten o'clock.'

'Sorry,' I said. 'If I'd known that was when you were meeting Hannah, I'd have reminded you. Please tell her how sorry I am for her loss.'

Christy was dropping loose coins into her purse. 'Hannah won't be there until later this afternoon to meet with Mort.'

It's like the woman's driving force was to keep me in a constant state of confusion. 'But you said—'

'That I wanted to be there with Celeste when she's prepared and cremated.' She snapped her purse closed. 'I'm hoping that if I'm a quick study Mort will give me the honor.'

'Of *cremating* her? You want to cremate somebody you *know*?' I think I nearly shouted it.

'Not necessarily, at least not yet.' Christy looked hurt. 'But I never even really met Celeste – not that I wouldn't be honored to perform this last service for her. But more importantly, I'm not qualified to handle the cremator. It takes far more experience than I have to do it right.'

Before I could inquire about the wrong way of doing 'it,' Sophie Daystrom trudged in from the side door.

'You're getting here late today,' I said, taking a mug from the rack. 'Did you sleep in?'

'I wish, but I was up all night. A stand-off, of all things, at the manor.'

'The dead versus the undead?' Sarah emerged from the back, arms held straight out in front of her like a zombie. 'Or maybe nearly dead.' The arms rotated down now, like she was inching ahead with a walker.

'That,' Sophie flopped into a chair, 'would be funny if it wasn't so close to the truth.'

'Oh, dear, has there been a death?' Christy was sounding far too eager for my liking.

I slid her to-go cup toward her so she could be to-gone, but Christy was busy digging through her pockets.

'No bodies,' Sophie said, holding up her hand, 'at least not when I left. So you can keep your cards right where they are.'

Christy's own hands dropped to her side.

'What happened?' I poured the brew of the day for Sophie and signaled for Sarah to deliver it to her table.

My partner living-dead walked it over. 'Zee zombie apocalypse, perhaps?' she lisped. 'Or maybe somebody looking for their mummy?'

Argh. 'Boris Karloff would roll over in his grave.'

'He can't.' Christy took the lid off her cup and sniffed the brew. 'He was cremated.'

Enough funereal fun facts for one morning. 'Didn't you say you're running late?'

'Oh, yes. With luck, Mort will let me help with something.' Her nostrils flared. 'Sweeping, even.'

Best hurry, then. I took the lid away from her and settled it on the cup so as not to slow the crazy little demon down. 'Off you go.'

'What can she possibly be that anxious to sweep?' Sophie was looking out the window as our neighbor rushed down the front porch steps.

'You don't want to know,' I said. 'So, tell me, what was going on at the manor last night?'

'I did tell you. A stand-off.' Sophie swiped at her forehead and the springy gray curls flew up and then settled right back down where they'd been. 'With the law, of course. If your boyfriend hadn't waved us through we'd still be hunkered down.'

'Pavlik?' I asked.

'You have more than one?'

She had a point. But speaking of 'boyfriends' . . . 'Where's Henry?'

'Barber shop. Nearly missed his appointment and, if he had, that guy next door would have been the reason.'

I frowned. 'The ex-convict?'

'Bingo. Couldn't wait until Tuesday.'

But I wasn't thinking of Sophie's death pool. Pavlik had said somebody they'd been looking for had showed at his brother's place. Could that be the senior home? The sheriff hadn't come back, so Sophie's stand-off might be the explanation. Or at least the explanation that was the most flattering to me.

But also the most risky for him.

'Is this stand-off still going on?' I asked. And then, without waiting for an answer, 'And is this guy – the brother – dangerous?'

'Brother?' Sophie asked.

I probably flushed. At least, it felt like I flushed. I try hard not to repeat what Pavlik tells me, even if he doesn't preface it with a 'Don't tell anybody this!'

And yet, I did. 'When Pavlik left, he said some guy that they were looking for had shown up at his brother's place. I had no idea – *have* no idea – whether he was talking about Brookhills Manor.'

'Well, now you do,' Sophie said dryly. 'And if Pavlik's "guy" came out of the same womb as our neighbor, I'd say he's a very bad man.'

Before I could ask for more details, the door flew open, sending the sleigh bells rappelling hard against the glass. I opened my mouth to scold some kid but then recognized one of Pavlik's deputies. Specifically, Detective Mike Hallonquist.

Hallonquist was Violent Crimes and, the last time I saw him, he was paired with Al Taylor of Homicide, not one of my favorite guys. In fact, it was Al's sarcastic ribbing that was partially responsible for Pavlik breaking up with me in the first place.

Now, though, Hallonquist was alone, his face pale as he swept the brimmed cap off his head. 'Maggy, the sheriff has been shot. You need to come with me.'

SEVEN

'**O**fficially, we notify the next of kin and emergency contact,' Mike Hallonquist said as we sped to the hospital. 'When I saw that you were down as neither, I thought I should get hold of you.' Hallonquist glanced sideways at me. 'I'm sorry.'

Sorry that Pavlik had been shot? Sorry his partner had been a jerk to me? Or sorry that I wasn't Pavlik's next of kin or emergency contact?

Whatever. 'Thank you.'

I thought to wonder who *was* Pavlik's emergency contact. I assumed his next of kin was his daughter, Tracey. She was just barely twelve, though, so it was unlikely she was his emergency contact. His ex-wife? Parents? It occurred to me that I didn't know a whole lot about Pavlik prior to his moving to Brookhills. For some reason that mattered a lot right now.

'How did this happen?' I mean, Pavlik was the sheriff, for God's sake. Shouldn't it be his deputies out there taking the bullets? I didn't have the grace to feel guilty about the thought. 'Pavlik said this guy you were hunting showed up at his brother's place?'

'Brookhills Manor. We've been sitting on the unit for a week.' Hallonquist signaled a lane change and checked his mirror before moving over. 'Not as easy as you'd think. Nothing gets by those old folks.'

I could imagine. 'Weren't you afraid somebody would tip off the brother?'

'At first, but it turned out to be just the opposite. Our guy posted at the front desk said folks kept wandering by, asking when we going to get rid of Andersen.'

If I was using our chat to do anything but distract myself, I'd have asked if Sophie had been one of them. 'Andersen is the brother?'

'Both brothers. Jack Andersen has lived at the manor for about a year – since he got out of prison.'

Just as Sophie had said. 'What was he sent away for?'

'Jack? Fraud. But it's his brother, Pauly, that we were waiting to nab.'

'And what did he do?' To my ears, my question sounded casual and almost disinterested. The kind of thing you'd ask about somebody at a cocktail party rather than the guy who just shot your . . . well, the man you loved.

'Convicted of bank robbery. He escaped while being transferred upstate to serve his sentence.'

Upstate to state prison. 'Transferred from Brookhills County Jail?' If so, the escape would have been on Pavlik's watch and the county sheriff would have taken it very personally. But Pavlik hadn't even mentioned it.

'Yeah.' Hallonquist was looking straight ahead, his expression tight. 'Got hold of Al Taylor's service revolver.'

Dear God. 'Is Taylor OK?'

'Physically, but . . . well, you've met him.'

Taylor played bad cop to Hallonquist's good one with gleeful swagger, but I thought I'd caught a brief glimmer of compassion in the man. Once. 'I imagine he's devastated.'

'Devastated, humiliated, angry, depressed – take your pick. I wasn't sure Al would come back from it at the time and now there's' – a swallow – 'this.'

Pavlik had been shot trying to recover the prisoner that Taylor had lost. The prisoner who'd taken the detective's sidearm. 'It wasn't Taylor's gun that—'

A single nod.

So Pavlik had been shot by his own detective's gun. I closed my eyes as the reality of the situation washed over me. Then I opened them. 'How did it go down?'

I imagined Pavlik rolling his own eyes at my 'TV cop-speak' and the fact that Hallonquist didn't do likewise gave me a twinge. 'Pauly must have managed entry by waiting in the woods by Poplar Creek and then leaving cover to blend in with a group that had just come back from a bus tour.'

The trip to the Mitchell Park Domes Sophie had mentioned. And the door Hallonquist was talking about would be the entrance Sophie had said was shared by the residential and rehab wings and faced the woods. It would have been a good plan. 'You didn't have anybody at the door?'

'We did, but by the time he picked Andersen out of the crowd he was already in and on the move to his brother's apartment.'

'And you couldn't stop him without endangering the other residents.'

A nod. 'Andersen barricaded himself in, using his brother as hostage.'

Now there's a sibling you'd want to share Thanksgiving dinner with. Yet, 'I thought Jack is a bad guy, too.'

A reluctant nod. 'But one who served his time and was now supposedly being held against his will.'

So they hadn't been sure of that and still apparently weren't. 'You had to treat it as a hostage situation, then, rather than two criminals in cahoots.'

This time 'cahoots' did earn me a trace of a smile. 'Exactly.'

'Sophie, the customer I was talking to when you came in, lives in the apartment next to Andersen.'

'I thought I recognized her. We were moving in when the perp fired shots through the walls into the corridor.'

The walls being none too thick, from what Sophie had said. 'One of them hit Pavlik?'

'Not then. But Pete Hartsfield took one to the chest and we all scattered for cover. Pavlik – Sheriff Pavlik – went in to pull Hartsfield out of the line of fire.'

'Did he?' To my ears the question sounded like polite conversation. Like, 'Oh, did he really? How nice.' When what I really meant was, *Did Pavlik have to take a bullet?*

Hallonquist answered the question I didn't ask. 'The sheriff dragged Pete around the corner so the EMTs could attend to him.'

'You said he was shot in the chest, too?' Pavlik, I meant.

Again, Hallonquist got it. 'Yes.'

'Was he conscious when he was transported?'

'Yes.'

I didn't ask if Pavlik had asked for me. Knowing he had would make me sad that I hadn't been there for him. Knowing he hadn't would make me sadder. 'Do we know . . . I mean, is there any word . . .'

'They took him in for surgery to remove the bullet is all I know.' Hallonquist turned the car into the hospital parking lot. I noticed the squads – not just Brookhills County Sheriff's Department but city police. Not just our city, but surrounding cities. And not just our county, but seemingly all of southeastern Wisconsin.

Hallonquist pulled into the physician parking by the emergency entrance. Leaving the flashing lights on, he came around and opened the door for me. 'We'll find out more inside.'

I climbed out of the squad and made for the sliding glass doors as Hallonquist closed the car door. I practically ran into the first automatic door and once that opened had to wait for the next.

It was as if the doors couldn't detect my presence – like the restroom faucet that you wave your hand under and get no water, the soap that won't dispense until you've removed your hand – but I couldn't blame the doors. I couldn't quite believe I was there either.

As I hesitated at the sight of a waiting room and corridor of uniformed officers, I felt a hand on my shoulder.

I turned, expecting to see Hallonquist, but it was Sarah. 'What are you doing here?'

For once, she didn't snap back as my terse question probably deserved. Truth was I was practically faint with relief at seeing my partner.

'I was in the back seat the whole way here. The deputy had to let me out. Those doors don't open from the inside, you know.'

I had no memory of her following me out of Uncommon Grounds or getting into the back of the squad. 'Thank you.'

'You're welcome. Now let's see who we can talk to find out Pavlik's condition.'

Some of the officers in the waiting room I knew, though it'd be hard for me to dredge up their names at that moment. As Sarah pulled me across the room, the uniforms seemed to part on both sides of us and I saw a blonde man in scrubs and a cap. He was standing with a tall brunette and a girl of maybe twelve who seemed to be doing most of the talking.

I stopped dead. 'That's Tracey and that must be Susan.'

'Pavlik's kid and ex-wife?'

'Yes. I've met Tracey but only seen a picture of Susan.'

'Well, you're meeting her now,' Sarah said, pulling me forward.

I was holding back, feeling awkward. 'I don't have any standing here. I'm just the girlfriend.'

As Sarah turned, likely to scold me or give me a pep talk, the girl broke away and ran up to me. 'Maggy, I'm so glad you're here.'

She gave me a hug and turned to her mother. 'Mom, this is Maggy. She and Dad are getting married.'

I didn't say anything but Sarah elbowed me anyway. And if her elbow could have spoken, it would have said, 'Go with it.'

So, I did. 'I'm sorry to meet this way. How's Pavlik?'

The doctor took it from there. 'I was just saying that he came through well.'

'The surgery.' Duh.

'Yes.' The surgeon pushed his blue cap up off his forehead. 'You can see him in recovery. Family only, of course, and just two people at a time.'

Pavlik's ex and I looked at each other. Not exactly a mirror image. I was wearing jeans, sneakers and an Uncommon Grounds T-shirt with a latte smooge on it. I smelled like coffee. Susan's jeans were designer, her boots high-heeled and her shirt was silk. No smooge. Oh, and she smelled like Joy. And no, not the dish detergent.

Given Susan had come here on short notice, too, I had to assume she always looked like this. Shopped like this. Worked in the garden like this. Hell, maybe she even slept like this. And if not, she probably wore something lacy with a matching robe, not something a hundred per cent cotton with a matching nothing.

But much as I wanted to engage in hate-envy, Susan had been married to Pavlik for almost ten years and was the mother of his child. And that child shouldn't have to walk into her dad's hospital room without her mom. 'You should go in with Tracey.'

But Susan shook her head. 'Jake will want to see you.'

'I—'

But Tracey was already pulling me toward the doctor, who was waiting for us at the end of the corridor. 'C'mon, Maggy.'

She apparently didn't think she needed her mother's support, so who was I to judge? And if I was not going to dissuade anybody from the idea that Pavlik and I were engaged, I might as well take advantage of it so I could see him.

I let Tracey zoom ahead into Pavlik's room and hung back to talk to the surgeon. 'Could you update Detective Hallonquist and the other officers in the waiting room?'

'Of course.' As he started past me back to the lounge, I put a hand on his arm. 'Pavlik is going to be OK?'

He smiled. 'The bullet broke a rib and did some tissue damage but no organ damage. The sheriff is going to be fine.'

I was glad I asked, because the sight of Pavlik lying in a hospital bed almost made my heart stop.

Tracey was already perched on the side of the bed. '. . . Going to bring Muffin in to see you.'

'I'm not sure how the docs would feel about that.' Pavlik flashed me a smile.

'Then I guess Frank wouldn't make the grade either,' I said. 'Though I can bring in a slimy tennis ball if you'd like.'

Tracey lit up. 'I'm dying to meet Frank. Daddy has told me all about him.'

I glanced over at Pavlik, who lifted a hand. I took it. 'He did, did he?'

'I did. You and he are my second favorite girl and dog combination, after all.'

'I take that as a compliment, since I know who number one is.'

Tracey giggled.

It seemed off, chatting like this with Pavlik lying in bed in a hospital gown, IV in one arm. He was always in control. Always doing something. Riding his Harley in his— 'Uh-oh.'

Pavlik squeezed my hand. 'I was going to tell you.'

'Tell Maggy what?' Tracey's freckled nose was wrinkled.

I pointed. 'Your dad's jacket.'

Draped over a vinyl upholstered chair was Pavlik's buttery leather jacket. It had a hole in it. And that wasn't the worst part.

'Cool,' Tracey breathed. 'Is that your blood, Dad?'

'Hard to tell,' Pavlik said. 'But probably most of it is Deputy Hartsfield's. At least what you can see.'

Meaning Pavlik's own blood would be on the inside.

'Ugh.'

Apparently your own dad's blood was cool. Somebody else's blood not so much.

'Have you heard what Pete Hartsfield's condition is?' Pavlik asked me.

'No, only that he'd been hit in the chest, too. And that you pulled him to safety.'

Now Tracey's eyes were big. 'Did you, Dad? You're a hero, just like in the movies.'

'Except those heroes never get shot themselves,' Pavlik said.

'Oh, they take bullets,' Tracey said, waving her hand as if it were nothing. 'You'll be back in action in no time.'

'Have they told you how long you'll be here?' I asked.

'No, but—' Pavlik broke off as a different doctor came in with a chart. 'Phyllis, thanks for stopping by.'

'Just don't make a practice of getting shot on my days off.' The doctor put her hand out to me. 'Phyllis Goode.'

'Maggy Thorsen.'

'Oh, you own Uncommon Grounds, don't you? I stop in sometimes with the gang from Goddard's. When I have a Sunday off, that is.'

'Hi, Doctor Goode,' Tracey chirped up.

'Hey, Tracey.' The doctor shook the girl's hand. 'You sure made it up from Chicago fast. Or were you already here visiting your dad?'

'Tracey and Susan have moved back,' Pavlik explained.

'Well, that's good.' The doctor flicked a curious glance toward me before continuing. 'I've missed you.'

Tracey, on the other hand, didn't miss a thing. 'If you're wondering, Doctor Goode, Maggy is my dad's *fee-ahn-say*.' Confusion crossed her face. 'Or is it *fee-ahns*? I looked it up the other day but now I can't remember.'

'Women are the double e,' Dr Goode said. 'Men are single. But they're both pronounced the same. *Fee-ahn-say*.'

'So, I was right,' Tracey said. 'Maggy is dad's fiancée. And he's hers.'

Pavlik threw a sheepish smile in my direction but didn't comment. 'Any word on Pete Hartsfield?'

Dr Goode shook her head. 'Still in surgery, I'm told. The bullet apparently nicked a lung, among other things.'

Pavlik grimaced, seeming to feel his deputy's pain. Or maybe some of his own.

The doctor noticed it, too. 'I can get you something. Now that the anesthesia is wearing off we want to keep ahead of the pain.'

Pavlik waved it off. 'I'm fine for now. When can I go home?'

'Not for a couple of days, at least,' the doc said, setting down the chart. 'After that, we like to get people out of the hospital as soon as possible, assuming there's somebody at home to care for them.'

'I can do that,' Tracey said. 'I'm a good nurse. And I can cook, too, right, Dad?'

'Best toaster pizzas in the land,' Pavlik said.

'I'm sure that's true, Trace,' Dr Goode said. 'But your dad is going to need somebody a little bigger to help him for a week or so. Otherwise we'll need to send him to Brookhills Manor.'

'Brookhills Manor?' Pavlik and I asked in unison.

'But that's for old people,' Tracey said. 'My great grandpa was there before . . .' She glanced over at her father.

'Before he died,' Pavlik continued. 'And that's not going to happen to me, sweetie. But you are right that Brookhills Manor is a senior facility.'

'With a new rehab wing,' the doctor corrected. 'It's not age-restricted and I know they have room.'

I could read the horror in Pavlik's face. It was bad enough to be shot and in the hospital with your fellow law enforcement officers waiting in the lobby. But having them visit you at the old folks' home?

And that's how Pavlik came to live with Frank and me.

EIGHT

'If the thought of Pavlik staying at your place weirds you out,' Sarah said back at Uncommon Grounds that afternoon, 'why'd you invite him?'

'I didn't say it weirded me out. It's just . . . well, it's a big step. And besides, I have one bed. Where should he sleep? With me? What if I roll over on him or something?'

'From what you told me, Pavlik's condition isn't that fragile. And it's not like you're some big lug like . . . Wait a second, are you worried about Frank?'

'Frank? I don't know what you mean.' I was running the cash register tape to get the day's totals so far.

'I mean that sheepdog that sleeps in your bed. Please don't tell me you're worried about kicking him out for Pavlik.'

'Don't be silly. Pavlik has slept over before.' I tore off the printed tape a little too aggressively, sending the remainder of the roll out of the register and across the room, unraveling as it went. 'Shit.'

'Easy, girl,' Sarah said, retrieving it.

'And, for the record, Frank sleeps on my bed, not in it.' I took the roll from her and rewound the paper on to it before slipping the roll back into the machine.

'Meaning he doesn't sleep under the sheet and blanket?' Sarah asked, watching me. 'Thank God. Though that's probably more a function of his needs than yours.'

I folded the printed tape in sections and paper-clipped it to our journal before turning. 'I heard the words but I have no idea what you just said.'

'I'm saying that Frank wears a fur coat so he's always warm. He's certainly not going to crawl under the covers with you. But I'm betting if he was hairless and came snuggling, you'd let him crawl between your sheets.'

I tried to imagine Frank as a hundred pounds of hairless. 'I'm pretty sure not.'

Sarah squinted, thinking about it. 'He would kind of look like a giant rat, wouldn't he?'

'Don't let him hear you say that.' But yeah. With longer legs. 'Back to Pavlik, though – I just can't imagine him rehabbing at Brookhills Manor next to Gloria Goddard.'

'And don't let Gloria hear you say *that.*' Sarah picked up a pot and poured the cold coffee in it down the drain.

'You know I love Gloria. But Pavlik would hate it. Besides, Tracey was looking at me like he was going to die if he went there.'

'Not your kid.' Sarah set the pot she'd just rinsed on the warmer before swiveling to face me with a wry grin on her face. 'At least, not yet.'

'If you want to know something that *does* weird me out, it's that Tracey thinks Pavlik and I are getting married. Why is that?'

'Because he told her, I assume.'

'Maybe he told her he was going to ask me.' I took the pot and gave it a thorough washing before placing it back on the warmer and pressing the brew button. 'I guess that makes sense. I mean, I'd probably run it by Eric before I asked somebody to marry me.'

'Yet you haven't told your son that Pavlik proposed.'

'Because I haven't answered.' I was already getting pressure enough from Sarah, thank you very much.

'And what about Pavlik moving in? Going to keep that a secret, too?'

'No.' At least, I thought I'd tell Eric. Assuming the subject came up before the week was over and the sheriff was back home. 'I wonder if Pavlik told Tracey he was going to ask me but didn't tell her I said no.'

'You haven't said no.' Sarah held up her index finger. 'You've said . . . maybe.' She let the finger go limp.

Enough.

Sarah must have read it on my face because she shifted gears. 'What happened to this Pauly guy? I wouldn't blame Pavlik's guys if they'd gunned him down on the spot.'

'Me neither. But Pauly Andersen escaped out of the window during the confusion that followed the shooting.'

'Are you telling me they weren't covering the back?'

'They were, but in the uproar . . .' I shrugged. 'We didn't get a chance to talk about it with Tracey there but I know Pavlik's not happy about it.' That was putting it mildly. And I wasn't happy about the guy that shot *my* guy still being out there somewhere.

'Oh!' I was waving my hand at Sarah like a kid waiting to be called on. 'Remember that gray-haired man who came out with the to-go cup when we were talking Sunday morning?'

'You mean the one you accused me of scaring away?' Sarah asked.

'That's the one. And now I wish you had. Pavlik says that's Pauly Andersen's brother, Jack – the one who lives at the manor. A detective followed him to our place and then back to his apartment, which they were already sitting on, of course.'

Sarah gave me the cop-speak eye-roll I deserved. 'The guy only bought one coffee, so his brother couldn't have been there yet.'

It seemed like a leap. After all, maybe Pauly Andersen didn't drink coffee. Or host Jack wasn't considerate enough to ask whether his brother wanted a cup when he picked one up for himself.

But as it turned out, Sarah was right. 'According to Hallonquist, Pauly didn't sneak in until the tour group came back from their trip to the Domes late afternoon. Though they think he was lurking in the woods before that.'

'What else do we know about the brothers grim?'

I tilted my head in appreciation. 'Brothers Grimm – good one.'

Sarah grinned. 'Thanks. I think it was the name Andersen that inspired it.'

Hans Christian Andersen. 'Did you know he wrote his own fairy tales while the Brothers Grimm were lawyers and academics who compiled folk tales and other people's writing? There's some thought that the Brothers' collection inspired Andersen. He never—'

The eye-roll was nothing compared to the disgusted look I was getting from Sarah. 'Are you done?'

Obviously not, since she'd cut me off mid-sentence. But I digressed. Mightily. 'Anyway, Pavlik said the two Andersen brothers couldn't be more different. Pauly, the younger, has a long rap sheet of mostly violent crimes. Jack is the smart one – a charming con man who has bilked people out of millions over the years, yet managed to stay out of jail until eight years ago.'

'Millions of dollars and he was in jail for less than eight years?'

'Good behavior, supposedly. Told you he was charming.'

Sarah shrugged. 'Could have fooled me. All I saw was an old guy with a pink face.'

'I'm trying to think if I've ever seen him in here before, maybe with the Goddard Gang?' Though why would I remember Jack Andersen any better than the rest of our customers?

'Not as far as I know.'

'So maybe it was just chance that he came here. Or maybe Jack left his apartment thinking the detectives would follow him and Pauly could sneak in unseen, but it didn't work.'

'And why not get a good cuppa joe while eluding the cops.'

'So the man is both charming *and* smart.'

'Talking about me again?'

Father Jim was on the other side of the service counter.

'No, but you are both of those things,' I told him.

'And sneaky,' Sarah added. 'It unnerves me when people just materialize in front of us like that.'

'It's my ninja stealth,' Jim said, striking a pose with hands held out flat. 'And the fact your chimes on the side door are gone.'

'What?' I circled out from behind the service counter and into the side hallway that led to the train platform and parking lot. 'Somebody stole our sleigh bells.'

'Maybe they thought they were helping us. You know, taking down the Christmas decorations.' Sarah had followed me. 'It is March, after all.'

'They're not Christmas decorations,' I told her for maybe the umpteenth time since I'd put them up on both doors. 'They're just bells.' That happened to be round. And tied with a red ribbon.

'And yet you insist on calling them sleigh bells,' Sarah said dryly.

'All I care about is that the sleigh bells ring—'

"'Are you listening?'" Jim's tenor rang out. "'In the—'"

I gave him a stern look. 'You're not helping, you know. You're supposed to be on my side.'

'Well, if you've got God on your side I'm out of here before I can be struck down.' Sarah was undoing her apron strings.

'You were leaving anyway. Your shift was over at three-thirty.'

'And I'm only a priest, not God,' Jim said. 'Though we *are* confused a lot.'

'It's the eyes.' She patted his check and handed him her apron.

'She's a trip,' Jim said to me as the now bell-less door closed behind Sarah.

'Yes, she is.' I took the apron from him. 'Can I get you a drink?'

'Not really. I've probably had enough caffeine today. Besides, I really stopped by to see if you are OK.'

'You heard about the shooting.' It wasn't a question, since everybody in Brookhills would know by now what had happened. 'And Pavlik.'

I heard my voice shake at the end and Jim must have, too, because he wrapped his arms around me. 'I'm sorry, sweetheart. Is there anything I can do?'

'No,' I said into his chest. Tears were suddenly streaming down my cheeks and I couldn't quite figure out why. 'I know Pavlik is going to be fine. I'm just being silly.'

'You're being human. It's only now hitting you that you might have lost him. Just thank God,' he let go of me to make the sign of the cross, 'you didn't.'

'Yes.' I dug into my apron pocket and came up with an Uncommon Grounds napkin to mop my face. 'Well, anyway, like I said,' a sniffle escaped, 'I saw Pavlik at the hospital and we should be able to bring him home in a couple of days.'

Jim didn't raise an eyebrow at the 'we,' meaning Frank and me. The priest knew the sheepdog and I were a couple and didn't judge. 'I'm glad to hear it. I stopped by his room at the hospital but the bed was empty.'

My heart gave a twist and I tamped it back down. What was with me all of a sudden?

Jim was watching me. 'I *meant* he was out of the room having tests. You sure you're OK?'

'Other than having watched too many bad movies with the "empty hospital bed means dead" cliché? Sure, I'm fine.' I made myself grin. 'Thanks for stopping by to see Pavlik. He's not even Catholic.'

'But he is a friend,' Jim said. 'Or at the very least, the friend of a friend. Besides, I was already there for Pete Hartsfield.'

Like Celeste and Nancy, I thought of last rites when a visit from a priest was mentioned. Talk about clichés. 'How is Pete doing?'

'Out of surgery but in the intensive care unit. Prayers are needed.'

'Done,' I said. 'You sure I can't get you a cup of coffee?'

'Thanks, but I need to go.' He checked his watch. 'I was due at the mortuary five minutes ago to discuss Celeste Bouchard's arrangements.'

'Has the day and time been set?' I asked.

'Not yet, but the cremation won't take place until tomorrow, so the funeral will probably be Thursday.' Jim was halfway out the door.

'But she was being cremated this morning. Or at least I thought that's what Christy said.'

'She must have confused the intake of the body with the actual cremation. That can't be done for forty-eight hours. Add that time to the actual procedure, cooling and packaging and—'

'Please.' I held up my hands palms out. 'I've heard enough from Christy on the subject to last me a lifetime.'

Or an afterlife-time.

NINE

I t had been a busy day, both death and injury-wise, and it wasn't over yet. The day itself, I mean. Hopefully the deaths and injuries were done, but one can never tell in Brookhills.

It was after nine when I got home, after stopping by the hospital to see Pavlik, who'd been downright ornery in comparison with earlier. I figured that was at least partially because whatever meds he'd been on after the surgery had worn off, only to be replaced by the regular painkillers. Which, of course, he'd delayed taking as long as possible, despite the doctor's advice to 'stay ahead of the pain.'

I also knew that he'd wanted to reassure Tracey after the shooting. With me, he could be himself. And growl. 'A prisoner escapes thanks to Taylor losing his gun? Another deputy is so rattled by the sound of gunfire and the call, "Officer down," that he deserts his post and lets Andersen get away for a second time? Talk about amateur time.'

'It's not like the Brookhills County Sheriff's Department has a lot of experience with shootings,' I said. 'Law enforcement here is different than in Chic—'

But Pavlik wasn't listening. He was too busy punching an email into his phone. 'This is my own damn fault, you know. I've been too easy on these guys.'

'What's going to happen to the brother – Jack Andersen?' I was trying to get him to focus on a subject that would require less self-flagellation than the second escape of Pauly.

'What's going to happen? Nothing. He claims he was a hostage and we can't prove otherwise. Another failure.'

Blessedly, visiting hours ended before he could take the blame for global warming and cancer.

'What do you think?' I asked Frank as he watched me pull the meat off a rotisserie chicken carcass I'd picked up at the grocery store. 'You OK with Pavlik coming to stay for a while?'

He growled and it took me a second to realize it was because I'd paused in dismantling the poor chicken and was waving a drumstick at him.

I dumped the chicken I'd pulled off into Frank's dish and added water and a scoop of dehydrated raw vegetable dog food that promised a well-balanced, holistic doggy diet. The stuff rehydrated into green goo and cost a fortune, but after both Frank and I had weighed in at a little over fighting weight at our respective doctors, I'd made a pact with myself that we'd eat better in the future.

I'd kept half the pact, at least.

Setting the dog's bowl on the floor, I poured myself a glass of red wine and pulled a sleeve of butter crackers and can of spray cheese out of the cupboard. The meal hit the major food groups, or would have if I'd added the vegetable sludge. Not an option, given the cost of the sludge.

Frank glanced up from his dish, wearing a green vegetable beard and a disgusted look.

'You win,' I said, setting down my meal. 'Pizza it is.'

'Since when do you go to funerals?' I asked Sarah the next morning.

We were sitting at a table in our own coffeehouse, enjoying lattes and sticky buns after the morning commuter rush.

'When it comes to the "Holy Hannah's Ladies of Ronny House," I'll make an exception.'

'Just what is your deal?' I took a sip of my latte.

'What deal?'

'I mean, why don't you like Hannah? She's a perfectly nice person.'

'Something's just . . . off.' Sarah pointed. 'You've got foam on your lip.'

I licked it off, lest it be wasted. 'Somehow I have a feeling the "something off" you're referring to is not my foam mustache.'

'Good call. I'm talking about little miss perfect.' She stuck a leftover pecan from the long-ago devoured sticky bun into her mouth.

'Hannah, because she took in her mother and her mother's friend?'

'"As anybody of good conscience would do."'

It took me a second to realize she was mimicking Hannah. 'Are you going to say nasty things about me, too, when Pavlik comes to stay?'

'I already say nasty things about you.'

It was true. Not that she meant them. Or so I thought.

'Besides,' Sarah continued, 'I know you're going to be busting your butt, working and playing nurse to Pavlik.' A sly grin. 'Though that doesn't sound half bad, come to think of it.'

I ignored her fantasy. 'I was thinking I might take a few days off.'

'Yeah, well, think again. But you're making my point. Exactly how has the lovely Hannah made a living while she was caring for the oldsters in the house Celeste bought?'

I shrugged. 'How do I know? Maybe Hannah works from home. Or has family money or something.'

'I think that's probably just it. She's living off her mother. But here's another thing. Why didn't Hannah have the power of attorney?'

Now she'd completely lost me. 'What do you mean?'

'This is what got me thinking,' Sarah said. 'Remember Christy telling us about the closing on the house?'

'What about it?'

'The way it works is if you can't be present at a closing, the papers can be overnighted to you to sign. Or you can give your power of attorney to somebody else and have them sign in your stead.'

'Which is exactly what Celeste did, according to Christy.'

'But to a lawyer, not her daughter. Don't you think that's strange?'

'What I think is that you're ornery that Christy sold your cousin's house on her own rather than have you broker the deal.'

'Ronny is *not* my cousin.' Sarah jabbed her finger a tad too vigorously at an errant flake of bun on the table, sending it off onto the floor.

'OK, your criminal cousin by marriage.' I retrieved the crumb with a napkin as the bells on the front door jangled.

I jumped up. Nobody likes to see their servers having more fun than they are.

'Sit, sit,' Langdon Shepherd admonished, his hand gesture identical to the one that signaled people to take their seats in the pews. It was customary in most churches for the congregation to sit for the sermon. But at Christ Christian it was also self-preservation. Langdon's record was an hour and four minutes.

'How is your sheriff doing?' he asked, leaning down to give me a one-armed hug.

'I saw Pavlik last night and he's good, thank you,' I said, wincing as he squeezed. The man was all bones. 'Fixated on work, of course.'

Which was true, as far as it went. It also reminded me that I'd better check my Internet provider to make sure I had enough bandwidth to handle Pavlik's phone, tablet and computer. All up and running simultaneously, even when Pavlik couldn't be up *or* running.

'And the other officer? Deputy Hartsfield?'

'No update last night. But Pete was in intensive care yesterday, according to Father Jim.'

'Oh, is the father here?' Langdon asked, glancing around like he expected Jim to pop out from under one of the empty tables. 'I wanted to share some ideas for a joint Easter celebration we've been discussing.'

'Just missed him by eighteen hours,' Sarah said, getting up to gather our plates and cups.

'Jim was in yesterday afternoon,' I explained, standing myself. 'You'll probably find him at the church, though.'

'I'll have to stop by. Easter will be here before we know it and we'll need to get the word out if we're going to do something. You know, social media, advertising, press releases.'

I did know, given I'd done corporate public relations prior to opening Uncommon Grounds. I was just surprised that Langdon was embracing marketing. Traditionally, his approach was more . . . traditional. Like church bulletins.

'I can't remember the two churches ever doing something together,' I said.

'An entirely new endeavor,' the pastor said as I ducked behind the counter to make his cappuccino. 'Despite our differences in doctrine we are united in the need to bring people into church.'

I reemerged at the ordering window. 'I thought Christmas and Easter were the two holidays people did come to church. Why do a joint service then? Won't you be taking away from your own attendances?'

'Oh, this wouldn't be on Easter Sunday itself. More of a festival on that Saturday, with the children.'

'Like an Easter egg hunt?'

'Exactly.'

Didn't sound like all that novel an idea, but maybe the real collaboration was not so much between the two churches as it was the Easter bunny and Jesus.

'Christmas, Easter, marry and bury, my father used to say,' Langdon went on, smiling a little painfully.

'Oh, was your father a pastor, too?' I picked up the portafilter and slipped it under the espresso grinder/dispenser, only to realize the bean hopper above it was empty.

'More agnostic, I'm afraid, laying out his parameters. My mother had to twist his arm to get him to attend church even for those milestones.'

Looking at Langdon, you'd imagine he came from a family with its roots in the bedrock of the church. 'Was it your mother who inspired you to become a pastor?'

Langdon smiled. 'Honestly, I think it was more my father's resistance than anything else. I was quite the contrary young man.'

Sarah appeared with a bag of espresso beans from the storeroom. 'That's hard to imagine.'

'That I was a young man or that I was contrary?' Langdon knew Sarah too well.

'Both.' Sarah grinned and dropped the five-pound bag of roasted beans on the counter.

'Did your dad ever forgive you for being holier than he?'

'I'm afraid not, though he did come to hear my first homily.' Langdon barely averted a roll of his eyes – an implied judgment I was sure he'd normally be loath to make.

'That was good, at least,' I said, using scissors to slice the bag so I could pour the beans into the hopper.

'I'll let you be the judge. He dropped a dime in the collection plate as it went around.' He held up his hands. 'Not that I'm saying God requires payment.'

'But . . .' Sarah was leading the witness.

Langdon allowed himself to look perturbed. 'My father was well enough off. To my mind, it was an insult. Like dining at a restaurant and leaving a penny as the tip for the waiter. It's worse than no tip at all.'

'And you were the waiter,' I said.

A wave of Langdon's hand said it was no matter. His face said otherwise. 'That's all in the past. But the fact is churches are in difficult straits because of people like my father, who partake but don't pay.'

'To be fair, your father didn't want to partake either,' Sarah pointed out. 'Or order, if you want to keep the dinner analogy going.'

Like Langdon, I thought maybe it was time to let this go. 'Is Christ Christian struggling financially?' I asked as I switched on the grinder.

'Most churches are,' Langdon said, not quite answering the question. 'Even at Angel of Mercy, which traditionally has done quite well, Father Jim says they're struggling.'

Since Jim was new to the church, that worried me. And mystified me as well. I'd go to Angel of Mercy to hear Jim if I didn't have to work Sundays, and I wasn't even Catholic. I couldn't say all that to Langdon, of course, so I said, 'Why do you think that is?'

'I honestly don't know,' Langdon said. 'Father Jim is a gifted speaker and has brought young people into the church. Actual attendance is on the upswing but collections remain stagnant. The key, we both feel, is to get people involved so they join the congregation and have a stake in its future.'

'So why Easter?' I asked, switching off the grinder and going to pull the shot. 'Like you said, that's one of the times the churches are full. Why not concentrate on increasing attendance during the downtimes?'

'Easter celebrations bring in young families, which is important for growing our membership basis. If we get them in for an Easter or Christmas event, maybe we can keep them coming.'

'And paying,' Sarah said, and then listened. 'Is that your phone I hear vibrating?'

The irony of 'hearing' vibration. But I heard it, too. I fished my phone out of my apron pocket, but the vibrating had stopped and it read 'missed call.'

'Good morning,' Clare Twohig called out.

The owner of Clare's Antiques was small – maybe five feet tall, with blonde hair cut short – but you couldn't miss her melodic voice or the vintage pieces she wove into her otherwise modern style.

She was also a 'double latte, skim milk, no foam', which she picked up on the way to the antiques shop every morning at about a quarter to ten.

Exactly what it was now.

I slipped my phone back into my apron and started Langdon's milk frothing. 'Morning, Clare. Can I get you your usual?'

'Please.' Today Clare was wearing a pillbox hat with jeans and a military-style blouse.

'I don't know how you do it,' I said, finishing up Langdon's cappuccino.

'Do what?' Clare was glancing around like she didn't know what I was talking about.

Which she didn't, of course, because for her the look was effortless. Me, I was lucky if I was wearing two of the same shoes. 'How you put together outfits like that.'

Sarah was passing behind me and backtracked so she could get a better look at Clare. 'Nice outfit.'

Not snide. Not sarcastic. A genuine compliment.

'Oh, this? It's nothing.' Clare tried to pirouette but fell out of it, giggling.

'It is very fetching, my dear,' Langdon said, taking the cappuccino and passing a five to me.

'Why thank you, Langdon,' Clare said. 'I thought since the pillbox hat that was so popular for women in the forties is believed to be inspired by military headgear, it would be kind of fun.'

'Well, I'm sure you wear the *chapeau* more beautifully than any soldier could have.' With that, Langdon bowed out. Literally.

'Did you all see somebody is moving into the building across the street from me?' Clare asked as she set her wallet on the counter.

'That's where Penn and Ink, the graphic design firm was,' I said, pulling a gallon of skim milk out of the refrigerator.

'Penn dumped Ink,' Sarah informed Clare. 'It got messy.'

Clare laughed. 'I bet. Any idea what kind of business is moving in?'

'No clue,' Sarah said, 'but customers have been complaining about the trucks blocking the street in that direction.'

Clare's nose crinkled. 'It's just the one lane, leaving plenty of room for cars to get around.'

'You're not from here, are you?' Sarah asked.

'No, Minneapolis. Why?'

'In most cities,' Sarah was saying, 'a double-parked truck is business as usual. In Brookhills, it's a reason to call the cops.'

Clare grinned. 'I do get a kick out of the police report in the *Observer*. Did you see the one last week where somebody reported they were sure they'd left their car windows down but, when they returned, they were up?'

'That was good,' I agreed, 'but my all-time favorite one was the guy who is allergic to poppy seeds calling the police because his wife bought three-seed bagels and he decided she was trying to kill him.'

'Ooh, that must have been before I moved here.' Clare's blue eyes sparkled. 'And I love the way they're reported. In a kind of "just the facts, ma'am" way.'

'That's the work of one of my original partners in Uncommon Grounds.' I poured milk into the frothing pitcher. 'Caron Egan. You might have seen her byline.'

'Caron Egan, of course,' Clare repeated. 'She wrote the article on the mortician, too.'

'Christy mentioned the article but I didn't realize Caron wrote it.'

'Front page this past Thursday. Either your friend Caron is a gifted writer or Mort the Mortician is fascinating.' Clare's eyes were bright as she leaned in to ask, 'Have you met him?'

'Sure.' I stuck the frothing wand into the milk and turned on the steam, moving the pitcher up and down to introduce air and get the froth the way I wanted it. 'He's part of the Goddard Gang that's here every Sunday morning.'

'Really.' She was thinking. 'I should come by to meet him.'

'You could go by the funeral home if you're really dying . . .' I stopped frothing. 'Sorry. Is this professional or personal?'

'You mean am I looking to date a mortician or hire one?' she asked with a smile. 'Neither. But what Caron called Mort's "thinking outside the box – or urn" in the article intrigued me. He believes both a funeral and a final resting place should make a statement about what was important in the deceased's life. Ashes sent up in fireworks' shells or stored in the departed's favorite brand of bourbon bottle. Rock and roll celebrations of life.'

'How about *Weekend at Bernie's*?' Sarah suggested. 'Now there's one I'd go to.'

'That's what I thought, too,' Clare said. 'Reading how creative Mort is, I thought my shop might have some . . . containers that might be perfect.'

'Have to be one big-ass antique to fit a body,' Sarah said. 'Steamer trunk, maybe?'

Clare was peering into the bakery case. 'Is that a sticky bun behind the muffins?'

'The last one.' I set the milk aside to rest. 'We had a run on them this morning.' And Sarah and I had eaten two.

'I was half hoping you'd be out of them,' Clare said ruefully. 'Save me from myself.'

'Better that you take it now than I take it home.' I picked up a pair of tongs.

'Says you. Anyway,' she continued, 'I have several items that would work for ashes. For example, a guitar for the rock and roll funeral. Or that vintage coffee urn you've been eyeing, Maggy, for the coffee lover.'

I stopped, tonged bun in hand. 'I said I liked it, not that I wanted to spend eternity in it.'

Clare chin-gestured for me to continue the roll's journey. 'But it is an interesting alternative to spending eternity in a plastic bag fastened with a twist tie, isn't it?'

It was indeed.

TEN

'Plastic bag and a twist tie? Really?' Sarah said as I slipped Clare's roll into a white paper bag, trying not to dislodge the pecans on top of it.

'Damn it!' A nut went flying.

'That's the way it's done, according to the article,' Clare's voice said as I ducked behind the counter to retrieve the pecan before it cemented to the floor or the bottom of somebody's shoe. 'A sturdy plastic bag, no doubt, and an industrial-strength twist tie.'

'That way the dead guy can't make a run for it.' Still bent,

I tossed the pecan into the trash basket and missed. 'And stays fresh, in the bargain.'

Resurfacing, I saw Mort Ashbury.

He was grinning. A curse on whoever stole my bells/early-warning system.

'Mort,' I said, 'we were just talking about you. Well, not you, but your—'

'Stay-fresh containers, I heard. And what could be better on a Tuesday morning than being the topic of discussion for three lovely women.' The smile stayed on his face as he turned to Clare. 'Morton Ashbury, at your service.'

Given the wink that accompanied his words – as well as what the mortician's 'service' was – I had to believe that Ashbury was in on the joke, even if his new loyal follower, Christy, wasn't.

Whether the name had spurred his decision to dedicate his life to burying and cremating people or the choice had been a pure coincidence, Morton Ashbury had decided to embrace it with a certain *joie de vivre*. Which Ashbury would no doubt term *joie de mort*.

The thought made me smile right back. 'Clare owns the antiques and flower shop next door. We were talking about the article on you in the *Observer*, and I was just saying that her shop might be the perfect place for people to find just the right . . . vessel for their loved ones.'

Of course, it had been the other way around – Clare had made the suggestion, not me – but I'd always found it more effective to have somebody else blowing your horn than to do it yourself. And you can take that any way you wish.

As for Clare, she threw me a grateful look before offering her hand to Mort. 'Clare Twohig. I must say that I'm fascinated by your idea of celebrating life, not mourning death.'

'I don't claim that it's a new thought,' Mort said. 'So-called celebrations of life are a dime a dozen in the funeral industry. The video presentations of a life well-lived, etc., etc. We try to go beyond that and – for cremations, at least – have the departed in a lasting reminder of that life. Now this shop of yours—'

A cell phone interrupted. Since I recognized the opening strains of 'Always Look on the Bright Side of Life,' I assumed it was Mort's.

As he went to answer it, Sarah said, 'I find myself disappointed his ring isn't "Another one Bites the Dust." You?'

'A little,' I admitted. 'But the man can't afford to be too obvious. He has a business to run.'

'It might come off as heartless.'

'You think?'

On the other side of the counter, Clare was looking on as Mort spoke into the phone. 'I'm so sorry. What a terrible waste. Yes, I'm sure there'll have to be autopsies, under the circumstances. I—' He listened some more. 'Yes, right now.'

My heart was thudding as he went to slip his phone in his pocket. Reaching across the counter, I stopped him. 'Autopsies, plural?'

Pete Hartsfield was in a critical condition. But a second? Could Pavlik's condition have deteriorated during night?

There was a missed call on the cell phone in my apron pocket. The hospital? Or Hallonquist with even worse news than he'd already given me? I knew I should pull out my own phone and see, but I was afraid.

Mort seemed agitated by his call, especially for somebody who dealt with death on an everyday basis. 'I'm sorry, but Peter Hartsfield has died. And this morning—'

My fingers tightened on his. Inside I was screaming, but I could barely whisper, 'Pavlik?'

I felt Sarah's hand on my shoulder as Mort's expression changed. 'Pavlik? Oh, no. I'm so sorry if I gave you that impression. The second deceased is not the sheriff.'

'Oh, thank God.' The relief that swept over me made me lightheaded as I let Mort's hand go. Sarah's hand back-stopped me.

I took a deep breath. 'I'm sorry. That was unkind of me, given Pete's death. And another family lost someone, too.'

Mort shook his head. 'I think you can be excused, under the circumstances.'

'Can we get you something to take with you, Mort?' Sarah asked.

'Thank you,' he said. 'Maybe just a black coffee?'

Sarah poured our brew of the day into a cup and fit the top on it.

As Mort fumbled for his wallet, I said, 'On us, please. You

go do what you have to do.' 'Cause you couldn't pay me enough
to do it. Be with people at the worst times in their lives? Over
and over again.

As Clare followed Mort out the door, I turned to Sarah.
'Thank you.'

'What for?' She was wiping the counter.

'You know what. Having my back again, literally. I thought
I was going to pass out.'

She turned, dishrag in hand. 'Doesn't that tell you
something?'

'That you're a good friend?'

'And you're an idiot. I mean doesn't that tell you something
about how you feel about Pavlik? Your world ended when you
thought he'd died. I saw it in your eyes.'

'You couldn't see my eyes.'

Sarah's own warning glance was enough.

'OK, you're right. I . . . Well, I couldn't breathe. Couldn't
even bring myself to look at my phone because I was afraid
that call I'd missed was . . .' I let it go at that.

'So, tell him.' Sarah tossed the rag into the sink. 'Or I will.'

'Duly noted.' I stepped out onto the porch and punched up
the missed call. It was from Pavlik. In fact, there were three
from him, all seemingly in quick succession.

'I heard about Pete,' I said when he answered. 'I'm so sorry.'

There were voices behind him in the room. 'Hang on a
second.'

Then, 'I wanted to get into the corridor.'

'Are you OK?' I asked. 'When Mort said there had been
two deaths, I was so afraid—'

'Mort?'

'Mort Ashbury, the mortician. He was here at the coffeehouse
when he got the call about Pete and somebody else. I was afraid
. . .' I was afraid to put what I'd thought into words.

'That it was me? No, I'm fine.' Pavlik's voice was flat. He'd
lost a man, and there was no getting past that.

'Then who was the other—' I had a thought. 'Did you
find Pauly Andersen?' Not that I necessarily wanted the
escapee dead, especially if it had been in a shoot-out with
law enforcement. But if somebody had to die, Pauly was

definitely the lesser of two evils. Or maybe, in this case, the greater.

'No, but we found a stolen car abandoned at the bus station in Milwaukee.'

'You think it's Pauly's?'

'We're working with the Milwaukee County Sheriff's Department to see if we can track him from there, but the timing works. The car was reported stolen from Brookhills Manor on Monday—'

I interrupted. 'Nobody was hurt when it was taken?'

'No, it was stolen from the back parking lot and turned up at the bus station fifteen miles away.'

'Then that's how Pauly got away.'

'It seems likely that it was during the confusion of the shooting.' Shot or not, Pavlik still wasn't happy about confusion on his watch.

'So if the second death wasn't Andersen,' I said, 'then it must be unrelated.'

'No.'

'No?' I think I looked at the phone.

'They took Pete Hartsfield off life support at eight forty-three this morning.'

'I know. And it's awful, but you did everything you could for—'

'At nine-oh-three, Al Taylor shot himself in the head.'

ELEVEN

'One way or another, I'm bringing him home tonight,' I told Sarah, who'd come out to sit with me on the porch as we waited for the last commuter train to arrive from Milwaukee so we could close.

I'd been to visit Pavlik and then come back to help Sarah. 'He needs to be away from that hospital and the media and even his own deputies. He's just so sad. It's all just so . . . sad.'

'Taylor blamed himself for Hartsfield's death?'

I nodded. 'I know Hallonquist was worried about him. First, his gun is stolen by a convict. A humiliation. Then not only does the guy escape but he uses the gun to shoot two of your fellow officers.'

'And one dies.' She sneezed. 'Sorry, I think I must be coming down with what that Nancy woman has.'

'Bless you.' I rubbed my face. 'Pete Hartsfield has a wife and brand-new baby girl. Apparently Taylor left a note and one of those Internet wills bequeathing everything to Hartsfield's family.'

'Hope it stands up in court.'

'I hope so, too, but I doubt that's anybody's priority right now. Pete Hartsfield is dead. Al Taylor is dead.'

'And Taylor wanted to make amends as best he could. You don't have to give me that "how can you be so insensitive" look.'

'And I'm not. OK, maybe I was, but this is such a tragedy all around.'

'And Pavlik feels responsible?'

'Of course.' I ran my finger along a line in the table. 'His department. His officers. His responsibility.'

Sarah pushed out her chair and stood up. 'I'll close for you. Go break your man out of the hospital.'

As it turned out, it was easier said than done.

By the time I got there, there was no doctor on duty to sign Pavlik out.

'I'm sorry,' the petite nurse on duty said, 'but Doctor Goode won't be in until rounds tomorrow morning. I'll be happy to ask her to stop by first thing, though.'

'Fine, but I won't be here,' Pavlik said flatly.

Once I'd floated the idea of bringing him home, he was totally on board. So much so that, under the circumstances, I wished I'd spoken to the doc first.

On the other hand, his eyes were verging toward blue again rather than the stormy gray they turned when he was upset. And I wanted to keep them that way.

'Couldn't you just call Doctor Goode?' I asked. 'Maybe she could just run by.'

'Out of town.'

'Well, what about the surgeon then? What was his name?'

'Doctor Warren's daughter is having a first birthday party tonight. You wouldn't want me to interrupt that, would you?'

The one-year-old probably wouldn't notice.

Pavlik was pulling on jeans. 'There must be an ER doc on. Maybe he or she would be willing to sign the release.'

'I don't know,' the nurse said. 'They've been awfully busy down there today.'

Pavlik was buttoning his shirt.

'Why don't we give it a try,' I suggested to the nurse.

In the end, we all came to an agreement. We got hold of Dr Goode, who agreed to call the ER doc, who agreed Pavlik probably wouldn't bleed out if he left. Pavlik agreed he'd sign a waiver just in case he did, and Frank and I agreed that peperoni pizza two nights in a row wouldn't kill us.

We were sitting in the bedroom, Pavlik propped up in my bed, a plate with a slice of pizza on his lap. Frank was on the floor, chewing. I was sitting next to Pavlik, cross-legged, doing likewise.

And sipping red wine. It had been quite a day.

'Thanks for getting me out of there,' he said.

'My pleasure. You're going to have to break it to Frank, though, that he needs to split his pizza with both of us for a while.'

'He'll be OK with that,' Pavlik said. 'We're buds, right, Frank?'

The sheepdog grunted and went back to chewing.

'See? You're not company anymore so you don't get the royal treatment.' I rubbed his right shoulder. The position of the bullet wound and resulting broken rib made doing anything with his left arm difficult and painful. The rib was wrapped and the wound was bandaged, but I was still worried that either Frank or I would jostle him during the night.

'You have to promise me you'll take it easy. I'm going to have to run into work tomorrow for a while and I don't want to find you on the floor "bleeding out" as that doctor so charmingly put it.'

'I'll make sure that if I do bleed out, I do it in the bed.' He put his good arm around me and kissed the top of my head. 'Easier to clean up.'

'But not so good for the bed. I'll go by your place and pack some things. Any special requests?'

His eyes danced. 'Yes, but I think that would make me bleed out.'

'I meant so you won't have to wear Eric's clothes.'

'What? You think they don't look good on me? He held out his arms so I could see the skin-tight Gap T-shirt in all its glory.

'It looks excellent on you,' I said. 'But he's going to kill both of us if you stretch out his clothes.'

'Fine. Just bring me some jeans and a couple of dress shirts and T-shirts. You know the drill. Oh, and a toothbrush and razor. Shorts.'

'I should probably stop at the grocery store, too. As you've no doubt noticed, I don't keep much food here.'

'Pretty much nothing that doesn't have caffeine, cheese or fermented grape juice in it. Unless it's for Frank.'

'I know I spoil him,' I said, snuggling back in. 'But he completes me.'

'And what about me?'

I froze, then felt myself relax. 'You complete me, too.'

TWELVE

'I'm so sorry,' Amy said the next morning.

'I know,' I said, pouring cream from the quart carton into our server. 'I have to say, she seemed fine yesterday, except for her attitude, of course.'

'And now she's gone.'

I nodded. 'It's for the best. Put an end to the suffering.'

Amy cocked her head. 'Hers?'

'Hell, no, mine. And yours. And anybody else who's around Sarah when she's not feeling well.'

My partner's sneeze of yesterday had turned into a scratchy throat and sniffles. In her mind, that meant she was getting sick. In my mind, it meant I was getting a week of grumpy partner, followed by a week of being sick myself. Not to mention all the customers we'd potentially infect, as well as my new house-mate. Pavlik didn't need to add that particular insult on his immune system to his current injury.

'I couldn't take it any longer and told her she should go home,' I continued. 'Thanks for coming in on such short notice.'

'I got the impression that you'd have gone it alone if I hadn't.' Amy screwed the top onto the cream pitcher and walked it over to the condiment cart.

'The sniffling was getting on my last nerve. And, every once in a while, she'd make this little whimpering noise.' I shuddered.

'Maybe she wanted you to send her home,' Amy said, circling back behind the counter.

'Believe me, I tried. Over and over again. Begged her for the sake of me and everybody else she was going to infect.'

'She hates being around people who are sick herself.'

Sarah routinely disappeared into the back to leave one of us to serve anybody visibly ill – or what she referred to as 'Patient Zero.' 'Yet she's happy to expose us when she's sick. The paradox that is Sarah.'

'She knows you have Pavlik to think about.'

'I did run out and take him lunch before you came. He and Frank were happily ensconced watching TV.' In fact, I'd been amazed at how relaxed Pavlik had been. And not a computer, notebook or phone in sight.

'Well, that's good. I'm sure Sarah didn't want to leave you in the lurch.'

Or herself without a sympathetic audience. On Amy's arrival, my partner had gone into the office, presumably to get her coat and go home. But now . . . 'Was that a whimper?'

Amy lowered her voice to match mine. 'A whimper?'

'From the office.' I stuck my head around the corner. 'Damn. The door is closed. She must still be in there.'

Amy's lips twisted in a smile. 'What are you going to do?'

'Nothing. Apparently containment is all we can hope for.'

'Well, you fought the good fight.' Her expression changed. 'I haven't seen you since Sunday, but I wanted to tell you how sorry I am about the sheriff and especially the two deputies who died. What an awful thing.'

'It's been a tough few days. Did you hear that Hannah's mother died, too? Last Sunday morning, when we were all here.'

'Christy told me when she was in. She says the mother's friend – Nancy, I think? – is not in good shape. Nearly beside herself with grief.'

'I guess they were very close,' I said. 'And had been for years.'

'"Two peas in a pod" – isn't that a great old-timey expression? Christy is just so cool and retro.'

In my mind, coolly retro and frozen in time were two different things. But who was I to judge? I was usually so late hopping on the bandwagon that I most often ended up chasing it. You've heard about Christy's new job?'

'At the mortuary?' Amy's eyes were big. 'Yes. Who knew she was such a . . .'

'Freak?' I said. Then added hastily when Amy's eyes widened, 'I mean that only in the nicest way.'

'Oh, I know,' Amy said, waving it off. 'Christy has a different way of going about things but she's very kind – have you noticed? Look at everything she's done for Sarah's cousin, his being in jail and all.'

'I think she's in love with him.' I got that icky feeling in my stomach at the thought.

'True, though I think that kind of developed, don't you?' Amy leaned on the counter. 'She started to visit him out of kindness and a need to do good and then fell in love. In a way, working at the funeral home is also providing a service to people in need.'

'Since the next step in her career path is sweeping out the cremators,' I said, 'let's hope she doesn't fall in love with somebody there.'

Amy stood up straight. 'Maggy, that's awful.'

'I know, but with Sarah in the office it seems up to me to make the inappropriate jokes.'

Amy cocked her head. 'Maybe next time it'd be better to just skip it.'

I'd take that under consideration. 'Well, anyway, I like Christy and I hope her new job makes her happy.'

As I said it, I spied Mort Ashbury taking the front porch steps to the door. He pulled open the door and let Hannah

Bouchard enter ahead of him. It was obvious she'd been crying.

As Amy turned to greet them, I heard the office door creak open and saw Sarah tiptoe out. Snagging a coffee mug from the counter, she filled it with hot water from the spigot on the brewer and snagged a salt shaker, all without acknowledging me. Then she disappeared again.

With a mental shrug, I poured milk into a pitcher to froth for Hannah's latte. Since Amy was handling the front of the house, it was the least I could do. 'I'll get your latte started, Hannah. And what about you, Mort?'

'. . . So sorry for your loss,' our barista was saying to Hannah.

'Double espresso,' Mort said, approaching the window. 'It's going to be a long day.'

It sure was. 'Three deaths in as many days. Unusual for a place the size of Brookhills.'

'Unprecedented in my memory.' Mort was rubbing his forehead. 'I'm sorry to have given you such a shock yesterday.'

'Detective Taylor and Deputy Hartsfield's deaths were a shock for everybody,' I said.

'Both relatively young and with full lives in front of them,' the mortician said.

'How do you do it?' I asked curiously.

'Do what?'

'How do you deal with death and grieving all day, every day? Psychologically, I mean.'

'In a way, living your own life is easier when you accept that death is the default position.'

I stopped mid-pour. 'What do you mean?'

He lifted his shoulders and let them drop. 'Just that death – ashes to ashes, dust to dust – it's what we all revert to. Nobody is immune.'

A sneeze from in the back.

I continued pouring as I thought about it. 'You're saying that *living* is the anomaly?'

'Exactly,' Mort said, nodding. 'We need to hang onto life with all we can, while we can. Because when we let go – whether it's because we're sick or hurt, tired or it's just time, we . . .'

I set down the pitcher. 'Revert to the "default."'

'Exactly, I—'

'We should take our drinks to go,' Hannah cut in. 'We told – what's her name, Mort?'

He turned. 'Clare Twohig.'

'Yes, we told Clare we'd be at her shop at ten and we're already late.'

I stuck my head out of the service window and looked up at the three oversized clocks above what had been the depot's ticket windows. Eight-ten, ten-ten and six-thirty – the first clock being Pacific Time, the second our Central time zone and the third – which was supposed to be Eastern – stopped, both hour and minute hands dangling at six. 'Clare usually comes by to pick up a latte on her way in just before ten but she hasn't been here today. Maybe she's running late as well.'

'Or she passed up *her* coffee to be there on time and here we are—'

'You *need* your coffee,' Mort said testily. 'As do I.'

'I'm sure Clare won't mind,' I said, pouring Mort's shots into a to-go cup and starting two more. 'In fact, if you'll wait a few seconds, I'll give you her drink to take to her.'

'Of course, happy to,' Mort said. 'Hannah is having a little trouble deciding where Celeste's ashes should be kept, and I thought Clare's shop might give us some ideas.'

'Is someone staying with Nancy?' Amy asked, and then blushed. 'I'm sorry. That's none of my business.'

'No, it's fine,' Hannah said, taking a tissue out of her bag. 'Doctor Goode gave her something to sleep.' She blew her nose.

Amy put her hand on the other woman's shoulder. 'The reason I ask is because Christy told me that Nancy is taking your mother's death very hard. If there's anything I can do, sit with her or whatever, please let me know.'

Amy really was too good for us, in so many ways. Kind and giving, with a love for the environment and an eye for marketing, she inspired Sarah and me to be better people.

So far we were fighting it, but maybe there was still hope.

'. . . Kind of you,' Hannah was saying, pushing an errant lock of hair out of her face. 'But I think we're fine. I tried to get her to come with us today to pick out the urn but she doesn't want to leave the house or even see anyone other than me.'

'She barely tolerates me.' Mort's smile was back. 'But I did think it important that Hannah get out and I thought she'd enjoy meeting Clare.'

'Clare's great,' I said, pressing the covers onto three to-go cups. 'Do you two think you can handle these or do you want—'

The sound of something akin to a cat choking on a hair ball interrupted me. Sarah in the office . . . gargling with saltwater?

I continued, 'A drink tray to—'

She hawked up something.

'Tell you what,' I said, untying my apron. 'Why don't I walk over there with you?'

THIRTEEN

C lare was grateful for the latte, though I had to admit bringing it personally was a poor excuse for escaping Sarah. And leaving Amy alone with her and her phlegm. Fact was, though, that our barista was far better – and infinitely more patient – at soothing the savage beast that could be Sarah than I was. I was hoping she'd soothe her right out of the door and home by the time I got back.

Clare showed Hannah around, stopping at the coffee and tea servers on the stairs. The shop smelled of lavender sachets and early-blooming fresh lilacs from the floral corner. The antiques themselves added a bit of a must and mildew, partly diminished by the fresh air wafting in from the front door, which Nancy had propped open with an antique flat iron – the kind heated on the stove and used to press clothes. Or so I heard tell. Ironing clothes, even in the age of electric irons, was not my thing.

The display of urns was as lovely as I remembered it, but I noticed for the first time that there was a velvet rope across the top of the staircase. Storage for the store, most likely, or maybe Clare had a private office or living space on the second floor.

'This is beautiful,' Mort said, pointing at an ornate two-handled urn set on a pedestal with four tiny ball-and-claw feet.

Clare smiled. 'You have a good eye. That samovar dates back to the seventeen hundreds.'

The urn, embellished with carved silver garlands of leaves and flowers, was a little gaudy for my taste. 'Is that a coat of arms?'

'Yes,' Clare said, lifting the thing. 'And there's a viscount's coronet here, too. Isn't it gorgeous?'

'It's the perfect size,' Mort said, taking it from her. 'Was your mother a tea-drinker, Hannah?'

'No – coffee-drinkers, both she and Nancy. They could go through pots in a day.' She was misting up.

Mort was admiring his find. 'I may get it anyway. It truly is the perfect vessel.'

It did look like something you'd put ashes in. Or maybe a genie. There was even a spigot for him or her to materialize from.

Hannah had moved on to the other side of the stairs. 'My grandmother had one just like this.' She indicated an engraved silver pot with handles and a spout.

'Another beautiful piece,' the shop owner said, picking it up to show her. 'Victorian.'

'Do you think Celeste would like that?' Mort asked, setting down the samovar to join Hannah.

Tears in her eyes, Hannah glanced at him and then down. 'I think she would.'

'Good,' Mort said. 'Then we'll take both of these.'

He lifted the samovar again and waved Clare and the coffee urn over to the cash register. 'Let's tally this up, and then can I get your business card? I'd like to put you on our list of recommended merchants.'

'Of course,' Clare said, picking one up from a porcelain dish on the counter. 'In addition to our antiques, we provide flowers for all types of . . .'

As the two talked, I focused on Hannah, who was still standing by the urns. 'How are you doing?'

She looked up like she'd forgotten I was there. 'Me? Sad. I feel like I'm losing both of them.' She reddened. 'First Mother and now Nancy to this sudden ennui. She's moody and angry, forgets things and seems to go in and out of focus. It reminds me of my mother sometimes, but not quite.'

'Triggered by Celeste's death, do you think?'

'That's all I can figure. It's like a switch has turned off in her.'

'Has Nancy been seen by a doctor?'

Her eyes flicked in my direction and then back. 'Not besides Doctor Goode, who Mort asked to give her something so she could sleep.'

'Professional courtesy,' Mort said, joining us.

A wan smile from Hannah. 'Neither Mother nor Nancy liked doctors. And hospitals are where people go to die. I guess I got some of that attitude from them. If Nancy doesn't want to see a doctor, I won't force her.'

'Even if she's not herself?' Mort asked. 'From what I've seen, she really is incapable of making those decisions at this point.'

'The dislike of doctors predates all this.' Clare's fists clenched at her sides. 'She – my mother, I mean – died peacefully at home. I'm grateful for that.'

'As am I,' Mort said with a little bow and checked his watch. 'Nearly eleven, my dear. You need to be at the attorney's office in twenty minutes and I need to get back to the mortuary with the urn if we're going to be ready for your mother's service at three p.m.'

'Today?' I asked. 'I thought it was tomorrow.' Hadn't Jim told me that?

'No, it's today at the mortuary,' Hannah said, checking her own timepiece. 'Oh, dear. I wanted to stop at the house and check on Nancy before I saw the lawyer.'

'Would you like me to run over to your house?' I asked. 'Or send Amy?' Better idea.

'That's nice, but—'

'It's no problem for me to stop by on my way to the mortuary,' Mort said. 'It's right next door and, as I've said, the old girl does tolerate me.'

'Not for long if you call her "old girl,"' Hannah said with a wan smile. 'But thank you.'

She turned to me. 'And thank you and Amy, too. It'll be better, though, if it's somebody she knows. I wouldn't leave her this long, but it's important I see the new lawyer and get to the bank, too, before the memorial.'

'Christy was saying how difficult dealing with the business side of death can be.'

'More so than I ever imagined,' Hannah said. 'And I, at least, have Mort to guide me. And the attorney, too, but he's being part of the problem. We have bills that are due and the funeral costs,' she glanced at Mort's back, 'aren't insubstantial. It's complicated because my mother's money is in a trust. Nancy is the trustee but she's so confused and distraught she's having trouble so much as signing her name.'

'I thought trusts were supposed to make things easier. At least that's what my lawyer friend Bernie is always telling me.' In truth, that's what he was always badgering me about. Not that I had anything to actually *put* in a trust.

'Bernie Egan?' Hannah looked surprised.

'He's a good friend and I worked with his wife Caron for years – both at First Financial and then in Uncommon Grounds.'

'He's the lawyer I'm going to see,' Hannah said. 'Small world.'

'Small town,' I countered.

'From what I can tell, his specialty is copyright law?'

'In the corporate world,' I said, wanting to reassure her, 'but now that he has his own practice he does a little bit of everything. Like I said, small town.'

'And a very nice one.' Mort slipped his credit card back in his wallet as Clare wrapped the urns in tissue paper and found a box to fit them in. I guessed the coffee urn would appear on Hannah's bill from the mortuary along with a markup.

'Well, I'd best be on my way,' Hannah said, stepping out of the door. She was already down the path and on the front sidewalk when she turned and called up to Mort: 'I leave the back door unlocked so just go around and let yourself in, OK?'

'Will do, my dear. And don't worry about a thing.'

Hannah turned back, nearly colliding with a man walking in the other direction. She zigged and he zagged.

Mort hefted the box. 'Thank you so much. Will I see either of you at the service?'

'I'll try, if I can find somebody to mind the shop,' Clare said.

'I'll be there,' I told him.

'That would be wonderful,' Mort said. 'Given the Bouchards

are new in town, we don't expect a large turnout. Hannah's afraid that nobody will show up at all.'

'Poor woman,' Clare said, watching Mort load the urns into a black Mercedes. Apparently the BMW wasn't his work car.

'You mean Hannah's mother?'

'Sadly, she's beyond sympathy now. I was talking about Hannah having to deal with all this.'

'She does seem anxious, doesn't she?'

Clare seemed surprised. 'Of course. Wouldn't you expect her to be?'

'I guess,' I said, watching Hannah's back disappear into the distance.

FOURTEEN

I left the antiques shop and walked slowly down the sidewalk toward Uncommon Grounds.

Hannah *had* seemed worried. Maybe even more worried than sad, but who was I to say? Like Christy had said, the emotional piece is only part of the puzzle you need to deal with when somebody dies.

But . . . if she thought Bernie only did trademark and copyright law – which he had at one time – why had she chosen him as her lawyer in dealing with the estate and trust?

I could hear Sarah's voice – probably raspy from her cold – saying in my ear, 'And why isn't Celeste's own daughter her trustee? Why Nancy?'

'I'll tell you why,' I said out loud. 'Because Nancy was her business partner, best friend and maybe more.'

A man getting up from a bench with an Uncommon Grounds' cup glanced over.

I touched my ear, like I was adjusting my Bluetooth earpiece, albeit an invisible one. He smiled and kept going, and it was only then that I recognized him.

Not only was he the man Hannah Bouchard had nearly

collided with going the other way, but I'd seen him before.
'Jack Andersen.'

The man turned. 'Yes?'

Now what did I say? The man was a released felon and may
have sheltered his prison escapee brother. In my book, Pauly
Andersen was not only responsible for Pavlik's injury but Pete
Hartsfield's and Al Taylor's deaths as well.

'You live at Brookhills Manor, don't you?'

'Yes?' The blue eyes above his now peeling nose were twin-
kling. 'Do I know you?'

'No, but my friends Sophie and Henry are your next-door
neighbors.'

He cocked his head and then his eyes narrowed just a bit.
'You're the coffeehouse owner.' He held up the cup.

'Maggy Thorsen. I think you stopped in on Sunday, too,
didn't you?'

'You know I did.' The voice and the eyes had turned cold.

'Jack,' a familiar voice called and the eyes snapped back to
friendly.

Vickie LaTour was hurrying up the sidewalk toward us.
'Maggy, I didn't know you knew Jack.'

'I didn't, really, until now,' I said truthfully, though I thought
I already had the man's number. Jack Andersen may play at
being charming but I'd wager that underneath he was as much
of a snake as his brother was.

Vickie hooked arms with Andersen. 'Isn't he handsome?
Do you know he does his own Botox? Aren't we just a match
made in heaven?'

Sure. I supposed a smooth brow and lack of expression was
handy for a con man.

'Glad two of my favorite people have met,' Vickie was saying.
'Maggy owns Uncommon Grounds, Jack.'

'So I just realized,' he said pleasantly.

'Jack and I were going to meet there on Sunday but we just
missed each other.'

'I was early, I'm afraid,' Jack said.

'And I was late.' Vickie smiled up at him. 'It's so us. We
went on a cruise to the Bahamas and Jack was always up with
the birds.'

'Seagulls, in that case,' he offered with a wide smile.

I laughed, since that seemed to be what was expected of me by the happy couple. 'Sophie mentioned you'd gone on a cruise.'

She wagged a finger. 'And don't you tell her I went with Jack or I'll never hear the end of it.'

'She doesn't like me for some reason.' Jack said it with a can-you-believe-it smile.

'I can't imagine why.'

I'd intended to just play along, but the words came out flat and Vickie gave me an uncertain glance. 'Oh, Maggy. You can't blame Jack for something his brother did.'

Yes, I could. And I did.

'That's not fair, my dear,' Jack said. 'Pauly has done some awful things. I've had to come to terms with the fact that sometimes I'm painted with the same brush.'

Vickie's eyes were as big as the Botox would allow. 'But you were held hostage, Jack. For hours.' The eyes swiveled to me. 'My Jack was a victim as much as your sheriff was.'

Now that was too much. 'Really? Was *Jack* shot? And why would Pauly have even come to the manor if he didn't think his brother would hide him?'

A nerve in Jack's jaw was jumping but he said evenly, 'I don't blame you for how you feel. But I can't control my brother or what he thinks. Believe me, I've tried.'

'We need to be away from him, go someplace where he'll never find you.' Vickie turned to me. 'I'm afraid that man is going to come through the window every night when we go to bed.'

Which meant that it was Vickie and Jack that Sophie was hearing through the walls between the two apartments.

'Botox Vickie's doing the convict, huh?' Sarah was sniffling.

We were just inside the door of Brookhills Mortuary. Despite her cold, Sarah had insisted on coming to the funeral with me rather than going home.

'Will you lower your voice,' I pleaded, looking around.

'Why? The place is a tomb. Literally. Helloooo . . .'

I shushed her. 'You realize you're shouting, right?'

'No, my ears are stuffed up. Besides, who's going to hear me anyway?' Sarah waved her arm at the empty hallway. 'There's nobody in the place except you and me.'

'Well, it's just quarter to three.' I stopped. 'Isn't that a song?'

'Isn't what a song?' She dug a tissue from her pocket and blew her nose.

'"Quarter to three." Isn't that Sinatra?'

'I don't know. Google it.'

'You say that when you want to shut me up.'

'But, alas, it doesn't work.' A half sigh, half sniffle. 'Are you sure it's today? Maybe you got me out of my sick bed for nothing.'

'You never even went to your sick bed. And if you had, I would have told you to stay in it. But no – you insisted on infecting everybody at the funeral.'

'Which is you.'

'Exactly my point.'

'I'm on antibiotics so I'm not contagious anymore.'

'Your doctor prescribed antibiotics for a cold?' I demanded. 'When? Your first sneeze was yesterday.'

'Actually, I realized it was Sunday. Remember I sneezed when we were outside unchaining the furniture?'

Unlike my partner, I didn't catalog each sneeze. But I did remember this one, because I'd nearly choked myself. 'That was Celeste's perfume, don't you think? But regardless, antibiotics aren't effective against viruses. You're—'

'Geez, will you relax? I had a few pills left over from last time so I took one. And you say *I'm* a pain in the ass.'

'Because you are.' I tapped a discreet card next to a doorway that read: Celeste Bouchard. I stuck my head into the room and saw a photo display at the back, the urn from Clare's the focal point in front. And, permeating everything, Celeste's floral scent.

I put my hand over my mouth. 'This is the place, though I don't see—'

'Maggy.' Hannah was approaching, arms wide, and enveloped me. 'Thank you for coming.'

'You're welcome,' I said, my face crushed up against the

shoulder of her tailored navy dress. 'You remember my partner, Sarah.'

Hannah turned on Sarah, who is not a hugger under the best of circumstances.

'You may not want to get too close,' I started to warn, but it was already too late.

'It's so kind of you to come,' Hannah said. 'You barely know us.'

'And yet you're hugging me,' came the strangled reply.

'I'm sorry,' Hannah said, stepping back. 'To be honest it's not my nature, but my first husband came from a big Italian family so I got into the habit of going into the clinch first to get it over with.'

'Preemptive hugging,' I said.

Sarah blew her nose.

'Are you sick?' Hannah seemed to notice my partner's red nose and watery eyes for the first time.

'No,' Sarah said, stashing the tissue. 'I always cry at funerals.'

'That's so sweet,' Hannah said, her own eyes filling.

Sheesh. 'We knew that you were new to town, so we didn't know how many—'

The door to the mortuary opened and two men came in, hefting large sprays of flowers. Vickie LaTour and Jack Andersen were behind them.

'Oh, how lovely,' Hannah said. 'Who are these from?'

Vickie linked her arm through the crook of Jack's arm. The happy couple had apparently decided to come out. At a funeral. 'The roses are from us.'

A speculative 'hmmmm' came from Sarah.

Vickie threw an uncertain glance my partner's way as she continued, 'And the lilies are from Brookhills Manor. We couldn't let your mother go out without a proper send-off.'

Hannah's eyes overflowed and she started to sob.

Jack Andersen took a neatly folded handkerchief out of his pocket and shook it out before handing it to Hannah. 'We're so sorry for your loss.'

'Hannah, I don't think you've met my beau, Jack Andersen?'

The bereaved woman tried to pull herself together. 'Thank you for coming.'

Jack gestured toward the photo display – an album flat on the table with framed photos surrounding it. 'Your mother was a beautiful woman. Was she a model?'

'At one time, yes.'

'That was before she opened the boutiques?' Vickie picked up a photograph of a well-endowed brunette in a bikini on the beach, arms flung wide.

'Yes, but that picture you're holding was taken less than twenty years ago. She was nearly sixty, if you can believe it.'

'Good genes,' Jack said appreciatively, taking the picture and studying it. 'An enduring beauty and successful business-woman. Vickie has told me what a good mind for numbers she had. It was kind of her to help the church.'

'Oh, no, dear,' Vickie said, putting her hand on his arm. 'That's Nancy. Celeste's friend.'

'Oh, I'm sorry,' Jack said, looking around. 'Is she here?'

'Nancy is resting in one of the anterooms. I . . . umm,' the tip of Hannah's nose tinged pink, 'thought I'd bring her in when the service starts.'

'Worried about another "accident," no doubt,' Sarah whispered to me.

I was impressed that she had the restraint to whisper rather than shout it, until I realized she was losing her voice.

'. . . A terrible loss for her,' Jack was saying as he set down one photo and picked up another to study.

There was something about the way the guy was studying a dead woman's glamour shots from long ago that gave me the heebie-jeebies. Hannah must have felt the same way because she took the photo. 'Oh, let me take that. I didn't mean for it to be out here with the others.'

As she tucked the snapshot away, I got a glimpse of two young women smiling and carefree, their arms linked. Probably Celeste and Nancy.

'Oh, there are Sophie and Henry,' Vickie said, waving.

'I thought you didn't want Sophie to know about . . .' I hiked my head toward Jack.

'Now that Jack's planning to make an honest woman of me, she can say all she wants,' the redhead said. 'I sure don't see Henry proposing anytime soon.'

'Jack proposed?' Because, of course, what else does one do when your escapee brother is on the lam after shooting his way out of your house?

I mean, if *that* didn't scream romance, I didn't know what did.

'There are quite a few people from the manor on their way,' Henry said as the two joined us.

'It'll take 'em a while,' Sophie said grumpily. 'All those walkers and canes.'

'We certainly can wait for them. Thank you so much for this.' Hannah gave Henry a kiss on the cheek and the man turned crimson.

'Sophie, Henry,' Vickie said, pulling the former convict over. 'You know Jack Andersen?'

'Know him?' Sophie spouted. 'His brother put a bullet through our wall and shot the sheriff. And the deputy. What's he doing here?'

'Jack is here as my guest.' She took his hand.

Sophie's eyes went wide. '*You*,' her index finger was tick-tocking back and forth between the two of them, like it, too, was trying to figure this out, 'are a couple?'

'We wanted to keep it quiet. You know how people gossip at the manor. But now that we're getting married—' Vickie shrugged.

'But, but . . . what about all the women in—' Sophie put her hand up to her mouth. 'That was you?'

Vickie simpered. 'I've always been a bit . . . noisy.'

'I'd say responsive, like a race car.' Jack draped his arm over her shoulder and they both laughed.

'But, but . . .'

I thought Sophie was going to explode all over us. 'Maybe we should take our seats,' I suggested. 'Henry and Sophie, why don't you sit with us?'

Sophie hesitated but Henry said, 'Come along, Sophie.'

Sophie relented and followed Sarah and me into the pew. 'This is just sick. The man is a felon. What can Vickie be thinking?'

'About what?' Christy was in the pew behind us, leaning on the back of ours.

'Just . . . umm, that particular shade of hair dye,' I said quickly. 'Sophie isn't a fan.'

'What I'm not a fan of,' Sophie said, 'is lonely women dating criminals.'

'I'm not lonely,' Christy said defensively.

'Well then, I must not be talking about you,' Sophie snapped.

'Oh, I guess not.' Christy sat back. 'Sorry.'

'Achoo!' came from Sarah on the other side of me.

'Why did you lie to Hannah about having a cold?' I asked, handing her a tissue.

'You're sick?' Sophie nudged Henry to move so she could slide away from me.

'Sarah's the one who's Typhoid Mary,' I told her as Sarah sneezed again. 'Not me.'

'Give it a day. You're probably already a carrier.' Sophie pulled a little bottle of hand sanitizer from her purse, squirting the goo into her palm before offering it to me.

I shook my head. The stuff smelled like rubbing alcohol crossed with the pink sawdust the janitor sprinkled on vomit in my elementary school.

'And you ask why I didn't advertise the fact I'm sick.' Sarah was searching through her pocket. 'Do you have another Kleenex? I blew through that one.'

'No. And I just think that warning people is the least you can do.'

'Or better yet, stay home.' Sophie sent a purse-sized pack of tissues sailing over my head.

Sarah caught it. 'I told you, I'm on antibiotics. Besides, the woman hugged me without permission.'

'And she apologized.' For hugging, for God's sake. 'Besides, her mother just died. Can't you cut her some slack?'

'Mine died, too, and you don't see me whining.'

I slid my butt back an inch into the space Sophie had vacated so I could turn to make better eye contact with Sarah. 'I'm sorry, I had no idea. When?'

'Last month.' Sarah sniffled, but I couldn't tell if it was from the cold or grief.

'Why didn't you say something?'

'She lives – or lived – with my sister.'

'I didn't know you had a sister.' Hadn't Sarah given me no end of grief last year because I'd never mentioned my reclusive brother? And she'd never mentioned her sister or her mother. 'Does she live in Brookhills?'

Sarah shrugged me off. 'In Milwaukee. And I don't get on with my mother or my sister, so don't make a big deal of it. Haven't seen them for years.'

Milwaukee was fifteen miles away. This went far beyond forgetting to call mom on Sundays.

'Is that why you don't like Hannah?' I asked, lowering my voice. 'She reminds you of your sister?'

Sarah turned on me. 'You're a psychiatrist now? Or is our omniscient, Christy, having visions?'

'Omnist,' Christy corrected from behind us. 'And I didn't know you don't like Hannah.'

Apparently I hadn't kept my voice down low enough.

'So I don't like martyrs,' Sarah snapped. 'Slay me.'

Two seats away, Henry chuckled.

FIFTEEN

'Why isn't her own daughter her trustee?' Sarah hissed in my ear. And, yes, her voice was raspy, just as I'd imagined it earlier. 'Why this Nancy person?'

'Nancy was her partner,' I said. 'It's not so unusual. Would your mother have made you her trustee?'

'Low blow.' Sarah snorted. 'But a good one. And no, she wouldn't have. My sister – that's another thing. And Ruth is the very last person my mother should have trusted.'

Lots of bad blood there and I wasn't about to wade in.

Luckily I didn't have to, because Sarah was still talking. 'I'm just saying that Celeste had better instincts. Remember? She gave the lawyer her power of attorney for the sale—'

'Shh!' Christy said from behind us.

I glanced to the front of the room to see Hannah guiding Nancy, dressed in a somber black maxi-dress and oversized vest today, to a seat in the front row. The older woman's face was drawn and tear-streaked, her gray hair limp.

'I feel sorry for her,' I said as Vickie and Jack made their way forward to pay their respects.

'Because of Celeste's death? Or because she's going to have to talk to those two?' Sophie asked.

'Now Sophie,' Henry said. 'Vickie is your best friend.'

'That was before she lost her mind. And we had to listen to her doing it every night.' She turned to me. 'Did she tell you how long this has been going on?'

'Not really. But she went on that cruise you mentioned with him. When was that?'

'Maybe two weeks ago? He must have been the one who filled her with all these ideas about retiring on a ship. And now she's going to marry the man, just like that?'

'Maybe Vickie and Maggy can have a double wedding.'

I kicked Sarah but it was Sophie who gasped. 'You're marrying the sheriff?'

I glared at my partner before turning back to Sophie. 'No, I'm not. Or at least I haven't decided.'

'Oh, I love weddings,' Christy said from behind us. 'Why don't you and Henry tie the knot, Sophie? We can make it a triple.'

'Good idea,' Sarah said. 'Add you and Ronny, too, and we have a movie title.'

I looked at her.

'"Four Weddings and a Funeral"?' Sarah wiggled an eyebrow at me. 'I'm surprised you didn't get that. It's one of your favorite movies.'

I do love me some Hugh Grant. But that was beside the point.

'People ask why Henry and I don't get married,' Sophie was saying, 'and I ask them why we should.'

'Not like you're going to have kids, I suppose,' Sarah said.

'That's what I say,' Sophie said. 'Shuts 'em right up. Though that probably won't work for you, Maggy. You're in your forties, right? These days women your age are still popping them out.'

'Not this woman. Eric, my one and only child, is twenty.'

I felt someone's breath on the back of my neck. 'Did you see the urn, Maggy?' Christy said into my ear. 'It was my idea to soak the doily underneath it with Celeste's favorite perfume. Mort seemed truly impressed with my suggestion. And did I tell you they let me sweep Celeste's ashes? Mort doesn't know, so keep it a secret.'

With pleasure.

'What about the sheriff?' Sophie was saying loudly into my other ear. 'Does he want children?'

Glad to turn my attention back to the living, even if they were haranguing me, I said, 'Pavlik already has a daughter. She's twelve.'

'Has he said he doesn't want more?' Sarah was being a huge help.

'No,' I said, letting them take that answer any way they wished. The truth was that Pavlik and I had never talked about having kids. Then again, we hadn't talked about marriage either, until he proposed. But having a baby at my age was so outside my—

Happily, Sophie had lost interest in my relationship and was digging into her purse. Coming up with an airplane-sized bottle of vodka, she held it up to Sarah. 'Kill a cold?'

Sarah ruefully shook her head. 'I can't drink on my meds.'

Or at least she didn't when I was around. Outside my orbit, I wasn't so sure.

'There's Clare,' I said, watching the little shop owner make her way to a seat halfway down. 'And Mort.'

The mortician had stopped at Clare's pew. As the two spoke, Hannah pulled Vickie and Jack away from Nancy to join them.

Sophie shook her head. 'I'm not surprised those two found each other. They're perfectly suited. He's obviously a player and Vickie is on men like white on rye.'

'I think it's white on rice,' I said.

Sophie sat back. 'Now what sense does that make?'

'I think it just means that rice is white, so you can't separate the white from the rice. It refers to two things being as close as they can be.'

'What about brown rice?' Sarah asked. 'Or wild?

'And what does that have to do with bread?' Sophie asked.

'It's not white *bread*—' I stopped myself and said, 'Google it.'

Sarah took out her phone but Sophie was still pouting. 'Guess she's part of the family now.'

There was a hurt tone to her voice, and I turned to see Vickie and Jack joining Hannah in the front pew. Mort was nowhere to be seen.

'Are you still thinking of moving from the manor?' I asked to change the subject.

'Henry won't agree to go. Though I'm starting to think just getting away from a round-the-clock version of Night of the Living Dead,' she nodded toward the procession of walkers, wheelchairs and portable oxygen tanks now making their way down the aisle to seats, 'might make the sacrifice worth it.'

'The sacrifice of Henry? Come on. That's not going to happen.'

'I suppose not,' Sophie said grudgingly as Henry slipped his arm around her shoulder.

'I am here, you know,' he said, giving her a peck on the cheek. 'And I'm not deaf like your last suitor.'

'Well, not *as* deaf,' Sophie admitted.

'You know what?' Sarah interrupted, raising her head from her phone. 'This rice thing makes no sense at all.'

'I told you,' Sophie said, sliding closer to see the small screen across my body. 'Does it say what white they're talking about, though? Is it bread?'

'Uh-uh,' Sarah said, holding it up.

'White is the absence of color,' Henry contributed.

'I think that's black.' Christy was leaning forward again, elbows on the back of the pew. 'Or is black the absence of light?'

'It depends whether we're talking paint color or—' I stopped myself as all four sets of eyes focused on me. This had all the trappings of a lose/lose, lose/lose argument.

So I just shrugged. 'Got me.'

It was almost as effective as telling them to Google it. Sarah went back to her phone and Sophie went back to her discussion with Henry. Christy just went back.

The service itself was short, but coffee and cookies had appeared in the foyer while we were in the chapel.

'I really couldn't have people at the house,' Hannah said, one hand at Nancy's elbow to steady her as they stood accepting condolences. 'And besides,' she lowered her voice, 'I had no idea so many would show up. Luckily Mort had boxes of cookies from the last funeral stashed in his storeroom and brought them out.'

'How many of these folks do you actually know?'

'Honestly, just you and Sarah, and Christy and Vickie, of course.'

'Had you met Jack before today?' I was keeping my voice down, too, since he and Vickie were just one mourner behind me in line.

'No.'

I read something in her expression. 'What?'

She shrugged. 'I don't know. He's just kind of pushy. Vickie is my friend, yet . . .'

'He acts like he's running the show,' I completed for her. 'For what it's worth, I don't like him either.'

She put her hand on my arm. 'Vickie told me your fiancé was shot. I'm so sorry.'

Then it was official. When I got home I'd ask to see the ring.

The person behind me let hunger outweigh speaking with the bereaved and stepped out of line to get a cookie. Jack stepped in.

'Again, very sorry for your loss.' Jack pumped her hand and then turned to the older woman. 'Nancy, is it?'

She squinted. 'Are you a doctor?'

'No, dear,' Hannah said. 'This is Vickie's friend. The doctor is the lady. The one who prescribed the pill to relax you?' She turned to us. 'I'm afraid she's taken to them a bit too . . . readily.'

'Do be careful about that,' Vickie said from behind Jack. 'Prescription overuse in the elderly is—'

'I don't like doctors or shots,' Nancy snapped. 'And I don't have a headache.'

'I'm glad you're feeling a little better,' I said to her.

I couldn't blame the woman for being testy. Everybody was talking about her like she wasn't here. Maybe Christy was right about people treating the elderly like they're invisible.

'I think my partner Sarah is coming down with something, too,' I told her on the theory that her misery would like a little company.

Hannah blinked. 'Is she really?'

'There must be something going around,' Jack said. 'Happily, it doesn't seem to last long.'

Nancy shifted her weight from one foot to another. 'Can we go?'

'Are you tired, dear?' Hannah turned to us. 'If you'll excuse me, I think we'll take a little break.'

'Would you like us to drop Nancy at your house, Hannah?' Vickie asked. 'Then she can lie down in her own bed.'

'Thank you, but she just needs to sit for a bit.' As she started away with her elderly charge, Hannah seemed to remember something. 'Oh, Maggy, when I saw Bernie Egan this morning he said to say hello. Maggy's friend is the attorney overseeing mother's trust,' she said by way of explanation to the other two.

'Bernie's a good guy,' I said.

'Yes, he is, and I'm sure a good lawyer, too. We're just running into a bit of trouble accessing the trust in order to pay,' she glanced self-consciously at Vickie and Jack, 'expenses.'

'Funerals can be terribly pricey,' Vickie said.

'We all need to pay the piper eventually,' her paramour contributed.

Cheery thought. But I was wondering why Mort couldn't give Hannah some sort of friends and family discount, given their relationship. Or maybe an EZ payment plan. I mean, even Pavlik cut me a little slack when I was a murder suspect. And I do mean 'a little.' Like enough to hang myself.

'I know,' Hannah said, reddening. 'And I'm sure we'll get it worked out. It's just that Nancy needs to come with me tomorrow and it's difficult for her. Just being here has taken its toll.'

Hannah's eyes were wide and moisture-filled. I thought any moment they'd burst like rain-heavy storm clouds. And so I made an Amy-like offer. 'I'd be happy to go with you and help, if you'd like.'

'Or we could, right, Vickie?' Jack offered.

'Well, I suppose—'

But Hannah wasn't having any. 'That's very kind, but Maggy is an old friend.'

'It's good that you have somebody here,' Jack said. 'Somebody who knows you well, I mean. I was but a stranger in town until Vickie came along.'

Sweet.

Of course, Hannah had meant that Bernie and I were old friends, not she and I. But neither of us enlightened Jack Andersen. It – along with most everything else in Brookhills – was none of his business.

SIXTEEN

Leaving the mortuary, I realized I hadn't stopped by Pavlik's place yet to pick up the things he needed.

Passing my house on Poplar Creek Drive, I continued south to Brookhill Road and then turned west out of town and toward the Brookhills County administration complex, which included the sheriff's office, as well as the county's court and jail facilities. Kind of one-stop shopping for criminals.

Just past the complex on Brookhill was Pavlik's two-bedroom Cape Cod-style house.

Crunching up the gravel driveway, I parked my Escape and climbed up the concrete steps. Fetching Pavlik's key from my purse, I turned it in the lock and stepped into the living room. The main floor consisted of this room and the kitchen behind it, and on the other side of the house were two small bedrooms with a bathroom between them.

Built in the early fifties, the place would be 'retro' in Amy's opinion. I kind of liked it because it reminded me of the house I'd been brought up in, but with none of the supposed 'updating' of subsequent decades. This house was fifties' kitsch with no apologies.

Looking around, I tried to remember what I was supposed to get.

Toothbrush, of course, since the only spare in my house was

Frank's, something I hadn't had the nerve to tell Pavlik after he'd plucked it out of the glass next to my sink and used it.

The toothbrush in his bathroom was worn, the bristles bent. I'd stop at the drugstore and pick up a new one on the way home. I did grab his tube of toothpaste. It was a different brand than mine. I preferred gel but Pavlik was a paste man. Can this relationship last?

We would see.

Pavlik would need a jacket now that his leather one was sadly destroyed. I sorted through the front hall closet and settled on a North Face that I laid across the back of the couch. Maybe I'd buy a new leather jacket for him. For us.

Moving to the bedroom, I found underwear and socks in one drawer. T-shirts in another. Jeans in a third.

I lifted out a pair. They looked like they'd been ironed. I sniffed. No. Could that be spray starch?

I collapsed on the bed. The made-up bed, I might add.

Don't get me wrong, I love a neat man. Ted had been a bit of a slob and Pavlik was fastidious by comparison. But . . . could I possibly take on the care and feeding of a man who starched his jeans?

Would Pavlik think I was a slob because I didn't iron my own jeans? Or even wash them each time I wore them?

Or every other time. They just started feeling comfortable after—

OK, Maggy, settle down. You are an adult. Pavlik is an adult. Neither of you is going to change your habits at this stage of life. And you're not expected to. For better or worse, you are now temporarily co-habitating.

Think of it as a fact-finding mission. A trial run. A weather balloon.

Yeah, that's it.

So reassured, I stood up and tried to think what else he might need. Absently, I pulled open the drawer next to the bed.

And closed it.

Then I opened it again.

A framed photo of Pavlik and Susan was smiling up at me. And he was wearing our leather jacket.

I pushed the drawer firmly closed, rocking the lamp on top.

I steadied it. So Pavlik had a photo of his ex in the night stand. Big deal. Susan had been a big part of his life. They'd been married for over a decade and were a couple longer than that. They had a child together.

And, I reminded myself, it wasn't like the photo was on the dresser or hanging on a wall. It had been put away.

In the night stand.

Why in the world had I looked in there anyway? Nobody keeps anything much in a night stand. Except things they need at night. Books. Sex toys. Pictures of their ex.

Argh. What was wrong with me? One moment I'm questioning our compatibility, the next I'm jealous. How exactly does *that* work? But . . .

Pavlik had moved to Brookhills, to this house, after his divorce. Wouldn't you expect that picture to have been packed away in a box somewhere? Why take it out?

Then again, maybe the night stand had been moved intact, drawers full, contents forgotten. I knew people who did that. Sure, that was probably it.

Or at least it was the explanation that would keep me from feeling . . . What was this I was feeling? Jealousy? Sadness? Or just plain ridiculousness? I mean, I probably had pictures of me and Ted laying around my place. Pavlik was likely stumbling over them willy-nilly right this very moment.

I moved to the closet to pick out a couple of dress shirts that Pavlik liked to wear with jeans, the sleeves rolled up. A pair of khakis. Sneakers.

Stuffing it all in a white plastic garbage bag, I let myself out of Pavlik's house, locking the door behind me.

'You didn't have to make a special stop to buy me one,' Pavlik said, holding up the new toothbrush. 'I know mine is trashed but I was fine using your spare. It's practically new.'

That was because Frank didn't brush regularly. 'It was no problem,' I said, pulling a bottle of wine out of the pharmacy bag.

Pavlik slipped an arm around my waist. 'You know, it's not like we haven't swapped spit before.'

Frank lifted his head from his water dish and we exchanged looks.

'I was getting ready to retire that toothbrush to clean grout,' I lied.

'A woman who cleans grout with a toothbrush,' Pavlik said, kissing me. 'Be still, my heart.'

I had cleaned grout with a toothbrush. Once.

I sniffed the air. 'Is that tomato sauce?'

'Yes, though pretty basic. All I could find was canned tomatoes, garlic powder and basil.'

I was surprised he'd found that. 'I had basil?'

'Behind the shriveled limes.'

'Oh, yeah. I bought that by accident when I had Sarah over for mojitos. I thought it was mint.'

'You didn't smell it?'

'Well, no. I was in a hurry.' See? It was already happening. I was making excuses for my perceived inadequacies. 'We substituted the basil and the drinks were pretty damned good, in fact.'

'It does sound good, actually,' Pavlik said, taking the wine. 'Want me to open this?'

'Can you do it with one arm out of commission?'

'I can try,' he said. 'If you'll keep the bottle steady for me.'

Maybe this living with somebody wouldn't be so bad after all. 'How was your day?'

Pavlik was rummaging in the drawer for the corkscrew. 'Shouldn't that be my line? You were the one off at work while I kept the home fires burning.'

'Oh, God,' I said. 'Please don't tell me you tried to use the fireplace. The chimney hasn't been cleaned for years and the flue—'

Pavlik was grinning up at me. 'Only an expression. Frank and I spent most of the day warming the couch.'

'Did you have any trouble with the Wi-Fi?' I said, holding the bottle so he could pull off the foil.

'I didn't use it.'

'Really?' I held out my hand for the foil. 'What a good patient you are.'

'Not really. I didn't have much choice. The county exec called to tell me I've been placed on leave.' He wasn't looking at me.

'Medical leave?'

'That's what they're calling it.' Now he met my eyes.

They were so dark that I couldn't read beyond them. 'But that wouldn't be unusual, would it? At the bank, if you were going to be out more than two weeks, I think it was, they had to put you on short-term disability so you got paid.'

'I know. Hold that.' He gestured to the bottle.

I wrapped my hands around it as he tried to turn the screw into the cork. 'What are you thinking?'

'I'm thinking that you'd be better off doing this by yourself.' He handed me the corkscrew.

I twisted it into the cork and pulled. 'You know what I mean. You were shot and the department has put you on medical leave. Do you think there's more to it?'

He slid out a chair and turned it around with one hand so he could straddle it backwards. 'I think there was a prisoner escape, a stolen police weapon and a shooting that left me wounded and a deputy dead. And God knows it could have been worse, given where it happened. And then, to top it all off, the detective whose weapon was stolen killed himself after refusing the psych evaluation I'd ordered for him.'

'Taylor was afraid he'd lose his job?'

'Or that they'd think he was becoming unhinged, which would have resulted in the same thing. Or maybe he'd just made up his mind and didn't want anybody to stop him.'

'From killing himself.'

Pavlik was gripping the back of the chair so hard his knuckles were white.

'We'll never know. Hell, if it were up to me I'd put me on leave.'

All the chatting about toothbrushes and spaghetti sauce – just bluster to cover what he was really thinking. 'It wasn't your fault. None of it.'

'Yes, I'm afraid it was. All of it.'

We drank the wine and ate the tomato sauce over noodles salvaged from a forgotten box of macaroni and cheese in the cupboard.

It wasn't a good night, but it was one I was glad we'd weathered together.

SEVENTEEN

'Frank jumped in bed with us at about three,' Pavlik said, pouring a mug of coffee the next morning.

Sarah and Amy were taking the opening shifts for the next week or so, since getting both me and Pavlik showered and dressed with only three good arms and one bathroom between us was time-consuming. I had, though, promised to meet Hannah Bouchard at Bernie's office at nine.

'Oh, really?' I was searching through my purse for the car keys.

'Really. And don't pretend you slept through a hundred-pound sheepdog leaping onto the foot of the bed and then shoving his way up between us like a battering ram.'

'I had no idea,' I said innocently. 'In fact, I was shocked to find that it was Frank's nose pressed against the small of my back this morning.'

'I hope you were both shocked *and* disappointed,' Pavlik said, coming up behind me. 'Frank doesn't have much of a nose.'

Frank raised said fuzzy muzzle from his breakfast.

'You'd be surprised,' I said, leaning down to give the sheepdog a rub. 'It's just hidden under all that fuzz.'

Vindicated, Frank went back to his food.

'Soooo . . .' Pavlik said, wrapping his arms around me. 'Does Frank sleep with you every night?'

'Not usually.'

Frank threw me a dirty look but didn't stop eating.

'Not *usually*, I mean,' I restated, 'when I have a sleepover.'

'Which is why I've never had a hairy butt in my face before.'

'You had the butt end?' I asked. 'He was the other way around this morning.'

'Only because I made him switch. Though his breath is no picnic either.'

'I know.' I turned in Pavlik's arms and gave him a kiss. 'And I'm sorry. But I let him up on the bed after the divorce, when . . .'

'You were lonely.'

'I was going to say when he was small. Or at least smaller. But yes, I was lonely, too. It's just kind of morphed since then.'

'Well, it's your house and your bed, so your rules,' Pavlik said, letting me go. 'But if there are going to be three of us we're going to need a bigger bed.'

A new bed? That was a big move. 'Frank will sleep on the floor tonight. Right, Frank?'

He pfffted, blowing the hair out of his eyes momentarily, and stalked out of the room.

'I'll buy you a doggy bed,' I called after him. 'You'll like that.'

'Sure he will,' Pavlik said. 'If it's a California king. Which would probably be a good size, come to think of it. Want me to look online?'

'Sure,' I said, despite being anything but that. 'I'd better go now or I'll be late meeting Hannah.'

I gave him a quick hug and then pushed back to study his face. 'How are you, really?'

'Are you asking if I'm going off the deep end?'

'I guess so.' I hesitated and then added, 'Do you think you should talk to somebody?'

'A shrink? Maybe.' He tipped my face up to study it. 'Are you worried that your suggesting it is going to send me to my gun, like Taylor?'

My stomach twisted. 'No. Well, maybe yes, I did hesitate because of that. But not seriously. I mean, you never would. Right?'

It was a mish-mosh of a statement/question but Pavlik got it. 'You don't have to worry. And as for the psychiatrist, the department will probably require it before they have me back, anyway. If they have me back.'

'Please,' I said. 'Don't worry about things that haven't happened yet.'

'Because there are enough to worry about that have?' Pavlik said. 'You're right. I just need to find something to occupy myself. Sitting around watching television with Frank will drive me batty.'

A harrumph from the next room. Somebody had gotten up on the wrong side of bed. Which was pretty much impossible, since he'd been smack in the middle and exited over the footboard.

'Maybe I'll call Hallonquist and find out what's happening in the hunt for Andersen.'

'Excellent idea.' I slipped my purse over my shoulder. 'By the way, his smooth-talking brother is dating Vickie LaTour.'

'Botox Vickie?'

'The very one,' I said, starting for the door. 'And I said dating, but Vickie is talking about an engagement. I'm worried.'

'You should be. The guy has bilked a lot of women out of a lot of cash.'

I stopped. 'So Jack Andersen was some sort of a gigolo? When I heard "fraud" I assumed he's a Bernie Madoff type. You know, getting wealthy people to invest in his schemes and then taking off with their money.'

'Pretty much, but change "people" to "women" exclusively.'

'Aw, geez,' I said, rolling my eyes skyward. 'I'm going to have to tell Vickie. She'll be crushed. And Sophie triumphant.'

'Sophie?'

'Daystrom. Her foul-weather friend.'

'Foul—'

'I'll explain tonight. I'm late already.' I opened the door.

Pavlik put his good hand on it. 'So how many sleepovers do you have? I mean, that Frank doesn't join.'

'Not nearly enough.' I removed his hand. 'And they're all with you.'

I was thinking this cohabitating thing wasn't so bad when I arrived at Bernie's home office door. Finding it locked, I knocked.

'What?' Caron Egan swung open the door.

'Good to see you, too,' I said, giving Bernie's wife a hug.

'Oh, Maggy, I'm so sorry but you couldn't have come at a worse time. I'm on deadline and if it's not Bernie's door, it's his phone. The man needs to get a separate office. And a receptionist.'

'Which you've been telling him for years.'

'And he's been ignoring.' She shoved a strand of light brown hair behind her ear. 'Because he's cheap. Are you here to see him? He's in with somebody right now.'

'If it's Hannah Bouchard, I'm supposed to be in there, too. I'm late.'

'Adding another partner?' Caron asked with a grin. She'd been my first partner in Uncommon Grounds, along with Patricia Harper, who hadn't survived our first day of business.

And no, I'm not talking figuratively.

As for Caron, she'd opted out when the first Uncommon Grounds had been destroyed. Sarah, luckily, had opted in. 'Heavens, no. Sarah is more than enough partner for anybody.'

Caron grinned. 'And you also have my fabulous barista find, Amy.'

It was true that it was Caron who insisted we hire our rainbow-haired, multi-pierced rock star of a barista. 'And she remains fabulous. I don't know what we would do without Amy.'

'I wish I had one of her here. Or two.' She pointed to the closed conference-room door. 'Do you mind letting yourself in? I have twenty-two minutes to send this story in and I'm only half done.'

'Still living on the edge, huh?' I called after her as she hurried down the hallway.

'Yeah, right,' floated back to me.

Caron wasn't a risk-taker by any stretch of the imagination, but she had strayed off the straight and narrow once that came to mind. And it had frightened her right back into line.

Rapping gently first, I stuck my head in the door and Bernie waved for me to enter.

He sat on one side of the rectangular-shaped conference table, with Hannah across from him and Nancy next to her.

Bernie stood and hugged me. 'Hello, stranger.'

'I know,' I said, taking the chair beside him. 'It's been too long.'

'Did you see Caron when you came in?'

'She let me in. Did you know your outer door is locked?'

'No, I didn't,' Bernie said, rising again. 'Let me go fix that right now.'

'Thank you so much for coming, Maggy.' Hannah looked like she hadn't slept. And was about to cry. 'I'm not sure how much help you can be, though. Nancy won't even write her name and Attorney Egan thinks we need to get a doctor to—'

'I don't need a doctor.' Nancy seemed shrunken in her flowy dress.

Hannah saw my look. 'She's not eating. I picked up some of those protein drinks but . . .' She shrugged helplessly.

Bernie rejoined us, running a hand over his bald head. 'Now, where were we?'

'You were saying we'd need a court order, and probably . . .' she glanced at Nancy, '. . . an evaluation in order for me to become trustee.'

'Right now, you're the successor trustee to the successor trustee, who is Ms Casperson here. You can only take over if she is unable or unwilling to act.'

I realized I hadn't known Nancy's last name. 'Can't Nancy just request that Hannah take over as trustee?'

'No,' Nancy said definitively. 'And I can't sign my name on that line.'

'And there you have the problem.' Hannah was leaning forward, fingers splayed on the table. 'Despite the fact that Nancy's not capable—'

'I am, though.' Nancy was looking out the window.

I addressed Hannah. 'From what both you and Vickie have said, Nancy was . . . is very competent. Maybe if she has some time to recover from the shock of—'

'We don't have time.' Hannah's hands were pressing so hard on the table that her fingertips were white. 'We have bills, payments due.'

It was sounding more and more like Sarah was right and Hannah's only means of support – visible or invisible – had been her mother.

'Perhaps Ms Casperson could sign checks,' Bernie said.

'No, she can't,' Nancy said stubbornly.

'Do you see the problem?' Hannah nearly shouted. The woman was obviously at the end of her tether.

'Who's the beneficiary of the trust?' I asked and then flushed. 'Not that it's any of my business.'

'The two of us.' Hannah hiked a finger at Nancy. 'Fifty-fifty. But it does me no good if I can't get access.'

Again, I wondered whether Nancy and Celeste had been a couple. And, if so, where and for long? Some states recognized common-law marriages but I didn't know if that also included same-sex couples. Or whether that would change anything.

Bernie was leaning forward to appeal to Nancy. 'As trustee, Ms Casperson, you have a fiduciary duty to the beneficiaries, which includes *both* you and Ms Bouchard here.'

Nancy just folded her arms.

'You see what I'm dealing with?' Hannah said.

'I do. But when your mother died, the trust became irrevocable and the terms can't be changed,' Bernie said. 'As I told you, you have a right to petition the court for removal of the current trustee. But that will take time.'

Hannah jumped up. 'Who are you – or the court – to make that decision? It's my mother's trust and I'm the one who hired you!'

Bernie stayed seated and calm. 'I represent the trust. And, in that capacity, I am responsible to your mother and her wishes.'

'You didn't know my mother. You have no idea what her wishes are. Were.'

'That's true. I only know what she put in the trust agreement. And Nancy Casperson is the successor trustee to your mother. If there's anybody I work for besides your mother, it's her.'

I couldn't be sure, but I thought Nancy Casperson smirked.

EIGHTEEN

'I'm starting to think you're right about Hannah,' I told Sarah when I got to Uncommon Grounds.

My partner was still sick but, germs or not, I was glad she was there. Not just because I didn't want Amy to have to open every day but because I was petty and wanted somebody to talk to about Hannah. Someone who . . . well, wasn't nice.

'That she has a martyr complex?' Sarah was dusting the shelves where we display coffee-related items for sale. Coffee makers, filters, cups and assorted bric-a-brac.

'Maybe that, but more that her mother was supporting the whole household.'

'Told you so. And now Mom's gone and Hannah of Brookhills gets the whole shebang.'

'Is Hannah of Brookhills supposed to be a play on Joan of Arc or Rebecca of Sunnybrook Farm?'

'The former,' she said. 'Would Joan of Brookhills have made the point better?'

'Probably.' And while we're talking about improvements, your dusting would be more thorough if you actually lifted something off the shelf.'

She held out the lambswool duster. 'Have at it.'

'No, thank you.' I'd been tricked before. Most notably when my ex had washed my whites with his red T-shirt so I'd never ask him to do the wash again. 'You're doing just fine.'

'Tell me what happened at Bernie's. Or can't you say because of lawyer/client privileges?'

I leaned back against the service counter. 'I think having a third person in the room – or in my case, a fourth – negates privilege. So we're good.'

'Did you learn that from Pavlik or on TV?'

'I honestly don't know. But I think it's true.'

'Good enough for me.' She ran the duster between two bone china cups, sending them both skittering sideways.

I didn't comment. On her dusting, at least. 'Can you believe Hannah had the nerve to tell me she thought Bernie was incompetent? Out of his depth is the way she put it.'

'Well—'

You know what I think? I think she went *looking* for an incompetent lawyer and is angry because she misjudged the little bald guy who works out of his house.'

'What did she want him to do?'

'Get Nancy to either hand over her role as trustee or sign checks so they can pay bills.'

'That doesn't sound so unreasonable,' Sarah said. 'I mean, if you discount the fact it's not Hannah's money and her mother gave it to Nancy in the first place.'

'Her mom made Nancy her successor trustee, meaning she controls the purse strings. The beneficiaries though are Nancy and Hannah, fifty-fifty.'

'Interesting.' Sarah jabbed the duster between the two cups again.

I grabbed them. 'Will you be careful? These are fragile.'

'Which is why nobody buys them. Who wants a tiny fragile coffee cup?'

She had a point.

'Anyway, Nancy may be a little unhinged by her friend's death but Hannah will have to prove that.'

'The old lady seemed OK to you?'

'Maybe not OK. She's very thin and Hannah says she's not eating. But there were a couple of times during the conversation that I thought she might be playing Hannah. Actually smirked when Bernie said he worked for the trust, and therefore Nancy, as successor trustee, was his client.'

'What does Hannah want Bernie to do? Decide that Nancy's incompetent and make Hannah the trustee?'

'That may be what she wants but it's not going to happen. According to Bernie, you must have a court order or appeal or something and prove the person can't fulfill their duties if they're not willing to step down.'

'Why did Hannah want you there in the first place? Did she think you could sweet-talk Bernie?'

'Maybe. She made a big deal about our being old friends. Or maybe she thought I could help sweet-talk Nancy.'

'How? You've met the woman twice.'

'I know. Better to take Vickie. At least she knows Nancy. Oh! Which reminds me – Pavlik says Vickie's new boyfriend is a gigolo. Romances women out of their money. I think we should tell her, don't you?'

'Of course,' Sarah said, setting down her duster. 'And I want to be there when you do. Just leave instructions for your funeral.'

'Vickie will be angry, no doubt. But—'

'I'll be angry about what?'

I swung around and there, sure enough, was Vickie.

'Bitten in the butt yet again by the sleigh-bell thief,' Sarah said with a grin.

'Yes, where are your bells?' Vickie asked. 'I noticed they weren't on the side door but now they're gone from the front, too.'

Damn it. I stalked to the door and swung it open. Nothing. Except the sound of it hitting the condiment cart behind it hard.

I steadied the creamer. 'Somebody took them. Who would do that?'

'I'm not sure, but they are pretty annoying,' Vickie said. 'I don't know how you stand them all day, every day.'

OK, if she was going to pick on my bells, I was going to pick on her beau. 'How much do you know about Jack Andersen?'

Sarah and the duster took their seats at the nearest table to watch the show.

Vickie lifted her chin. 'I know that Jack loves me. That's all I need to know.'

'Did you have a tuck, Vickie?' Sarah asked.

'What?' Vickie said, distracted.

'Your chin. I can see it really well from down here and it's not wattly.'

'Wattly?'

'Like a chicken,' Sarah said. 'The skin looks tight.'

'Oh, well, thank you.' Vickie patted the place where wattle had lived. 'Last week Jack had a peel and I did a laser treatment. Do you think it helped?'

'I do,' Sarah said. 'No more jiggling. And speaking of jiggle-ohs, Maggy?' She swept her hand toward me in a 'your turn' way.

I took a deep breath. 'Jack Andersen is a gigolo who romances rich women and takes off with their money.'

Vickie burst into laughter. 'That's ridiculous. I'm not rich.'

There was that. 'Are you sure? Maybe a pension or something?'

Vickie was shaking her head. 'Sorry. Jack loves me because he says I embrace life with both hands. At this point in my life, I'm game for anything.'

As witnessed, at least aurally, by Sophie and Henry.

'Vickie, this is a man you've known less than a year. He's

served jail time for bilking women out of their money. Why do you think you're different?'

'I told you, I don't have any money. Jack says we're in the same boat, sink or swim.'

'Telling Maggy about our cruise, honey?'

Yup. Jack. With no warning. Maybe I would be better off belling the people rather than the doors.

But Vickie, for one, looked like she'd scratch my eyes out. 'Maggy isn't interested in our trip, though she'd probably be surprised that you paid for it.'

'Really?' Jack draped his arm around his 'honey's shoulders and smiled. 'Don't you think my Vickie is worth it?'

'I think *you* think she's worth it.' The man set my teeth on edge for no good reason. Except the 'his-brother-shot-my-guy' thing. 'I'm just not sure why you think it.'

'Really.' Same word, different intonation. 'That's a rather rude thing to say about somebody who considers you a friend.'

'I *am* Vickie's friend,' I said, balling up my hands and planting them on my hips, a la Wonder Woman. 'Which is why I'm concerned about her well-being.'

'You don't have to—'

Jack interrupted Vickie's protest, moving closer to me. 'Her well-being doesn't need to concern you. You have your injured sheriff, who has his own problems. I'd save my concern for him if I were you.'

I started toward the jerk, even as Vickie put her hand on his chest and Sarah jumped to her feet, duster at the ready.

Jack held up both hands. 'I don't mean to start an argument. I was just defending my woman, much like you'd defend your man against any and all charges.'

'What charges are you talking about?' Sarah was pointing her duster at him.

'Not legal charges, of course. At least, not for now. But there are some who think the sheriff's decision to raid my apartment put innocent people in danger, including myself.'

'From *your* brother.' My teeth were so tightly clenched the words barely came out.

'Again,' the hands were up once more, 'not trying to start a fight. I think it's kind of you to open your home to the sheriff, like Hannah did for her mother and the other woman. I'm afraid I've forgotten her name.'

'Nancy,' Vickie said.

'Of course,' he said, pulling her close with an embarrassed laugh. 'I saw them driving home and waved, but I'm afraid I've met so many women of a certain age since moving here that it's hard to keep them straight. Except for my gal Vickie here, who stands out in a crowd.'

He gave her an appreciative look that made me queasy.

Vickie, though, seemed delighted. 'Oh, you charmer. Bet you say that to all the ladies.'

'Lady killer and lady chiller,' Sarah said under her breath.

Jack would have had to be deaf not to hear, but he chose to address Vickie. 'Not true, my love. And you are the only woman in my life right now who counts.'

The woman in question giggled.

Jack gave her a squeeze. 'I'm not in the mood for coffee after all. You?'

'Maybe just a cup to go?' She stood on tiptoes to add in a whisper, 'I don't want to offend my friends.'

'No offense taken, Vickie,' I said. 'You know you're always welcome to come and go as you please here.'

'Without question,' Jack said pleasantly. 'It *is* a public train station, after all.'

'True,' I said. 'And I'm hoping to see you in another public facility very soon.'

The mask slipped a bit. 'I'm sure you would like that. But you and your friend have a glass house for accommodations. Maybe I have the rocks to bring it down.'

'Jack!' Vickie said. 'I'm sure Maggy only meant—'

'I *meant* exactly what he and his "rocks" think.' Anger could make me ballsy, too. Or was it just plain stupid? 'And just what glass house problem do you think I have, Jack? I'm not the one who's an accessory to a crime.'

Jack set Vickie aside to lean in close. 'You're not, huh? Well, play nice and maybe no one else needs to know better. *Capisce?*'

Capisce.

NINETEEN

'Lady killer and lady chiller? Truly?'

Sarah and I formed a united front, standing shoulder-to-shoulder at the front window as Vickie LaTour and Jack Andersen retreated down the front steps to the sidewalk.

'Lady killer is self-explanatory. And "chiller" like on ice. I thought it was kind of clever. And apropos, as it turns out, given the *capisce* thing. The guy's a mobster.'

The adrenaline had ebbed; now fear was seeping in. 'Let's sit down before my knees buckle.'

'You were great,' Sarah said, following me to the high counter that faced the window.

I pulled out a stool and climbed up, watching the two move out of sight. 'He did threaten Pavlik and me, right? I mean, I didn't just imagine that?'

'The "glass house" and "rocks" thing was pretty clear, I think.' Sarah hiked herself up on the chair next to me. 'And what exactly was it that he whispered to you before the *capisce*? I missed it.'

Sure. This had to be the only whisper that nobody else heard. 'Something about playing nice and maybe nobody would have to know better.'

'About what?'

'Accessory to some crime. I have no idea what he means. And why bring Pavlik into it?'

'Could it have something to do with the reason they put him on leave?'

'Medical leave,' I said. 'Pavlik is a hero. He only got shot because he tried to save Pete.'

'I know that,' Sarah said. 'But you know how it is. Everybody has their own version of the truth.'

'I don't buy that. A fact is a fact, by definition.'

'And it's a fact that Jack Andersen thinks he's got something on you and Pavlik. Maybe when you go home to your house hubby you should find out what that is.'

'I honestly have no idea.'

I'd found Pavlik sitting at the kitchen table, a computer in front of him.

He sat back now. 'The bus station is a dead end so far. The security camera in the parking lot hasn't been working for a month, so we don't even know when the Chrysler was dumped. We do have a camera at the ticket window inside.'

'But no Pauly?'

'Nope. And not on the cameras on the surrounding buildings either. It's possible he jumped a train without a ticket, of course.'

'You said the stolen car was a Chrysler?'

'Yes.' He hit a few keys. 'And you, my dear, know the owner. Dark green Chrysler belonging to Gloria Goddard. Report filed Monday afternoon by Oliver—'

'Benson.' Small world, indeed. 'Well, that sucks. Gloria had a stroke, which is why she's at the manor in the first place, and now her car was stolen?'

'From the rehab wing,' Pavlik said, nodding. 'She and Benson used the car on Sunday—'

'To come to Uncommon Grounds.'

'I didn't know that.' Pavlik made a note. 'You do have a finger on the pulse of this town.'

'Only the arteries that run by my coffeehouse.' I settled on the chair across from him. 'Are you back on the case?'

'Not officially, no.' He punched some keys.

'But you talked to Hallonquist.' I gestured at the folder next to the computer.

'One of my friends on the Milwaukee PD, since the train station is there. I decided I'd be putting Hallonquist in a bad position by asking him to keep me updated. I'm his boss – or at least was – so he'd feel an obligation even if he was instructed not to.'

'You think he's been instructed not to?' I asked.

'It's an ongoing investigation. More than one ongoing investigation. Pauly Andersen is one case, then there's Taylor's suicide, and also the question of whether the shoot-out at the manor was reckless.'

'You didn't start that – Pauly did. And you had evacuated people from the surrounding apartments. What were you supposed to do? Let him go?'

'I know. But a complaint has been filed so they have to investigate it.'

I frowned. 'Who complained?'

'Well, that's another interesting thing,' he said, leaning back in his chair. 'Vickie LaTour.'

'Who happens to be Jack Andersen's girlfriend.'

'Which I only know because you told me. And I thank you for that.'

'It's what I do.' I was chewing on this new information. 'Do you think Jack put her up to it?'

'I wouldn't be a bit surprised.'

'But Vickie is my friend,' I said. 'Why would she do this?'

'I doubt that she's thinking of it as something she's doing to you. And even if she is, she wouldn't be the first woman Jack Andersen convinced to abandon her friends as well as her scruples.'

'Geez, what's this guy got?' I asked. 'I just don't see it. The only things in his face that move are his eyes. And you should have seen them change when I challenged him.'

'You obviously pushed the right buttons. If you were one of his "ladies," he'd make that seem to be your fault.'

Like an abuser, who only hit you because you asked for it. 'And revert to charming, I suppose. Until the next time.'

'Exactly.'

I'd seen the chameleon-like change in the man. 'Could he be abusing her? Physically, I mean?'

'It's not his M.O. but there are other methods of abuse. Isolating somebody from their friends, for one.'

Or turning her against them. 'Do you think that's the leverage he thinks he has on you? Vickie's complaint?'

'Petty stuff for a guy like Andersen. Besides, a complaint would be public record. What's there to expose?'

'I don't know, but he said I had a glass house problem and he had rocks.'

Pavlik's lips twitched. 'He really said that?'

'He did.' I got up and opened the kitchen cabinet. 'Glass of wine?'

He nodded. I poured two glasses and handed one to Pavlik. 'For what it's worth, Hannah Bouchard likes Jack Andersen about as much as I do. Says he insinuates himself in situations and she's absolutely right.'

'What do you mean?

'For example, he offered to come to the lawyer with her instead of me. Who does that?'

'A con man.'

I'd been about to take a sip of wine but stopped mid-air. 'You think he's decided Hannah is a better mark than Vickie?'

'From what you've said, she's got money – or will, once she gets hold of it. That's one of his pre-requisites.'

'But Hannah is probably in her early forties. If Mort is twenty years older, tack on another ten or fifteen for Jack.'

'Age-appropriateness is *not* one of his requirements. One of his victims was in her thirties.'

Yikes. 'I guess at least he'd leave Vickie alone.' And likely heartbroken.

'And destroy Hannah instead.'

'True. Though I think she's more able to take care of herself. Besides, Vickie is a friend.'

Pavlik's eyebrows went up. 'I thought Hannah was a friend, too.'

'A very new friend, so if I had to rank her on my concern-o-meter she'd have to be below Vickie.'

The sheriff grinned. 'Good thing you didn't go into law enforcement. You'd have to serve and protect people you didn't even know.'

'Oh, I would if I swore to.' I looked over his shoulder. 'What are you doing now?'

'Checking the layouts of the bus station and adjoining buildings to see if we missed something.'

'Somewhere he could have disappeared to.' I sat down. 'Didn't you say the Milwaukee police are on this?'

'They are, but I can provide an extra brain and set of eyes. I've studied Pauly and—'

My phone rang but I sent it to voicemail. 'Sorry.'

'Anyway, the MPD is happy to have me helping and it gives me something to do, which makes me happy.'

'And me.' I reached across the table and put my hand on his mouse. Which was where *his* hand was. 'I—'

The phone rang again and this time I glanced at the readout. 'Christy – both times.' Then, 'Hi, Christy,' I said into it.

'Maggy, did you hear? It's just the saddest thing. Nancy Casperson has died.'

'Died of what? I just saw her this morning.'

Pavlik's chin gestured, *What's going on?'*

I lifted my shoulders.

'I know you did, which is why I was sure you'd want to know. Hannah brought Nancy home after your meeting and then ran over to see Mort about the funeral expenses and all. When she got home an hour later, Nancy was dead.'

'She died in her sleep?'

'Yes, isn't it awful? Just like Celeste. *Déjà vu.'*

Or a horror version of the movie *Groundhog Day*. Except at Hannah's house, fewer and fewer people were waking up each morning.

TWENTY

'So, Hannah finds out she can't remove Nancy as trustee, at least easily. A few hours later, Nancy is dead.'

We'd moved on to the second course of our meal, from the wine to peanut butter sandwiches.

'Convenient, but maybe too much so.'

I stopped smoothing my chunky spread onto the bread. 'Too obvious, you mean?'

'I mean she'd have to be an idiot to kill Nancy and think she'll get away with it.' Pavlik appropriated the knife and jar of Skippy from me. 'Is she?'

'I don't think so. But she is desperate.' I gestured at his sandwich – more a mutilated piece of bread. 'Can I please help you with that? Spreading peanut butter one-handed is not working.'

'Fine.' He passed the peanut butter to me and I took his plate. 'You don't have any Jif, do you?'

Jif brand peanut butter, instead of Skippy? Sacrilege. What was next? Pepsi over Coke? Decaf over regular?

But I just said, 'Sorry, no.'

'Or cracked wheat bread?'

Them's fighting words. 'Peanut butter on cracked wheat? That's un-American.'

'Not for this American,' Pavlik said, getting up and swinging open the refrigerator door. 'You have any decaffeinated Diet Pepsi?'

'Nooooooo . . .'

Frank raised his head and then cocked it, the doggy version of, *What the hell are you doing?*

Pavlik just asked, 'Was it something I said?'

'No, I'm fine. And I don't have any Diet Pepsi that's de—' I choked on the word, 'decaffeinated. But I can get some, if you like.'

'Nah.' Pavlik sat back down with a Diet Coke and popped it open one-handed. 'I just wanted to see what you'd say.'

I passed his sandwich of Chunky Skippy on white bread, thank you very much, to him. 'That was mean.'

'But kind of fun.' He put his hand over mine. 'I know that two people of our ages thinking about blending households . . . it isn't an easy thing.'

'But,' I ran my index finger down his palm, 'it's kind of fun.'

'I did mention to Pavlik,' I said to Sarah the next morning, 'that—'

'Wait,' she said, waving a dishtowel in my face, 'was this before or after sex?'

'Who said we had sex?' I snatched the towel.

'Your face.' She snatched it back. 'And your laid-back vibe.'

'I'm always laid back.' I opened the dishwasher and started to load in the dirty cups from the morning rush hour.

'That's clean,' Sarah said.

'Oops, guess we'd better run it again.' I added soap, closed the door and pushed the power button.

'See?'

'See what?'

'See how chill you are. Non-sated Maggy would have been ticked off at whoever didn't empty it, then ticked off at herself, for not checking before she put in the dirty cups.'

'I—'

Sarah held up her hand. 'I'm not done. Then you would have debated leaving the cups and taking out the clean dishes around them. Taking out one, you'd have sighed, put it back, finally slammed the door and re-started the machine.'

'You make me sound demented.'

'You are.' My partner was feeling better, with just the occasional cough to show she'd been sick. She chalked it up to the antibiotics. I just figured germs didn't stand a chance against her.

'Anyway,' I said, 'I told Pavlik that you and I both questioned Hannah's . . .'

'Martyrdom?'

'Exactly.'

'What did he say?'

'He seemed more inclined to give her the benefit of the doubt.' I felt myself blush. 'But then we kind of got off the subject and didn't quite get back to it.'

'I'm sorry I brought it up.' Sarah hiked herself up on the kitchen counter.

Not sanitary practice, but what the hell.

I did the same.

'Returning to our regular G-rated programming,' Sarah said, 'what does Nancy's death mean for Holy Hannah?'

'Poof goes the problem of accessing the trust, for one thing.'

'That's awfully convenient.'

'Plus, they both died in their sleep? How lame is that?'

Sarah bobbed her head. 'To be fair, probably a lot of old people die in their sleep. If they're lucky.'

Since when was my partner fair? 'You have a point, but I'm not going to give up on mine.'

'I didn't think you would.'

'So Celeste dies . . .'

'In her sleep . . .'

'Or at least while napping,' I continued, 'on Sunday while Hannah is away.'

'And the same thing happens to Nancy four days later,' Sarah continued. 'Also when Hannah is away again.'

'You know,' I said, 'someone like Christy or Amy—'

'Somebody with a heart?'

'Well, yes,' I admitted. 'They'd say Nancy died of a broken heart.'

'Sweet,' Sarah said. 'And I'm sure it happens, but it's just too convenient. Don't you think?'

'I do. I asked Pavlik to see if there was an autopsy on Celeste.'

'Will he?'

'He would and he did. Believe me, Pavlik's looking for anything and everything to keep him busy.'

'And?'

'As he suspected, there was no autopsy, given her age and all.'

'Old people die.'

'They do. And the body's been cremated, so there's no going back.'

'What about Nancy?'

'You mean will there be an autopsy? Yes.'

'Then Nancy's death is considered suspicious?'

'Pavlik might have suggested that it might be.' I shifted my bum on the hard counter.

'You said he wasn't in touch with his department. That it wasn't fair or something I didn't quite understand.'

'Not fair for him to press his detectives – Hallonquist, in particular – on the shooting, which involves Pavlik and is still under investigation. He had no problem letting them know about the trust and what Hannah has to gain.'

'Which you told him.'

'I did.' I couldn't resist a satisfied smile. 'All of a sudden, we're like Nick and Nora, trading theories. It's kind of nice.'

'Don't get used to it. He'll be back to being sheriff and shutting you out in no time.'

I hopped down. 'True. But right now I'm enjoying having him around.'

'Aww.' Sarah tipped her head. 'Are those wedding bells I hear?'

I heard them too, except, 'Those are my sleigh bells!'

Mort Ashbury came around the corner dangling two red ribbons with bells attached. 'Look what I found.'

I took them. 'Where were they?'

'In the dumpster in the parking lot.'

Sarah slid off the counter, too. 'What were you doing in our dumpster?'

Mort looked surprised at the abrupt question. 'Well, I . . .'

'Don't mind Sarah,' I said. 'We've had trouble with people dumping things and then we're charged for the removal.'

'Get your own damn dumpster, I say,' Sarah said.

'Not you, Mort,' I said. 'I'm sure the mortuary has its own trash removal service.'

'And who knows what you put in it,' Sarah added.

Thankfully, Mort didn't enlighten her. 'To answer your first question, Sarah, I had an old to-go cup in the cup-holder in my car and dumped it to make way for the new one.'

Getting the hint, I set down the bells and picked up a cup. 'Today's brew is Sumatran.'

'Sounds good,' Mort said. 'It's going to be another busy day. Both the Hartsfield and Taylor services are scheduled for tomorrow.'

I assumed Pavlik would want to go. 'They're not at the same time, are they?'

'No, no. The Taylor service is at one o'clock at Angel of Mercy and the Hartsfield funeral will be at four in our chapel. We knew people – especially law enforcement – would want to attend both.'

'Christy called to tell me about Nancy,' I said, pouring his coffee.

He sighed. 'Another tough one. The elderly die, of course, but so soon after Celeste? It's very hard on Hannah.'

'I bet,' Sarah said, the inflection somewhere in the wasteland between sympathetic and sarcastic. 'We hear there's an autopsy.'

'This morning,' Mort confirmed. 'It's unnecessary in my opinion, given she'd been ill and under Doctor Goode's care. But for whatever reason, it's been ordered.'

Pavlik and I were the whatever. 'Is Hannah worried?'

'I think more relieved than anything.' He opened his wallet and took four dollars out.

Sarah's head went up. 'Relieved that Nancy is dead?'

'Oh, heavens, no. That an autopsy is being done. She feels responsible, I think, and an official cause of death will give her closure. Well, thank you for this,' he continued, picking up his cup, 'and just put the change in the tip jar.'

'Thank you,' I called after him as he hurried out of the door. Then I turned to Sarah. 'That's interesting.'

'What do you mean?' She'd picked up the dishtowel and was wiping the ring Mort's cup had left.

'If Hannah killed Nancy, why would she be grateful for an autopsy?'

'Maybe she just told him that to cover her tracks. Or maybe he's in on it and he's just saying that.'

'Both possible, I guess.' I chewed on my lip. 'It's curious that Mort said Doctor Goode was Nancy's doctor when she'd only seen her once. And that time, according to Hannah, only to prescribe a sedative after Celeste died.'

'Maybe that's all it takes.'

My phone jangled. 'Would you please get a clean towel? You're just smearing around coffee smooge with more coffee smooge.'

Sarah looked skyward, and then went to the backroom to do as she was told. For once.

I checked my phone and saw that it was Pavlik. 'Hi, there.'

'The autopsy results are back.'

'And?'

'And there are petechiae in the eyes.'

Small hemorrhages. 'Nancy was strangled?'

'Suffocated. There were no ligature marks or bruising.'

'She'd been sick – a cold or the flu. Could congestion have caused it?'

'Struggling to breathe causes the petechial hemorrhaging, so theoretically, yes. But there's something else.'

Sarah had returned with a fresh cloth and held it out to me.

I punched up the speaker on the phone so Sarah could hear and mouthed, 'Pavlik.'

'Yes?' I said to the sheriff. 'You said there was something else?'

'We – or Hallonquist and his new partner – think a pillow might have been used to smother her and there's a pillowcase missing.'

'The killer took the pillowcase?'

'A yellow flowered pillowcase, according to Hannah Bouchard.'

'Maggy,' Sarah whispered.

I waved her off. 'Why take the pillowcase and not the pillow?'

'Something on it, I assume. Something that didn't penetrate to the pillow, which was hers in the first place.'

'So finding Nancy's DNA on the pillow would mean nothing.'

'Most likely.'

'So why—'

The towel came flying across the room and fell at my feet.

Except it wasn't a towel. It was a pillowcase covered in yellow daisies. And with a red lipstick stain on it.

'I'll call you back,' I said into the phone.

TWENTY-ONE

'**N**ancy wasn't wearing lipstick when I saw her,' I said for the third time.

'Oh, good,' Sarah said. 'The pillowcase isn't the murder weapon and we're off the hook for touching it.'

'You touched it,' I said, holding the thing by the wooden tongs we used for getting stuck toast out of the toaster. The sticky bun tongs were in the dishwasher. 'And I kind of doubt that a pillowcase would hold fingerprints anyway.'

'Good,' she said. 'Let's throw it in a dumpster. Mort's got one and who'd want to dig through that?'

'The last thing we need is for somebody – or some camera – to catch us disposing of it,' I said. 'We're not guilty. Why act like it?'

'Then why not tell Nick, Nora?'

I didn't think that was such a good idea, either. 'Pavlik may be on leave but he's not going to withhold evidence.'

'Yet we are.'

'Because it's evidence against *us*.'

'You might want to lower your voice,' Sarah said. 'Unless you want people walking down the street to hear us discussing this.'

I rubbed my forehead. 'How did it get here?'

'Well, there were no bells on either door. If we were behind the service counter or in the front of the store, somebody could come in the platform door and go right into the storeroom without us ever seeing them.'

'OK, so there's the how,' I said. 'And I don't want you ever to complain about those bells again, once I put them back up. But what's the why?'

'Why would the killer plant evidence on us? Got me. You're the one arguing with the Scandinavian mob.'

Jack Andersen. 'You think this is a crime that I was supposed to be accessory to? Maybe it had nothing to do with Pavlik.'

'Then who's the friend?'

'What friend?' I was casting about for somewhere to put the pillowcase.

Sarah shook out a plastic garbage bag and held it out. 'Here.'

I dropped the pillowcase in. 'Your fingerprints will be on that bag.'

'Then we'll dump out the pillowcase and take the bag with us. At least we're protecting the evidence.'

'I think the police use paper bags. Or is that just for wet things?'

'Wouldn't you put wet in plastic?'

'It can degrade the evidence, I think. But this isn't wet.' I looked inside the bag. 'At least, I don't think it is.'

'Is the lipstick considered wet?'

'I'm not sure.' I had a different question on my mind. 'Why would somebody put lipstick on Nancy and then suffocate her?'

'It's evidence. They wanted to pin it on us and it's the only thing they could think of.'

'It's so cruel, though. Poor Nancy having this crazy person

applying lipstick on her?' I had a thought. 'Speaking of crazy, maybe Pauly Andersen had a hand in this.'

'If he's still in the area after being responsible for two cops dead and one being wounded, he *is* crazy.'

'And it runs in the family, from what I've seen of Jack. He just has a shiny candy-coating over the rot.'

'I think you're making a mistake.'

'Not calling Pavlik, you mean?' I'd been hunkered over the bag and now I stood up.

'No, I'm fine with that. I think it's a mistake letting Hannah off the hook. She's the one who benefitted from both Celeste and Nancy's deaths.'

'True.' A lightbulb went off. 'Maybe she's the friend.'

'What?'

'You asked who the friend Jack referred to was, if not Pavlik.'

'Yeah, when he said something like "you and your friend have a glass house."'

'I assumed he was talking about Pavlik, since he had just come to stay at my place. But maybe Jack was talking about Hannah.'

'He thinks you and Hannah killed the old ladies?'

'That's the only thing that makes sense.'

'Hannah, I get. We suspect her, too. But why you? You barely know the woman and have no motive.'

'Maybe because Hannah wanted me to go to the lawyer with her and not him?' I had a thought. 'He threatened me. Maybe he's blackmailing her.'

'Hannah?'

'Yes, maybe that's why she's so hot to get her hands on the trust. She said she needed to pay Celeste's final expenses. Including blackmail?'

'If he's blackmailing her, that means she killed Celeste. And then, following that logic, she also had to have killed Nancy to get access to the money.'

'That means she's the one who put the pillowcase here. But why frame me?'

'She could be framing me,' Sarah said. 'Or isn't that in the realm of your possibilities?'

'Oh, for God's sake,' I said, picking up the bag with my toast tongs and holding it out to her. 'Are you jealous? Because if you want to be framed, it's fine with me.'

'I just don't like to be dismissed.'

'You have as much of a motive as I do, which is none. Yet somebody stashed Nancy's lipstick-stained pillowcase with our towels.'

'They folded it first.'

'So? Being neat doesn't preclude you from being a murderer.' I didn't understand any of it. 'I'm going to ask Pavlik to find out if Nancy's body had lipstick on it.'

'I thought you didn't want him to know about . . .' she gestured at the bag I was still holding, '. . . that.'

'I'm hoping I can finesse it.' I pulled out my phone with my free hand. 'Can you hold down the fort for a while?'

'If you do something with the evidence,' she said. 'Has it occurred to you that whoever framed us wants it found? The police or sheriff's department could be on their way as we speak.'

'Shit, no answer,' I said. 'OK, I'm going, but I'll hide this on my way out.'

'Are you going to see Pavlik?'

'No. I need to think about how I'm going to approach him on the lipstick thing. I don't want to invite questions.' I dropped my phone into my purse. 'I'm going to see Bernie.'

'Ah, the lawyer. Maybe you'll see Hannah there.'

'That's just what I'm thinking.' Taking my tonged garbage bag with me, I left through the side door.

TWENTY-TWO

But nobody was in Bernie's office, except for Bernie.

'Hannah called me this morning.' He waved me into a guest chair. 'But I can't tell you anything beyond that. And you know it.'

'I do.' I sat. 'But I was hoping you might bend the rules, since I was here with Hannah and Nancy just . . . Geez, was it just yesterday?'

'It was.'

'And now she's dead.'

'So I understand.'

'C'mon, Bernie,' I said, leaning forward to put my elbows on his desk. 'This has to smell as fishy to you as it does to me. Yesterday, Nancy was blocking Hannah's access to the trust. A few hours later, she's dead. And Hannah's already called here, presumably to get access to the trust to pay "expenses," right?'

'It would be within her rights.' He was my friend, but he was also her lawyer now, which meant he was measuring his words.

'Nancy was murdered.'

'What?' That had gotten his attention. 'By whom?'

'The autopsy says she suffocated.'

He was literally on the edge of his chair. It squeaked. 'Suffocated, or *was* suffocated.'

Potatoes, potahtoes. Lawyers and their words. 'Technically, she suffocated.'

'Geez, there you go again, Maggy. It's always got to be murder. An elderly woman died of suffocation. Maybe she choked on something.'

'Yes, a pillow. Then after she was dead she took off the pillowcase and stuck it in my storeroom.'

'Holy shit.'

'Yeah.'

'Are you hiring me?'

Since I'd just blabbed, I was torn between 'I don't need a lawyer' and 'yes, please,' which would get me confidentiality for a mere $400 per hour.

Then came a pounding at the door, which I'd locked behind me. 'Hello? Is anybody in there?'

Hannah. Bernie and I exchanged looks, and I had to assume my eyes were as big as his.

'If she hires you to represent her and I'm here, does that give me confidentiality about what I just told you?'

'What?'

'The pil—'

'Shhh.' He held up a hand. 'I don't know what you're talking about.'

Good enough for me. 'Should I let her in?'

Bernie threw out his arms. 'Why not?'

I opened the door.

'Oh, Maggy, did you hear? Poor Nancy was murdered and they think I did it.' She threw her arms around me and burst into tears.

I just stood there stiffly and let her cry it out on my shoulder, before leading her into Bernie's office.

After all, the woman might have killed two women and tried to frame me for one of the murders. No hugs for her.

Bernie poured a glass of water for her and then sat back down. 'What can I help you with, Hannah?'

'Didn't you hear me? Nancy was suffocated and I'm a suspect. The investigators are crawling all over everywhere looking for a pillowcase.'

Bernie's eyes flicked to me and then back. 'A pillowcase.'

'It's missing off one of the bed pillows. The pillow itself was next to Nancy on the bed. I noticed it when I got home and wondered where the cover was, but . . .'

'You have to believe me,' she continued to Bernie. 'I didn't do this. I would never do this. She was . . .' She started to sob again.

The woman was in worse shape than when her mother died. I guess a murder rap hanging over your head could do that.

I was feeling none too chipper myself. 'Are you being blackmailed, Hannah?'

'What?' from both she and Bernie.

'How can you ask me that?'

There had been the slightest hesitation after the word 'how.' Had she started to ask how I knew?

'Just a feeling,' I said, watching her. 'Jack Andersen is a sleazeball and he gives me the creeps. I think you feel the same.'

'And so he must be blackmailing us? For what?' Her words were defensive but there was fear in her eyes.

'I'm not sure. Something about your mother's death, I think.'

That seemed to score, but maybe only half a point. 'I . . . I came here for help. Not to be accused.'

'If you're being blackmailed, you're the victim,' I said. 'Maybe Bernie and I can help.'

Bernie's face said he didn't want any part of this, but he kept quiet.

'I don't need your help. I came here to see my lawyer. In private.' She stood up.

I gestured for her to sit down and got up myself. 'I'm sorry. You're absolutely right. I'll go.'

When I got to the door, I turned. 'But when you said, "he must be blackmailing us," who is the "us"?'

'She didn't answer me, of course,' I told Pavlik over Chinese that night. 'And if looks could kill, Bernie's would have dissolved me right there and then.'

'Essentially, you just stirred her up and then left him to deal with her.' He was trying to get fried noodles out with chopsticks and the box kept moving away from him.

I took it and pushed a tangle of noodles onto his plate. 'I did. I called later and apologized.'

'Thanks,' he said. 'And I assume you also tried to worm more information out of him.'

'Would you expect any less?' I helped myself to orange chicken. 'But, alas, all he told me was that he'd recommended a criminal attorney and that was pretty much that.'

'Bernie's a good lawyer. I'm sure after he'd gotten over his initial astonishment at the idea that his client might be a murderer—'

'Who might also be being blackmailed,' I interjected.

'He went back into professional mode. Did you get any sense of whether she was able to access the funds in the trust? If so, Andersen could get his money and be in the wind along with his brother.'

I was enjoying having Pavlik egging me on, rather than lifting his leg on my ideas. 'You think I could be right about the blackmail then?'

'A man like Andersen is always on the lookout for a new opportunity to make money. If he stumbled on information that made him think Hannah had something to hide, sure I believe it. I just don't know why he seemed to be threatening you as well.'

'For some reason, he believes that I'm in this with her. Whatever this is.'

'The "us."' Pavlik scored a piece of chicken off my plate. 'Could it be Hannah and Nancy?'

'They killed Celeste for her money? But if they're in collusion, why did Nancy refuse to let Hannah have access to the trust?'

'She wanted it all for herself maybe.'

'The woman fell apart after Celeste died – mentally and physically.'

'Guilt can do that.'

'True.' Greed and guilt wouldn't make good bed partners. 'I wish we knew how much is in the trust.'

'Bernie would be disbarred if he told you that. And rightfully so.'

'Could a trust be subpoenaed?'

'Not a trust, because it's an entity. But a trustee probably could. There would have to be cause, though.'

'The trustee is Hannah now. I assume they're looking at her seriously for Nancy's murder.'

'More seriously, if they could find the pillowcase.'

I put down my chopsticks. 'What would that prove that the pillow can't? From what Hannah said, it was Nancy's pillow – and pillowcase – so her DNA will be all over them.'

'There could be a stain or something that didn't soak through to the pillow. But more than that, it's the absence of the pillowcase that's important. Somebody was there and took it for some reason.'

'Maybe to frame somebody else?' I leaned down to put my plate on the floor so Frank could slobber up the rest of my rice.

When I sat back up, Pavlik had an odd look on his face. 'Why would you say that?'

I tried for casual, but not push all the way to nonchalance. 'Like you said, taking the case only raised suspicion in the first place. Why not leave it and hope Nancy's death passed for natural causes?'

'I didn't say that, but it's a point. The case could also have traces of the assailant on it, meaning he or she would have been forced to take it.'

'What kind of traces? A pillowcase wouldn't show fingerprints, would it?' I wanted to confirm what I'd told Sarah.

'Not likely, but there could be blood, sweat, hair, that sort of thing. Thing is, if Hannah is the killer, those traces – except for the blood, probably – are easily explained by the fact she lived in the house.'

'And probably made the beds,' I added. 'Which is why, I guess, I was thinking there was another reason for removing the pillowcase.'

'We'll know when and if it's found.' He was studying me. 'You wouldn't know where it might be, would you?'

'Me? How could I know that? Oh, by the way, I saw Mort this morning. Did you know Al and Pete's funerals are both tomorrow?'

Pavlik's face dropped and I felt ashamed for changing the subject to the loss of his officers. Not that he could ever forget, but when we'd been discussing the case he'd been distracted and, seemingly, happy.

'Hallonquist told me when we talked,' he said. 'He'd be willing to come pick me up if you have to work.'

'That's nice of him. But I'd like to go with you. If it's OK with you?'

'Better than OK,' Pavlik said. 'Thank you.'

He took my hand and I felt ashamed all over again. This time for lying to him about the pillowcase.

TWENTY-THREE

I took the opening shift the next day so I could leave at noon to pick up Pavlik for the funerals. He was waiting at the door in full dress uniform when I pulled in.

'How did you get into that all by yourself?' I asked as he climbed into the Escape. 'I should have come home early so I could help you.'

'I can move my left arm, you know. It just,' he rolled it and winced, 'smarts a bit when I do this.'

'Then don't do this.'

Pavlik threw me the look the old gag deserved. I knew that it smarted more than a bit. I also knew he'd deny it.

'You know,' I said, backing out of the driveway, 'I was thinking last night—'

'When was that?' Pavlik asked. 'Before Frank jumped up and sat on my head or after?'

'After. Anyway, if Hannah is being blackmailed by Jack, like we talked about, that would have to be for Celeste's murder.'

'We don't know that Celeste was murdered.'

'And never will.' I pointed the car south on Poplar Creek Road toward Angel of Mercy, where Al Taylor's service was being held. 'But if Jack has something on Hannah—'

'Which he also thinks he has on you—'

This was the downside of being with – and trying to keep things from – somebody as smart as the sheriff. Pavlik knew stuff. And figured out other stuff to go with it. I could almost see the sheriff slotting 'missing pillowcase' right up there next to 'Jack's leverage on Maggy.'

'It has to be something that pre-dates Nancy's death,' I continued.

'I'll give you that. Turn here.'

'But the church is on the next street down.'

'I know, but we'll park behind the church with the squads.'

I followed directions. 'But if our theory is that Hannah was already being blackmailed for Celeste's murder, she certainly wouldn't kill Nancy and give him even more of a hold on her.'

I expected him to correct 'our theory,' but he surprised me. 'When I hit a roadblock in a case, I step back to the various forks in the road and rethink my assumptions. Maybe we're wrong about the blackmail in the first place. Or it has nothing to do with the deaths of Celeste and Nancy.'

Like I said, he knows stuff. 'Other than that Hannah moved here with them in December, I don't know enough about her to guess what else Jack might have on her.'

'Who would?' Pavlik asked, unclicking his seatbelt as we pulled up next to a Brookhills' County squad car.

'Christy, maybe.' I shut off the engine. 'She sold Hannah the house here. Or, better yet, Mort. They're dating.'

'Mort and Hannah?'

'Yup.'

'That's interesting.' Pavlik had gone to open the door and now he sat back. 'Mort will be here today.'

'Want me to talk to him?'

'Let me,' Pavlik said, swinging open the door. 'You take Christy.'

'I'm not sure she'll be here,' I said, getting out and coming around the car.

'I am.' Pavlik pointed to the back door of the church, where Christy was talking to her boss. 'We'll divide and conquer, but not necessarily now. We have all day and two funerals. You catch Christy alone and I'll do the same with Mort.'

'Sheriff.' It was Mike Hallonquist. He was in full dress uniform, too.

'Mike.' They shook hands. 'You know Maggy Thorsen.'

'Of course. Good to see you, Maggy.'

'Same,' I said. 'I'm so sorry about Al.'

'He could act like a jerk but he was a good cop.'

I smiled. 'And here I always thought you were the one playing the good cop, to his bad.'

'It was our shtick,' Hallonquist said with a matching grin. 'We tried it the other way around, but I couldn't cut it.'

'I bet.' I shook my head. 'Despite Al's hard-ass act, I never questioned his heart, at least once I got to know him.' Which admittedly had been a rocky time.

As we approached the back door, Mort and Christy finished their conversation and Mort went inside. Christy started down the sidewalk toward us.

I thought I had my opportunity to talk to her, but Pavlik took my arm and said, 'Wait.'

Whether it was because Christy seemed in a hurry or Hallonquist was with us, I didn't know, but I followed his lead. 'Hi, Christy.'

'Oh, hi, Maggy. I'm running back to the mortuary to help prepare for the Hartsfield service. Will I see you there?'

'You will. You remember Jake Pavlik, and this is Mike Hallonquist.'

'I'm so sorry for your losses,' Christy said. 'We will do right by your officers. Mr and Mrs Taylor are inside if you'd like to greet them before the service.'

She hurried away with a sympathetic smile.

'She really has taken to this,' I said.

'To what?' Hallonquist asked.

To dealing with death was what I was thinking, but I said, 'Christy just started with the mortuary after years of teaching piano. It seemed quite a leap at the time.'

'They're both service industries, I guess,' Hallonquist said. And then, 'What the hell?'

We had rounded the corner to the front of the church.

'Now that's interesting,' Pavlik said.

I followed their gazes and saw Jack Andersen in a dark suit amidst a sea of blue uniforms. As we were watching, Vickie LaTour came out to meet him. 'Oh, that's not good.'

'Actually,' Pavlik said, 'it could be. Let's go say hello to your friend.'

I assumed he meant Vickie. Facetiousness wasn't Pavlik's thing.

'Oh, Maggy,' Vickie said, looking relieved to see a familiar civilian face. 'I'm so glad to see you.'

She seemed so adrift and panicked that I gave her a hug. And I'm not much more of a hugger than Sarah is. 'What are you doing here?' I whispered into her ear.

'Jack insisted,' she whispered back. 'To pay our respects. I'm . . . I'm appalled.' The woman was visibly trembling.

'Andersen.' Pavlik didn't take the man's proffered hand.

'Sheriff Pavlik.' He turned to Hallonquist. 'And Detective . . .?'

'Hallonquist,' Pavlik supplied. 'Al Taylor's partner.'

'Of course,' Andersen said. 'I'm so sorry.'

'If you're so sorry, tell us where your brother is so we can put him away for life,' Hallonquist said.

As he spoke, I saw officers stepping back. It took me a second to realize that if trouble started, they wanted time to react.

And get a good shot off. Out of the corner of my eye, I saw Father Jim move out of the narthex and, if not into the fray, near it.

Pavlik had seen him, too. 'Now, Mike, that's not fair. I'm sure Father Jim here would say that Andersen's not his brother's keeper.'

But Father Jim shook his head. 'I'm afraid that was

what Cain said when God asked him where his brother Abel was.'

'That's right.' Pavlik cocked his head. 'And hadn't Cain killed his brother?'

'He had,' Jim said. 'Beyond that, though, we should all be our brother's keepers. In that light, Cain's denial was both against doctrine and an outright lie.'

'Because he knew very well where his brother was,' I said.

Pavlik nodded. 'Or at least where he'd left his body.'

Silence. One, two, three beats. Then, 'I killed my brother? That's the analogy you're going for?' Jack Andersen was smooth.

'Parallel, analogy.' Pavlik shrugged. 'Take your pick.'

'And why, in this work of fiction you're weaving, would I do that?'

'Money?' Pavlik ducked his head. 'I'm sorry to say that your brother Pauly is violent and uncontrollable. None too smart, either. You, on the other hand, are very smart. You plan, you pick your mark, you execute. But with him on the loose, you never know when he's going to show up and ruin one of your schemes. Like with Vickie here.'

Jack put out his hand and pulled Vickie toward him. 'There is no scheme this time. Vickie and I are in love.'

I wasn't sure that was true on either side, at least anymore. But she said, 'Let's get out of here, Jack. Please.'

Andersen held up his hands. 'What about it, Sheriff? Are you going to arrest me? Oh,' the hands went down again, 'I forgot. You're not sheriff anymore, are you?'

'He is as far as we're concerned,' a voice from somewhere in the blue-uniformed crowd said. 'All he has to do is say the word.'

'No, Andersen's right,' Pavlik said. 'I'm not in a position to take him down. Yet.'

'C'mon, Jack,' Vickie said, tugging at him.

Finally he relented and let her pull him away. As they did, the blue sea parted to let them through.

'What was that?' I whispered in Pavlik's ear as we sat waiting for the service to start. 'Are you telling me you knew Jack killed his brother all this time?'

'Of course not,' Pavlik said. 'It came to me when I thought of the Cain and Abel story.'

'Really?' I sat back. 'That's pretty cool.'

Pavlik tipped his chin. 'It is, assuming it's true and he takes the bait.'

TWENTY-FOUR

Detective Al Taylor's service was short and sad. Taylor was divorced with no kids and his mom and dad, both in their seventies, seemed to be surprised and overwhelmed by the support from his fellow officers.

'But he took his own life,' his mother whispered to Pavlik in the receiving line afterwards.

'Al was one of my best detectives,' Pavlik said. 'He could be a pain in the butt, if you'll excuse me for saying—'

Next to his wife, Mr Taylor cracked a small smile. 'Nothing we don't always know, right, Helen? Remember all the trouble he gave us growing up? Always had to have the last word.'

She nodded once and a tear rolled slowly down her cheek.

'But we always knew he had our backs,' Pavlik said. 'He felt he let us down and didn't seem to want to hear otherwise.'

'And so he had the last word.' Mrs Taylor held up a shaky finger. 'One more time.'

Pavlik smiled. 'Your son was a good man.'

His father was folding and refolding the order of service. 'He left what he had to that poor widow and her daughter. I think . . . I think that was a very honorable thing to do.'

'Yes,' Mrs Taylor said, her voice breaking. 'Al did his best.'

'Now we'll do the same, Helen,' her husband said. 'And get through this. He never wanted us to hurt like this.'

We walked to the car in silence.

'Is it wrong for me to hope that Pauly Andersen is dead?' I said, getting in. 'And that he suffered as much as Al Taylor and his parents? And Mrs Hartsfield and,' I looked across the center console, 'you.'

'That's probably a question best asked of Father Jim. I'm more of an eye-for-an-eye man.'

'Don't give me that,' I said. 'You believe in justice, not vigilantism.'

'You don't know that. Maybe I'll go rogue if I'm not reinstated.'

I had no fears of Pavlik going rogue, but the fact he was thinking of life after sheriffing broke my heart. 'Fighting for justice. Does this mean we're going shopping for a bat spotlight and a cape?'

'Please. I'm not a follower. I'll develop my own alter-ego.'

I grinned. 'Speaking of altars, I saw you talking to Father Jim.'

'Your old boyfriend? Yes, I was asking him for your hand.'

I swatted him.

'Ouch,' he said, wincing. 'Wounded, remember?'

'I'm so sorry.' I was mortified. 'Is it OK? Did I rip any stitches?'

'No, but my ego has sustained a terrible wound.'

'Your ego is just fine.' I put out my hand palm up.

He took it. 'Only if you marry me.'

'Maybe I will,' I said. 'Now tell me what you really were talking to Jim about.'

'First, I wanted to explain why I brought him into the discussion with Jack.'

'Which was?'

'I wanted Jack – and maybe Vickie, even more so – to know Father Jim was there listening.'

'It probably would give Vickie pause,' I said, taking my hand back and using it to turn the ignition key. 'Not only is she Catholic but she works for Father Jim. Jack, though, is another thing. He's perfectly brazen in front of fifty-plus law enforcement officers. Why would a priest make a difference?'

Pavlik pulled the seatbelt across and clicked it in. 'You never know. Maybe Jack was an altar boy. Or just has good old Catholic guilt, which is the other thing Jim and I talked about.'

'You have Catholic guilt?' I was waiting for traffic to clear behind me, so I could back out. 'But you were brought up Jewish.'

'We have the corner on guilt,' he said. 'But Jim was showing me a note that somebody put in the collection plate.'

I shifted my eyes from the rear-view mirror to Pavlik's face. 'Some kind of threat?'

'Just the opposite. An apology. For stealing.'

I sat back. 'Somebody receiveth rather than giveth when the plate passed by? That's pretty low.'

'And pretty hard to do without somebody seeing. Father Jim does say it explains why collections have been down.'

Which Langdon Shepherd had mentioned.

'Does Jim think it's an inside job?' I asked. 'I mean, one of the elders or the people passing the plate? It's obviously somebody inside the church.'

'He doesn't know but he gave me the note.' He reached into his suit pocket and held out a folded sheet of paper.

'Fingerprints?' I asked, hesitating.

'All over it, from what Jim told me. The elder who found it passed it around before giving it to him.'

'This person used cutout words,' I said, examining it. 'They probably wouldn't go to all that trouble and be stupid enough to leave prints.'

'My thought, too.'

I felt a twinge of gratification and looked down at the note. *We took money from collections. Will replace. Please forgive me.*

I handed it back. 'First "we," then "me" – did you notice?'

'I did. Interesting, though crooks don't necessarily have good grammar, especially when piecing together a note like this quickly.'

'Was this found in the collection plate on Sunday?' I asked.

'Today, but—'

'Well, that narrows things down. It has to be somebody here for the funeral.'

'Not necessarily.' Pavlik twisted his head around. 'I think you can back out now.'

I shifted into reverse. 'Why not necessarily?'

'Watch out.'

I was backing out of a parking spot amidst dozens of squad cars. Believe me, I was watching out, but apparently not enough.

'Maybe give it a minute,' Pavlik suggested. 'Anyway, the elder found it in an empty plate before today's service.'

Hmm. 'The pilfering might have been going on for a while. Vickie said she and Nancy were trying to track down some sort of discrepancy in the books. Maybe this was it.'

'When was this?'

'It would have been Saturday night, because Vickie mentioned it on Sunday morning. Nancy had just taken over the books from Fred Lopez. Maybe she was on to something.'

'And what? Fred killed her?'

'I think he's been deported, so probably no. Besides, Fred's a great guy with a family.'

'Great guys with families sometimes get in financial trouble and become desperate. But Fred or not, if Nancy and Vickie found this discrepancy on Saturday night why wait until Thursday to kill her? And what about Vickie?'

I shook my head. 'I don't know.'

'Do you know if we're ever going to back out? Because we're going to miss Pete's service if we don't.'

'Oh, right.' I put the car in reverse and this time pulled out successfully. 'I need to talk to Vickie. Without Jack around.' I shifted verbal gears this time. 'Do you really think Jack pulled a Cain on his Abel?'

'It's entirely possible.'

'The bait you mentioned. It's Jack knowing that you're on to him?'

'And doing something in reaction, like making sure the body is hidden or the weapon is properly disposed of.'

'How will you know? You're still on leave.'

'The department still has officers sitting on Jack Andersen's place in case his brother shows up. If Jack heads off into the woods around Poplar Creek to move his brother's body, for example, we'll know it. Or Hallonquist will and he'll tell me.'

The woods stretched the length of Poplar Creek from behind Brookhills Manor past the mortuary, Hannah's house and beyond. 'Has the area behind the manor been searched?'

'Not for a body.'

'Your theory is that Jack killed Pauly in the woods and then stole Gloria's car and abandoned it at the station to make us think he'd left the area.'

'Pretty much.'

'Your guys checked the trunk, right?'

Pavlik gave me stink eye. 'A little credit, please? And it was the Milwaukee PD, since the train station is in Milwaukee.'

I grinned and turned north on Poplar Creek Road to the mortuary, where Pete Hartsfield's service would start in twenty-five minutes. 'And the trunk of Jack's car?'

'Doesn't have a car, according to him. There's nothing registered in his name.'

This was the suburbs and public transportation except for the occasional bus from the city was nearly non-existent. How did the man get around? 'You said the MPD scanned the security footage around the bus station for Pauly. What about Jack?'

'Their focus was Pauly, though they should have had Jack's picture, too.'

'Maybe somebody picked him up. If a car pulled up at the front and Jack ducked out the door and into it quickly, they might have missed it.'

'You're thinking the somebody might be Vickie?'

'You mean is she Bonnie to Jack Andersen's Clyde? Got me. But she has a car and you say he doesn't.'

'Any idea what kind of car?'

'White Kia Soul.' I glanced sideways at him. 'I think she's scared. Didn't you get that impression?'

'Honestly, yes. And eyes on the road. Please.'

I complied and Pavlik continued, 'Question is whether she's afraid for herself or for him.'

'Or both.' We passed my house. 'I wish we had time to stop and let Frank out.'

'I could cut you a doggy door. That's what I did for Muffin.'

'You know Frank. You've slept with Frank. If you cut an opening big enough for him to get through, there'll be no door left.'

'Yet he manages to squeeze himself into the two inches between us in the middle of the night.'

'I know. He's like a memory foam mattress. Arrives small and then splat, he's all over the place. Here we are.'

The mortuary driveway had a rope across it and Christy was directing traffic. 'Sorry, Maggy, but the lot is full. You can park at Hannah's if you like.'

'She's not home?' I asked.

'She's staying with Mort,' Christy said, waving to another car. 'The house is so empty now.'

'Happens when you kill off all your housemates,' I said as I pulled up the driveway.

'You're ruthless, you know that?' Pavlik said.

'More cynical, I think. I just think bad things. Mostly, I don't even say them except to you and Sarah.'

Pavlik braced himself on the dashboard as we hit a pothole. 'Why us?'

'Sarah's even more ornery than I am. And you, I love.' I stopped in front of a white frame house with green trim.

'See, did that hurt?' he asked, getting out. 'And you said it twice now in less than a week.'

'Trying to get used to it.' I went around the car and snuggled into his arms. 'You do know I care about you, right?'

'I do. And I think you're even getting used to living together.'

'Scary as that is, yes.' We started down the driveway hand in hand. 'Though technically you're living with me.'

'You're right. Living together demands more than one dresser drawer and just space enough on the bathroom counter for my toothbrush.'

'It is a little tight. Ouch!' I held onto his good shoulder to rub my ankle.

'Turn it?' Pavlik asked.

'Just a little – it'll be fine. This driveway needs to be paved,' I said as we started down it again. 'The house itself looks nice enough but it's set so far back into the tree line. We could have parked at my place and walked back from there easier.'

'Not to mention let Frank out.'

'Yup, thereby averting a possible doggy emergency.'

As we approached Christy again, I said, 'I'm going to stop and talk to her. Save me a seat?'

'Sure.'

Pavlik continued on up the hill to the mortuary while I waited for Christy to finish giving instructions to a driver in a blue car.

'There seems to be more of an equal number of civilian and law enforcement cars at this service,' I said.

'I know,' Christy said. 'I don't think Detective Taylor had as many non-police friends or much family. I didn't stay but I imagine it was terribly sad.'

'It was. As Pete's will be.'

'Such a young family.' She sighed deeply.

'Is this getting to you?' I asked. 'All the deaths, I mean. Celeste, Pete, Al and now Nancy, all in less than a week.'

'Five days, actually.' Christy blew a lock of hair out of her face. 'Celeste died Sunday and Nancy on Thursday. Today is Saturday.'

I saw my opening. 'That's right. It was Monday when I almost made you late getting to the mortuary for Celeste. Were you able to help with the cremation?'

Her face lit up, God help us. 'I was, in fact. I just observed the body preparation and loading. But the technicians actually let me help sweep.' She frowned. 'I told you that, didn't I?'

She had, but I wanted to clarify what day the cremation was. 'Sophie was jabbering in my other ear.'

'Oh, yes, at Celeste's funeral. It was lovely, wasn't it?'

'It was. I haven't heard what arrangements have been made for Nancy.'

'The cremation is scheduled for tomorrow so the service will likely be Monday afternoon. I can let you know, if you like. Though I'm sure Hannah will tell you, since you're friends.'

Why did everybody think Hannah and I were friends? Even Jack Andersen had—

Andersen's name in connection with Celeste's funeral rang a bell. Hannah had said, 'Maggy is an old friend,' meaning I was an old friend of Bernie's. Jack Andersen, though, had misunderstood and assumed Hannah and I were old friends.

Neither of us had corrected him at the time, me figuring it was none of his business. But if Jack did think we were long-time friends, he might assume that I knew something about her that I clearly didn't. Maybe something that dated back to before she came to Brookhills.

'. . . Like to do them around one o'clock, but—'

'Why so long?' I interrupted.

'What's so long?' Christy asked, not understanding.

Not that I necessarily did. Which is why I was asking. 'Celeste was cremated the day after she died, but Nancy died on Thursday and isn't being cremated until Sunday afternoon. Why so long?'

I purposely didn't mention the forty-eight-hour waiting period Jim had told me about, wanting to see what Christy would say.

'Excellent question, Maggy. It is an interesting business, isn't it?'

Fascinating. Answer the question.

'There was an autopsy on Nancy, but that fell within the forty-eight hours we have to wait before cremating a body anyway. The extra day delay was because the Hartsfield service was being held here.'

Good of them not to smoke out the funeral guests. 'But what about the forty-eight hours for Celeste? She was cremated the next day.'

Christy's nose wrinkled. 'I know there are exceptions for special circumstances, so she must have fallen into that category.' Her handbag was hung over the fencepost and now she pulled out a paper and pen. 'You know what? I'm going to ask Mort about what exactly the special circumstances were.'

'No need to do it on my account,' I said hastily. If there was something hinky, I didn't want to tip him off.

'Oh, no bother,' Christy said. 'I need to know these things if I'm going to be in the business.'

She lowered her voice and beckoned me close. 'Don't tell anybody, but I think I'm going to go all the way.'

OK, it was an old-fashioned way of putting it. But then, like Amy said, Christy was retro. 'All the way with Ronny?'

'What?' She giggled as she got what I meant. 'Oh, Maggy, don't be silly. Ronny's in prison. No, I meant I'm really going to commit to this new career.'

'And that means?'

'I'm going to become – wait for it – a mortician!'

A booming organ signaled the start of the second funeral of the day.

TWENTY-FIVE

'**N**o Jack Andersen at this service,' I said to Pavlik as I drove us home.

'Hopefully he's busy burying the body.' He checked his cell phone. 'No messages to that effect, though.'

'I assumed he'd be a little stealthier. Like do it in the dead of night, perhaps?'

Pavlik was texting.

'I'm glad Jack wasn't at Pete's service,' I continued, 'but I was hoping maybe Vickie would be there alone.'

'She sounded like she wanted nothing to do with either funeral.'

'I'm sure she'll be at Nancy's. But that won't be until Monday from what Christy said. Oh!'

Pavlik looked up from his text. 'What?'

'Both she and Father Jim told me that there's a forty-eight-hour waiting period before a body can be cremated. Nancy's cremation is tomorrow.'

'OK.' He was back to texting.

'But Christy also said that Celeste's body was cremated on Monday morning – less than twenty-four hours after she died. That apparently there are exceptions to the rule. Is that true?'

'I can check.'

Switching from texting to Googling, he punched it up. 'Here it is. The Wisconsin statute on cremation. No person may cremate the corpse of a deceased person within forty-eight hours after the death, or the discovery of the death, of the deceased person unless the death was caused by a contagious or infectious disease.'

I frowned. 'I don't think Celeste had an infectious disease. Or at least I hope not, or we were all exposed to it on Sunday.'

A chill went up my spine as I thought about Sarah getting sick, too. 'Could that be what also killed Nancy? A disease from Celeste?'

'Only if that disease causes pillowcases to disappear.' Pavlik was still studying his phone. 'It says that cremation requires a permit signed by the coroner or medical examiner, so the mortuary would have had to obtain that before proceeding.'

'No autopsy was done on Celeste,' I said.

'Not unusual if the death isn't suspicious. A doctor could pronounce death, too, and provide that information for the permit and the death certificate.'

'I don't know who might have done that in Celeste's case. Hannah said that both she and Nancy hated doctors and refused to see them. Though she did,' I drummed my fingers on the steering wheel, 'have your doctor—'

'Doctor Goode?'

'That's the one. Mort said Nancy was under her care, which seemed a stretch since Hannah said all she'd done was prescribe a sedative.'

Turning the car into my driveway, I turned off the engine. 'Doctor Goode is a friend of Mort's and part of the Goddard Gang.'

'My family practice doc is in a gang?'

'You know what I mean. It's what the group of people who used to meet at Goddard's for coffee – and now Uncommon Grounds – call themselves. They're pretty tight.'

'You're insinuating that Phyllis Goode did what?'

'Not insinuating. Just suggesting that Mort might have asked her to sign off on Celeste's death to save Hannah the heartache of having to have an autopsy. Celeste was old and apparently ill. It's not all that different than her calling the ER doc for us and having him sign you out of the hospital.'

'For one thing, I wasn't dead. For another, I was in my rights to sign myself out.'

'I know,' I said, patting his hand. 'But I didn't really want the liability of bringing you home like that. What if you'd bit the big one overnight?'

'What?' Pavlik put down his phone. 'You were afraid—'

'Water over the bridge,' I said, waving him off with a grin. 'But my point is that people bend the rules for friends. And maybe Doctor Goode bent the rules for Mort and Mort bent them for Hannah.'

'What about the permit required for the cremation? Mort certainly would have to have that.'

'True, but what's to stop him getting the permit for the cremation and then not waiting the forty-eight hours?'

'But what's to be gained by cremating a body a day early? Destroying evidence? Of what?'

I knew Pavlik had to be exhausted after the funerals of two of his men, so I just shrugged. 'I don't know. What's say we go in, build a fire and have a glass of wine?'

'Sounds good,' Pavlik said, swinging open the car door. 'But first we'd better let Frank out before he goes firehose on us.'

Excellent idea.

Storms woke us up that night. Or first woke Frank, who then stepped on me to launch himself over Pavlik and off the bed.

'Ouch!'

I used to be a side sleeper, but since I'd let Frank on the bed I'd become a pretty-much-any-position-that-gives-me-a-few-inches-of-mattress-and-a-shred-of-blanket sleeper. My legs got more sleep than I did, since they were usually trapped under one of Frank's furry body parts and needed resuscitation in the morning. Add Pavlik to the equation – and the bed – and . . .

'Oooh, cramp, cramp.' I was frantically grabbing at my leg.

'What, what?' Pavlik was blinking.

'Charley-horse in my calf. Frank was laying on it. And it went to sleep.'

Pavlik sat up and gave it a rub. 'Was that thunder I heard?'

'Yes. That's what woke Frank up and set off this chain of events.'

'I didn't hear him.' He was working his thumb into my calf muscle.

'Mmmmm. That's because he sailed over you when he used me as a springboard to jump off the bed.' A flash of lightning followed by . . . one one-thousand, two one-thousand, three one-thousand, four one-thousand, five one . . . a crash of thunder. 'Five seconds, so the storm is five miles away. I love a good thunderstorm.'

'Actually, that's not true.'

'I don't love thunderstorms?'

'No, I'm sure that you do. But it's not true that each second between the lightning and thunder means the storm is one mile away. Since it takes roughly five seconds for the sound to travel one mile, you need to divide the seconds you count by five.'

The theory behind it was beyond me at that time of night, but I could do the math. 'Five divided by five – so just one mile away, not five.'

'You got it.'

'A lifetime of storm-counting, shattered in an instant.' Stretching, I pointed my toe and the cramp seized again. 'Oww, oww, oww.'

'Who knew you were such a baby,' Pavlik threw a sideways glance my way, 'about leg cramps. You're so . . . stoic about other things.'

'Good attempt at bailing yourself out,' I said, giving him a pat on the cheek. 'But I'm not stoic about anything.'

He grinned. 'As I recall, you don't scream too much when facing down a python. Or an alligator.'

'Paralyzed with fear is a real concept. That's good,' I said as the cramp let up. 'Thank you.'

'You're welcome.' He lay back down. 'Can we go back to sleep now?'

'Not quite yet,' I said.

'Ohhh?' His eyes darkened playfully. 'What do you have in mind?'

Not that. At least, not right that second. But I needed Pavlik to find out something for me without tipping him off that I had the pillowcase. 'I was wondering do they remove makeup during an autopsy? It seems like they would in case it was concealing bruises or something, right?'

Pavlik groaned. 'I probably deserve this.'

'Deserve what?' I asked apprehensively.

'Your being fixated on something like that in the middle of the night. I probably did it often enough to Susan.'

Way to bring up the ex-wife.

He sighed and sat up. 'But in answer to your question, in my experience they would take photos and then make a careful examination, which I believe would include removing makeup. Why? Do you think Nancy was being abused?'

Since that was exactly what I hoped he'd think I was getting at, I said, 'Maybe. Do you think you could ask tomorrow?'

'About signs of abuse on the body? It would have been in the autopsy report.'

'Also the makeup itself. You know, whether she still had on foundation or eyeliner or lipstick.' Nancy had been wearing none of those things in Bernie's office, something that Pavlik couldn't know since he wasn't there. 'It might give us an idea how long she was home after she died. You know, did she have time to take off her makeup?'

I thought it was a masterful sleight of hand on my part, especially at 1:10 in the morning. But Pavlik's eyes narrowed. 'If I know you, you're after something else.'

He did know me. But I also knew him. 'Me?' I said innocently, slipping back down onto my pillow. 'Well, maybe a little something else.'

As I pulled Pavlik down to me, Frank resignedly settled on the rug next to the bed.

TWENTY-SIX

Sunday was my day off, so Pavlik and I had breakfast together.

Which meant I made coffee and he made toast from the last of the white bread. 'Do you have butter?'

'Of course. Who doesn't have butter?' I swung open the refrigerator door. 'Well, maybe not.'

I was saved from his expression, since he was working on getting the heel of the bread out of the toaster.

'I have some wooden tongs,' I started to say and then realized they were at the shop. Or, more specifically, under the shop, along with the garbage bag containing the pillowcase. 'Or I had. Whatever did I do with those?'

'Probably hiding with the butter,' Pavlik said, unplugging the toaster and turning it upside down to shake. 'We need to do some grocery shopping. Or easier, just raid the fridge and cabinets at my place.'

Why did I get the feeling he had no plan to return to 'his place' any time soon? At least to live.

'You're getting crumbs all over,' I pointed out.

'But the crust came out.' He held it up. 'Which is good, because it and this,' he indicated a full piece of toast on a plate, 'are the only things we have to eat.'

Sure, if you discounted green sludge dog food and spray cheese.

'Tell you what,' I said, slipping my arms around him, 'I want to go by Brookhills Manor and talk to Vickie, so I'll run out to your place first for food and then stop at the manor on my way home.'

'Is it going to take long with Vickie?' he asked. ''Cause there's some really good ice cream in my freezer you could snag, assuming you don't plan on grilling the witness so long it melts.'

'I'll make it quick.' I let go of him and swung open the cabinet door. '*Voila!* Grape jelly.'

'It'll do,' he said, taking it. 'But why don't you grab my lingonberry while you're at my place.'

Lingonberry. Really? Next he'd be wanting cheese that didn't come in an aerosol can.

Pavlik's cabinets and refrigerator were admittedly a treasure trove of treats. And cheaper than a grocery store. First, I snagged the lingonberry jam and a loaf of bread – cracked wheat, naturally. Or unnaturally, as far as I was concerned. Also, a pound of butter, a jar of Jif and, much as it pained me, a twelve-pack of caffeine-free Diet Pepsi. Sensing that somebody who craved cracked wheat bread might also eat vegetables, I checked out the crisper. The bag of lettuce I found there was wilted so I tossed it. But the broccoli and carrots looked fine and Frank would eat the carrots if nobody else did. I also grabbed some Fuji apples, a Frank favorite.

Standing in the middle of the kitchen, I felt like I was missing something. The ice cream.

Sliding out the freezer drawer, I found two. Madagascar Vanilla and Bittersweet Chocolate. Yum.

And no need to decide. I'd take both. And hope I could catch Vickie at her home and be back at mine before the ice cream melted.

I found a brown bag from Schultz's market under the sink and loaded everything into it, ice cream on top.

Driving to the manor, I thought about how I should approach Vickie. And where.

'Call Sophie,' I told my cell phone, which was lying on the center console.

It beeped and that's it. Stopping at the signal on the corner of Brookhills Road and the manor, I scrolled to Sophie's number.

'Do you know if Vickie is home?' I asked when she answered.

'How would I know that?' she demanded. 'I'm at your shop.'

Well, that was good, if not helpful. The light turned green.

'Why don't you call her?' Sophie continued.

'I wanted to drop in unannounced. And when Jack Andersen is not around.'

'That'll be tough. From what I've been hearing next door, she's living with him.'

Damn. 'You don't think I can catch her at her own apartment?'

'You can try. Do you know the number? Eleven, which is the other side of Andersen's from us. Henry, I told you—'

The line went dead. Turning left into the Brookhills Manor parking lot, I pulled around back to the section closest to Poplar Creek. Getting out, I scanned the tree line. No sign of Andersen dragging a body, of course. Nor sheriff's deputies combing the area for that body, either. I was happy, though, to see Vickie's white Kia parked in the last line of cars, closest to the woods.

The rehab wing was to the left when you entered the building and the residential one was to the right. I knew Sophie and Henry's apartment was on the ground floor of the residential wing and had a door leading to a small patio facing the Poplar Creek woods. I had to assume Jack Andersen's set-up was the same, meaning he could have taken Pauly's body out that way and avoided the communal hallway and lobby.

As I went to lock the car, I hesitated, eyeing the ice cream on the passenger seat. It was already softening up. I probably should have dropped it off at my place but I'd been too busy talking to Sophie as I'd passed. Maybe I would take it in with me. If Vickie was home, I could stash it in her freezer as we talked.

I was in luck. As I stepped into the lobby, Vickie was coming out of the small store which also served as the post office.

'Maggy,' she said, seeing me. 'Why are you carrying two cartons of ice cream?'

'I didn't want to leave it in the car but I needed to ask you a few things.' I glanced out of the lobby window and saw Jack Andersen walking through the parking lot toward the entrance. 'Could I stick these in your freezer so they don't melt?'

'I guess so.' She looked none too sure that she wanted to talk to me, much less store my frozen treats. 'But I don't know that I can help you.'

I was pretty sure she could. What I wasn't sure about was whether she would. I did know, though, that if I had any chance of prying any information out of her, I had to keep her away from Andersen.

'Can we get it in right now?' I asked, making a show of juggling the cartons. 'It's going to drip all over.'

'I guess so,' she said again, leading me down the hallway. We passed Sophie and Henry's number nine. There were bullet holes in the walls across from ten, so no question who lived there. Each hole was circled and numbered.

I noticed Vickie didn't look at them as we passed, instead searching through her purse. 'I know the key is in here somewhere.'

Finding it, she turned the key in the lock and I made it in just as Jack rounded the corner. Hopefully he was just heading to his apartment next door and hadn't seen us. If he had and had something to hide – something he didn't want Vickie to share – we wouldn't have much time.

'Sorry the place is such a mess.' She pushed some foil and a plastic bag aside to get at the microwave, which was flashing 12:00. 'The electricity must have gone off last night.'

'I'm not surprised – it really stormed. You weren't here?'

She finished resetting the clock. 'I've slept here all of two nights in the last month. Jack and I are talking about my giving it up and moving in with him.'

'This is it?' I put the two cartons down on the kitchen table. 'You're in love?'

If doubt does have a shadow, I saw it cross her face.

'Now why didn't I put these dishes away?' she scolded herself, plucking silverware from the dish drainer next to the sink and opening the drawer to put it away.

She was nervous, but with Jack in the hallway I didn't have the time to schmooze her. 'So do you think you're in love? Is that why you're sticking with him against your better instincts?'

'Maggy, it's sweet of you to be worried about me but you need to just . . . stop.' She pulled a large serrated knife out of the drawer and brandished it. 'For your own good.'

I backed up. 'What are you going to do with that?'

'This?' She looked at the knife like she hadn't realized she'd been holding it.

Yes, that. The big-ass frozen food knife in your hand. 'Please put it back in the drawer before you cut yourself.' And, more importantly, me.

'Uh-uh.' She gestured with the knife for me to move away from the table.

I stayed where I was. 'Pavlik knows I'm here.'

'So?' The gesture again, the tip of the knife drawing a circle in the air.

I say tip, but the one on this knife was a two-pronged stabby doo-hickey. I had a feeling it would hurt. More. 'I told him your Soul was in the parking lot. He wondered whether Jack has been using it?'

Vickie seemed surprised and the knife dipped a bit. 'Occasionally.'

'Any odd . . . smells?'

'Smells?' Her nose wrinkled. 'You and your imagination. It's amusing when you're talking about somebody else, but I must say you're getting downright annoying. Now will you move?'

This time I did, sliding right toward the patio door. 'Where are we going?'

'I don't know about you, but *I'm* not going anywhere,' she said. 'Jack will be here any minute.'

'Vickie, please—'

'I can't believe you think he killed his brother. Not that life wouldn't be simpler without Pauly around.' She shook her head.

Yeah, murderous future in-laws are a bitch. 'You heard what Pavlik said at the funeral. He believes Pauly is dead. And Pavlik is no fool.'

'No, unfortunately he's not.' Vickie was thinking.

It was better than stabbing me. 'He knows that you picked Jack up at the bus station in Milwaukee.'

That startled her. 'How does he know that?'

'He's the sheriff.' I said it simply, the implication being that Pavlik was all-seeing and all-knowing. Like, for example, he saw that Vickie had a knife and knew to send in the troops.

Though, at the moment, the sheriff had no troops. I decided to ignore the knife and play it the way I would with my friend Vickie, who I believed was being duped. 'What was Jack doing at the bus station anyway?'

'Well, that's where they dropped him off, of course, after they questioned him.'

'Who?' I'd noticed a panic button – the kind Sophie had been grousing about – on the other side of the refrigerator/freezer. I'd have to reverse course to reach it.

'Your sheriff's detectives, of course. Jack texted me after all the ruckus that they had a few questions and he was going to the station with them.'

I ignored the reference to the double shooting as a ruckus. 'The bus station?'

'No, of course not. The sheriff's station.'

'But Pavlik's detectives are with the Brookhills County Sheriff's Department west of here. Why would they drop him fifteen miles east at the Milwaukee bus station?'

'Why . . . I don't know.' Vickie's eyes were uncertain and even her Botox couldn't keep her brow from furrowing this time.

I shook my head. 'That's not what happened, Vickie. Jack stole Gloria Goddard's car and drove it to the station to make it look like Pauly had abandoned it there.'

'Stop, Maggy. I don't want to hurt you.'

I froze as, with one swift movement, she lifted the knife . . .

And plunged it into the knife block on the counter to my left.

I put my hand up over my heart, which was thumping wildly. 'You . . . umm, you just wanted to put the knife away.'

'Of course,' she said. 'It doesn't belong in the silverware drawer. What did you think I was doing?'

She didn't want to know. But maybe I should tell her anyway. 'I thought you were going to stab me.'

Her eyes went wide and filled with tears. 'I would never hurt you. I never meant to hurt anybody.'

Odd way of putting it. 'What do you mean, Vickie? Who got hurt?'

'It was only meant to be temporary, you understand? I—' She was nervously moving between the kitchen table and the refrigerator and back again. 'Oh, dear. Your ice cream is melting all over the table. Let me just put them—'

'Leave them,' I said. 'And tell me what was meant to be temporar—' A knock at the door interrupted me.

'Vickie?' Jack's voice called. 'Are you home?'

'We need to leave,' I whispered to Vickie. 'Now.'

'But what about the ice cream?' she asked, lowering her voice to match mine. 'Do you still want me to put it in the freezer?'

'Vickie.' I put out my hand as she picked up the Madagascar vanilla. 'We're going out the patio door. You won't have to explain. He'll never know we were in here.'

'Fine,' she said, not looking toward the door where Jack stood on the other side. 'But first let me—'

She swung open the freezer door and dropped the vanilla.

Pauly Andersen's head was staring back at us, wrapped in aluminum foil.

TWENTY-SEVEN

My first thought was that Pauly must not have fit into the zip-lock.

My second was *get the hell out of there*.

Vickie was still staring open mouthed at Pauly and he at her. She moved first, backing away as Jack knocked on the door again. 'Vickie, sweetheart? Can I come in, baby?'

I grabbed her arm. 'Does he have a key?'

She nodded but I could have answered the question myself. The key was already turning in the lock.

'Come on.' I pulled her toward the patio door.

She resisted. 'We have to call for help.'

You think? 'No time. We can't get caught in here with him.'

'But—'

Enough. I yanked her toward the door as the hall door swung open. Jack Andersen may have been all sweetheart and baby for the benefit of people in the hallway, but as he moved into the room and took in the still-open freezer door, he slipped a gun from his waistband.

Parole violation, of course. But nothing compared to stashing a foil-wrapped bro-head in the freezer. 'Don't move.'

I'd learned many things from Pavlik. One of them was never obey a bad guy. The second was never let them get you alone. Third was that it's tougher to hit a moving target than a stationary one.

So I moved. One hand still on Vickie, I flipped the lock on the slider and tugged.

I'd assumed Vickie would keep it locked, so I was unlocking it.

I was wrong. Or maybe Jack, being a killer, had left it open in case he needed a little fresh air as he was sawing apart his brother with the frozen food knife.

'Jack,' Vickie said, like the man didn't have a gun in his hand. 'I was just showing Maggy the patio.'

I flipped the lock the other way.

'Nice try, but you forgot to close the freezer.' He gestured at Pauly with his gun.

With one movement, I slung open the door and used that momentum to sling Vickie out like a game of crack the whip.

She went flying across the patio and onto the grass. I was halfway out the door when a hand gripped my arm.

'Maggy!' I heard Vickie scream.

'Run!' I told her as he dragged me back in.

'Couldn't mind your own business, could you?'

Cliché. And though it probably wasn't the right time, I said, 'Cliché, much?'

'What?'

He shoved me against the kitchen counter and I flinched as

the edge bit into my hip. 'Couldn't I mind my own business? C'mon, Jack. You're a con man, Jack. Can't you do better? Even your glass house and rocks was more original than that.'

'And yet you ignored it.'

'I did.' I was inching away from him in the direction of the refrigerator.

'Stop moving.' He was following me, gun pointed at my chest. The pistol was a semi-automatic like the one Pavlik carried and I saw no silencer. Which meant Jack would rather not shoot me right here. I kept going.

When my foot touched the ice-cream carton on the floor, I kicked it toward him and made my move for the panic button, slapping it hard.

Nothing happened.

Andersen's hand grabbed my shoulder.

Truly panicked now, thanks to the non-functioning panic button, I gave Andersen a hard shove, hoping the ice cream on the floor had melted sufficiently.

It had.

Jack Andersen took one backward step and then skidded. He was hitting the floor as I high-tailed it through the door into the hall and pulled the fire alarm.

TWENTY-EIGHT

'Those panic buttons don't work,' I told Sophie, who'd come out of her apartment when the fire alarm went off. We were sitting on a picnic bench, watching the county's big crime-scene van pull up.

There was a freezer full of evidence for them to collect.

'Those things buzz in the office,' Sophie said. 'What did you think? They go off like the fire alarm just did? You'd give people heart attacks.'

'Even more heart attacks,' Vickie said, joining us.

I was hoping I hadn't done that. Though I thought maybe I could be excused. 'Detective Hallonquist finished with you?'

'For now,' she said. 'He doesn't seem to think I had anything to do with Pauly and the . . .'

'Dismembering,' Sophie supplied. 'How in the world did that man kill, butcher and package his brother in your apartment without you knowing?'

'He said he had to use the bathroom,' Vickie said. 'And don't you look at me like that, Sophie Daystrom. You said yourself how hard it is to get by with the one bathroom in these units. And you know how men are.'

'I'll give you that,' Sophie said. 'Can't jackhammer Henry off that toilet sometimes.'

Interesting, but I was thinking about Jack Andersen being led off in handcuffs, one pants leg creamed with Madagascar vanilla . . .

'What are you smiling about?' This voice was Pavlik's.

I stood up and hugged him as Vickie and Sophie thoughtfully moved to the next table. 'How did you get here? You're not supposed to drive.'

'Hallonquist picked me up. Are you all right?'

'I'm fine. But Jack Andersen is one bad dude. I never should have come here alone.'

Now Pavlik laughed. 'You're saying that so I can't say it first?'

'Yup.'

'Well, I wasn't going to. You had no reason to think you'd be in danger talking to Vickie here at the manor. And who knew he'd stashed his brother's body in the fridge?'

'Oh,' I said, my nose wrinkling. 'Not just the freezer?'

''Fraid not,' Pavlik said. 'Pauly was a big boy. He's even in the crisper.'

'Meat-keeper?'

'A little.' Pavlik held up his thumb and index finger, about two inches apart.

I laughed. 'Pauly dead and Jack, I assume, going away for a very long time. I'm good with that.' I chin-gestured to where Vickie and Sophie had been joined by Henry. 'What about Vickie? Will she face accessory charges?'

'It'll depend on where the investigation takes us. And what Jack tells us.'

'Do you think he'll try to pin it on her?' I hadn't thought of that.

'Andersen is slick,' Pavlik said. 'But don't worry; he's not going to get a deal on this.'

'I still don't understand what he thought I had to hide,' I said. 'I suppose I should have asked him that.'

'While he was holding a gun on you?' Pavlik said. 'That kind of thing only happens in movies. Or books.'

Right. Along with being framed by a pillowcase. 'Did you ever find out from the coroner if Nancy was wearing lipstick?'

Pavlik's head jerked quizzically. 'What made you think of that?'

'I don't know – loose ends? Remaining murderers on the loose?'

I wasn't sure Pavlik was buying it but he answered anyway. 'Nancy Casperson was wearing lipstick, though no other makeup.'

'Was the lipstick smeared?'

'Wildly. But she was smothered, so that's not surprising. Aren't you going to ask me if we found the pillowcase?'

I made my eyes widen. 'Did you?'

'No.'

'You keep saying "we." Did something happen on the inquiry?'

Pavlik's face darkened a tinge. 'Just old habit. I'm still on leave.'

'With Jack in jail and Vickie out from under his thumb, I'm sure she'll drop whatever complaint she filed.'

'We'll see,' Pavlik said, rolling his shoulder back and forth. 'Are you ready to leave?'

'Sure,' I said, standing up. 'Let's stop and get ice cream on the way home.'

TWENTY-NINE

I opened the next day. Despite it being Monday, I knew the core of the Goddard Gang planned to show up, likely thinking they'd get the lowdown on what happened yesterday from the horse's mouth. Me being the horse.

Meanwhile, I'd been doing some thinking of my own and had decided the gang's attendance would save me the trouble of rounding up the suspects.

And, yes, I know that only happens in books.

Christy was the first to arrive. 'Are you coming to Nancy's service?'

'Wouldn't miss it,' I said truthfully. 'What time is it scheduled?'

'One-thirty. Mort let me help with the cremation yesterday. The sweeping and packaging.'

'Congratulations,' I said. 'How did it go?'

She looked around the empty store before answering in a low voice. 'Challenging. At the last moment we were told implant removal was needed.'

'What?'

She leaned over the counter and whispered. 'Silicone. Thank God it was caught in time.'

I'd bent over to hear her and now straightened up in surprise. 'Nancy had breast implants?'

'Yes,' Christy said. 'Nobody told us or we would have removed them earlier.'

'Then you must have removed Celeste's, too.'

'Celeste? No, she didn't have breast implants.'

Nor a communicable disease that would have required disposing of the body before the forty-eight-hour waiting period. Interesting.

Christy left for work before the rest of the gang showed up. First, Mort and Hannah, then Vickie – blissfully single – and Henry and Sophie. I was about to convene my planned meeting of the murder club when Father Jim arrived.

Vickie jumped up. 'I want to confess.'

I thought a priest would take confession in stride, but Jim backed up a pace. 'Excuse me?'

I had an inkling of what was coming, since Vickie had started to confess to me before all hell broke out with Jack.

'I'm the one who took the collection money. It was only a loan, and we were already paying it back with Jack's inheritance.'

'Inheritance?' I couldn't help myself. 'The man's in his seventies. Who was he inheriting from?'

'I don't know,' Vickie said, turning to me. 'Jack said it was an estranged relative.'

'Like Pauly?' Had Pauly given Jack the money from the bank robbery for safekeeping while he was in jail? If so, it explained why Pauly had shown up at the manor – and why he'd never truly left.

Vickie's eyes widened. 'I don't know. After you told me he was a gigolo, I started to think Jack had made it all up. That's why I left that note in the collection plate. I knew I'd been duped like all those other women. But instead of giving Jack my money, I gave him the church's.'

The woman fell to her knees and grabbed Father Jim's hand. 'Can you ever forgive me?'

For the embarrassment, probably not. 'Ah, well, we'll talk in private,' Jim said, pulling back his hand and awkwardly patting her on the head before moving away. 'There will have to be restitution, of course.'

'Of course,' she said, following him on her knees. 'I can't tell you how—'

'Oh, for God's sake,' Sophie said. 'Will you get up? You're making an idiot of yourself.'

As Vickie got to her feet, I decided to make a fresh pot of coffee and give Sarah a call.

She wouldn't want to miss the fun.

'What's the plan? Sarah asked.

'Refills,' I said, gesturing with the pot in my hand.

'And then what?' she hissed. 'Here's your coffee and would you like a jail term with that?'

'I like that,' I said. 'But given I don't know who did what, I probably shouldn't threaten them. Yet.'

'You know Hannah did something.'

'Something, yes,' I admitted. 'I'm just not sure it's everything.' I took a deep breath. 'Here I go. Wish me luck.'

'Luck,' Sarah said, and then took up the prime viewing spot behind the service window.

Hannah was at a table with Mort, Sophie and Henry. Father Jim and Vickie, who was trailing him like a remorseful puppy, were at the next with Phyllis Goode, who'd just arrived with a woman I didn't know.

'Refill?' I asked, my pot hovering over Hannah's latte mug. While many of the gangers initially ordered espresso drinks, when time for refills came around they were happy to switch to free coffee.

'You're right,' I said. 'What we're left with is two women – one is rich and has breast implants. The other is of more modest means and has none.'

'But,' Sarah piped up from the window, causing everybody to turn her way, 'the bodies were just the other way around, right?'

'Right.' They twisted back my way. 'It made me wonder if it really was Celeste who died on Sunday. We'll never know, of course, because Mort cremated the body before the forty-eight-hour period.'

'Mort?' This was from Dr Goode. 'Is this true?'

'Well, I . . .'

'He put you in a tough position, didn't he?' I asked. 'Apparent natural death of an old woman, family just moved to town. Why wouldn't you agree to sign off on the death certificate when an old friend asks you to?'

'Because I wasn't an idiot.' The doctor's eyes were shooting daggers at her old friend. 'But apparently I am. How could you put me in this position, Mort?'

'There was nothing suspicious about my mother's death.' Hannah had finally decided to enter the fray.

'But there was.' Quietly, from Vickie at the next table.

All heads swiveled.

'No!' Hannah said. 'She's just saying that because her "friend" was trying to blackmail me. But all I did—'

'No.' Mort put a hand on hers. 'All *we* did was . . .' He seemed not to be able to articulate it.

I could. 'You switched them. It was Nancy who died on Sunday and Celeste on Thursday.'

'But why?' This was from Dr Goode's friend, who seemed to be getting into it.

'Money, what else?' I nodded toward Hannah. 'Your mother was wealthy but had everything tied up in a trust with Nancy as the successor trustee. You needed money.'

'We all needed money,' Hannah burst out. 'My mother was fine with spending it on herself – on her clothes and wigs and cosmetic surgery – but she had no idea how much it cost to run a house. And then, to make matters worse, she started to lose it mentally.'

'Alzheimer's?'

She flung out her hands. 'Dementia of some kind, I assume. Not that she would see a doctor.'

'Did you really want her to?' I asked. 'Or were you fine with your mother just fading away mentally? Except there was the money.'

'I loved my mother.'

'Wait.' Sophie was waving her hand. 'We saw Nancy at Celeste's funeral.'

I smiled. 'You should be able to answer that one, Sophie. You're the one who told me all old ladies look alike.'

The hand went down. 'I did.'

'Think about it,' I said. 'Dress Celeste in a shapeless dress, no wig, no makeup.'

'She'd be Nancy,' Sophie said. 'You're right.'

Damn right, I was right. 'With the dementia progressing, Celeste couldn't even tell us who she was. And if she had, we wouldn't have believed her. At the funeral she confused Jack Andersen with Dr Goode, who'd prescribed her a sedative.'

'I didn't prescribe anything,' Dr Goode said.

'I just said that,' Hannah said, 'to explain mother's confusion.'

'Nancy had been a sharp woman. You used the drugs and grief to explain why she wasn't herself. And succeeded, largely. But then you were blackmailed.'

'By Jack,' Vickie said. 'Though I'm to blame.' She looked like she'd throw herself at Jim's feet again if she weren't sitting across the table from him.

'How did Jack know the identities had been switched?' I asked, and then it dawned on me. 'You'd been to the house and seen the real Nancy and Celeste the night before. In fact, you were the only person who'd seen the two women, right?'

'They were pretty much housebound,' Father Jim said. 'Or so we were told.'

Hannah shrunk under his glare. 'It's true that my mother wasn't well and Nancy didn't like going out. You have to believe that none of this was planned.'

Sarah was not going to let me forget this. She'd had Hannah pegged from the very beginning.

'When I found Nancy dead and called Mort to come over,' she was saying, 'he wasn't certain at first whose body it was.'

'And that gave you the idea.'

She hung her head. 'With Mother dead, we'd have access to the trust.'

'And with Nancy alive,' Sophie said, 'you'd also get her social security. A two-fer.'

'Well, yes.' The head didn't go up.

'You went along with this, Mort?' Dr Goode couldn't believe it.

'I . . . well, Hannah asked me to.'

'Doesn't hurt that she's twenty years younger than you, I'll wager,' Sophie said.

Henry sighed. 'Many a man has been led astray by a younger woman.'

Sophie slapped him.

But back to our dramatic reveal. 'After Celeste's death, things started to go awry. First, Jack and Vickie tried to blackmail you.'

Vickie looked about to object and then thought better of it. The woman had stolen from a church and been a co-conspirator in a blackmail scheme. Not a good day.

Hannah nodded. 'Jack called Sunday night and said he knew it was Nancy who was dead. He also knew that she was wealthy.' Hannah threw a dark look at Vickie. 'He demanded fifty thousand dollars to keep his mouth shut.'

'Which is why it was so important that I go to the lawyer with you and convince Bernie to let you get into the trust fund. Only problem was Bernie is ethical and Celeste was stubborn. She refused to sign Nancy's name.'

'So, after all this, Hannah couldn't get access to the money?' Father Jim had finally been sucked in.

'Nope,' I said. 'Not as long as "Nancy" lived.'

'She had to die.' This from Vickie.

All eyes – including Mort's – turned on Hannah. She held up her hands. 'I didn't kill my mother. I would never do that.'

'Yet she was murdered,' I said. 'Smothered with a pillow and the pillowcase was removed from the crime scene. It had lipstick on it.'

A single tear ran down Hannah's cheek. 'Mother loved her lipstick. First thing she did when I brought her home after our meeting at Bernie's was sit down at the vanity and try to put it on.'

So the lipstick hadn't just been part of the attempt to keep me quiet. But something else Hannah had said bothered me. 'Jack called you on Sunday night?'

'Yes.' She took a handkerchief from Mort.

'But there had been no funeral – not even the cremation.' I swiveled to Mort. 'Who would have seen the body?'

He sat back. 'Only me and one of my people who's been with me for years.'

'Then how could Jack know it wasn't Celeste who had died?'

Vickie wouldn't look at me.

The redhead said she'd seen Celeste in the living room the night she'd met with Nancy. Even that Celeste was all decked out – a fashionista, I thought she'd called her.

When Celeste/Nancy saw Vickie and Jack at the funeral, she mistook him for a doctor. Why?

'So Jack was with you that night?' I asked Vickie. 'The night you met with Nancy about the Angel of Mercy's books?'

This seemed to be news to Father Jim. 'You met with Nancy to go through the books the night before she died?'

'She . . . umm, she left you a message about some discrepancies and I . . . um, happened to see it. I went there to try to set her mind at ease.'

'By killing her?' Sarah asked.

'No, of course not.' Vickie's face was as red as her hair.

'Wait,' Jim said, holding up his hands. 'The money you've confessed to stealing was cash from the collection plates. There would be no discrepancies – the money just wouldn't be there. Are you telling me you pilfered more?'

She nodded, and tears slipped over and ran down both cheeks.

'How much?'

'Umm, maybe twenty?'

'Twenty . . .?'

'Thousand.'

'You stole twenty thousand dollars from my church?' The fire and brimstone in Jim's voice would have made God (the Old Testament, testy version) proud.

I held up my hand. 'I'm not sure that's the worst of it, Jim.'

'You think they killed Nancy?' Hannah asked, looking relieved at being off the hook for this part, at least. 'But how? She was alive after they left.'

There was Celeste/Nancy's comment about a doctor at the funeral. Something about shots and headaches? 'Did you give her something?' I asked Vickie. 'A shot?'

'No, not me.' She was sniffling. 'But Nancy had a headache and Jack said he had something that could help.'

I felt my eyes go wide and my brow, thankfully, furrow. 'He injected Botox? I turned to Dr Goode. 'Could that have killed her?'

The good doctor seemed to be wondering what she'd stepped into. Her friend, on the other hand, was having a grand time. It was she who answered. 'In high enough doses, yes.'

'Who are you?' Sophie demanded.

'Pharmaceutical rep,' the woman said. 'Botox – in addition to its cosmetic use in low doses – is very effective in treating headaches. Like any other drug, though, it can be deadly if misused.

'What would the symptoms of overdose be?' the doctor asked.

Botulinum toxin is systemic, so it enters the bloodstream and spreads to all the muscles. It takes a tiny needle, so it can be injected anywhere.'

'Making it hard to find the site?' Mort asked.

'Yes. And the other thing is that it could take hours or even days for the victim to die. Symptoms would include things like weakness, blurred vision, trouble swallowing and breathing, maybe hoarseness, loss of bladder control—'

'Bingo,' Sarah said.

'Then it might present as natural death?' Dr Goode looked both relieved and horrified.

'And one following a flu-like illness.'

'But you must have known,' Hannah said to Vickie. 'You might not have realized what he was doing. But after the fact, and when he started to blackmail me, why didn't you speak up?'

Vickie's own Botox couldn't fight the lines in her face. 'I was so scared.' The words barely came out. 'And the blackmail – well, you were a criminal, too, switching those two old women.'

'And that made it OK?' Father Jim demanded.

'No, of course not.'

'What about Celeste?' I asked. 'I mean the real Celeste. Did he kill her, too?'

'I think so.' Vickie's voice was raspy and low. 'He said he'd seen Hannah drop Celeste off at home and go on to the mortuary. He knew somehow that the back door would be open. I think . . . I think maybe he snuck over.'

That day at Clare's, Hannah had called back to Mort that she'd left the back door unlocked, before nearly colliding with Jack. He would have heard.

'But why?' Hannah asked. 'Why kill my mother?'

Vickie swallowed hard, blinking back tears. 'When she mistook him for a doctor at the funeral, he decided that she had seen him inject Nancy. I tried to tell him that she was just a confused old lady and nobody would pay any attention to what she said, but he . . . he called her a loose end.'

A strangled sob from Hannah.

'So he killed her,' I said.

'And tried to frame us,' Sarah added, 'by stashing the case from the pillow that was used to smother her in our storeroom.'

'Oh, dear,' Vickie said, hand to her throat. 'I didn't know about that, either. He asked me a lot of things about you, Maggy. You have to get leverage on people, he said, because you never know when you'll need it.'

'Did he ask about me?' Sarah asked, looking a little miffed.

'No. And I didn't tell him any—' Vickie was trying to stand. The chair beneath her was wet.

'Call nine-one-one!' I yelled.

Pavlik joined Father Jim in catching her as Vickie toppled to the floor.

THIRTY

'**B**otox.' Pavlik was shaking his head. 'Who knew?'
We were sitting on the couch in front of the fireplace, Frank at our feet and wine, yet again, in our hands.

'Vickie's drug of choice,' I said, 'and it almost killed her.'

'Good thing the good doctor, Doctor Goode, was there.'

'You didn't really say that.'

'I did.' He pulled me toward him. 'And I'm deeply ashamed.'

'If you're next line is "don't you want to punish me?" it's over between us.'

'Then I won't.' He rested his chin on my head. 'Now tell me about this pillowcase.'

When I'd called Pavlik from the shop, inviting him and the driver of his choice to my impromptu 'round up the suspects' party, I knew I'd have to own up to having the pillowcase. And, more importantly, to not telling him I had the pillowcase.

'I'm sorry I didn't tell you. But I knew that if I did, you'd have to relay it your guys.'

'You're right.'

I hesitated. 'That you'd be honor-bound to let them know?'

'Yes, and you were also probably right not to tell me. It would have made me crazy, but the only thing I could do, in good conscience, I wouldn't have wanted to do.'

'Rat on your sweetie?'

'Rat on my sweetie.' He kissed the top of my head.

'I'm still not sure why Jack went to the trouble of trying to frame me.'

Pavlik shrugged. 'The man's a con. He plays all angles and he prepares to play all angles.'

'I was just another angle?'

'And maybe somebody new to blackmail.'

'Me?'

'Or me. If I knew about the pillowcase, for example, and *didn't* pass it on.'

'Sheesh, I'm glad I didn't tell you then.' I snuggled down under his arm and then sat right back up. 'You know, I bet he was the one who snagged my bells. That first day we laid eyes on the man at Uncommon Grounds I remember something was jingling in his pocket as he went down the porch steps. I assumed they were keys. I can't believe I didn't recognize the sound of my own bells.'

Pavlik wasn't following. 'Your bells?'

'On UG's doors. First the ones from the trackside door were missing, then the front.'

'Maybe somebody got sick of hearing them all day, every day. Have you canvassed your neighbors?'

'I'm serious,' I said, turning to face him. 'If Jack played all the angles and prepared for all eventualities, like you say, he might have figured he'd have a reason to sneak into the shop. Which he ultimately did, to plant the pillowcase. Has the lab finished with it?'

'They have, but there was nothing on it beyond what you'd expect on a pillow.'

'Celeste's hair, lipstick. Any DNA?'

'We think so, though that will take more time. We have samples from the autopsy, which we can match with samples from her room and inside the wigs to make an identification.'

'Something you can't do for poor Nancy. What in the world was Hannah thinking?'

'It's fraud but thankfully it's not murder. I prefer to save that charge for Jack Andersen.'

'Along with money laundering through a church. He's worse than his brother, in my book.'

'I don't disagree.'

'Even though his brother shot you?'

'At least I knew what I was up against. Jack Andersen preys on people. He's a snake.'

'You should have seen him at the funeral, pretending he was confused about who was Nancy and who was Celeste. To Hannah, of course.'

'The woman he was blackmailing about the identity switch.'

'Which he only knew about because he'd killed Nancy that

night, not Celeste. The man had the nerve to go to his victim's funeral and taunt Hannah. No wonder she was desperate.'

'I'm not sure Hannah deserves your pity,' Pavlik said.

'Oh, she's not getting that,' I said. 'I'm just trying to understand.'

'Don't,' he said. 'When you understand evil it's too easy to become it.'

'Ooh, nice. Original?'

Pavlik squinted, trying to remember. 'Probably an old movie?'

'Old movies and books were the inspiration for my rounding up the suspects, you know.'

'To be fair, you didn't really need to round them up,' Pavlik pointed out. 'They show up at your place every Sunday morning.'

'True, but this was Monday. And speaking of showing up at my place, I'm glad you're here.'

'Me, too, although the circumstances could have been better.'

'Like not getting shot?'

'For one.'

I knew he was also thinking about Al Taylor and Pete Hartsfield.

'I'm so sorry,' I said. 'About the deaths of Al and Pete, of course. But also about your being placed on leave. It's been a tough week for you and it's not fair.'

He pulled me down to him and kissed me. 'Thank you. In one bit of good news, pending medical clearance from the good doctor—'

'Don't say it!' I held up a warning finger.

'Anyway, I have an appointment tomorrow. If all goes well I should be able to go back to work. And my house.'

I felt an unexpected twinge. 'But I'd grown accustomed to your face on the pillow next to me each morning.'

'If it was this morning, that was Frank. I was in the bathroom. Right, Frank?'

Frank grunted agreement.

'OK,' I said, trying to scoot up again. 'But what I'm trying to say is . . . that I like living with you. And maybe your idea of our getting married isn't too crazy.'

'That may be the worst acceptance of a proposal I've ever heard.'

'I know. Sorry. Not that we have to do it right now, you understand.'

'You just said yes. Are you getting cold feet already?'

'You press your jeans,' I blurted out. 'And starch them.'

'I do,' Pavlik said. 'Old habit from the military and pressing my dress uniforms. I kind of enjoy it.'

'But they're *jeans*.'

'The bottom hem gets all bent. Doesn't that bother you?'

I thought about it. 'No.'

'Well, it does me. And as long as I have the iron out I figure I might as well do the rest.' He wrapped his arm around me and pulled me against his chest. 'Is this a deal breaker?'

I laughed. 'Honestly, I find it kind of endearing. It's just . . . I guess I'm afraid I won't measure up. I mean, if your jeans have to be perfect—'

'Will I iron you when you get wrinkled?' He settled his chin on the top of my head. 'No. Nor will I suggest Botox. Personally, I'm looking forward to getting old and wrinkly together.'

What does a girl say to that?

'We did pretty well living together,' Pavlik continued. 'So, let's continue taking baby steps. For example, I'd like you to meet my parents.'

'What?' My head snapped up, smacking him in the chin. The word 'baby' had nearly freaked me out but meeting the parents was scary, too.

'Damn,' he said, rubbing it. 'You could just say no.'

'No?' I tried.

Pavlik's face fell.

'It's not that I don't want to meet them,' I pleaded. 'It's just kind of . . . abrupt.'

'Abrupt? We've been dating for two years, I've lived here for a week, I've proposed and you've accepted. We've survived the pressed jeans crisis. How much longer do you think we should wait?'

He had a point. 'But don't they live in Chicago?'

'Yes. An insurmountable ninety-minute drive.'

I sighed. 'OK, I know I'm being silly but it sounds so . . . formal. Meeting the parents.'

Pavlik gathered me back against him. 'Maggy, I know you've

been skittish about getting married and I respect that. But we're both adults – it's not like we need their permission to get married or not to get married. I just . . . well, I just want you to meet my parents.'

'You haven't met mine,' I pointed out.

'Your parents are dead.'

There was that.

Even so, it didn't seem fair for him to get off so easily. I opened my mouth to a put up more of a fight but realized I was being silly. From all accounts – which meant, essentially, Pavlik – his parents were nice people.

'Fine. Why don't you find a date that works for them and we'll go down and have dinner.' Ninety-minute drive there, two-hour dinner, ninety-minute drive back and we'd be done.

'I have a better idea,' he said, kissing the top of my head. 'How about I book a room in the Lakeshore East area for next weekend. Maybe the Blu or the Sofitel. We can have dinner with my folks on Saturday night, and then we'll have the rest of the weekend to ourselves.'

I perked up. I did love Chicago. Museums, parks, Michigan Avenue, me and Pavlik alone in a hotel room. What's not to like?

'Your parents wouldn't expect us to stay with them?' It had been a requirement with Ted's parents, which meant sleeping in twin beds in his childhood room when we were married and on opposite ends of the house before that.

Apparently it never occurred to them that if we were looking to fornicate we'd more easily be able to do it at home.

'My parents?' Pavlik said, eyebrows raised. 'No way. They've lived in a two-bedroom apartment on the fortieth floor of the Randolph since the building was built in the sixties. Once I was gone they turned my room into an office just so they can't have guests.'

My kind of people. I cranked my head around and up so I could see his face. 'And that includes you?'

'*Especially* me.' Pavlik grinned. 'I love my folks and they love me, but as adults we do not cohabitate. Besides.' He nuzzled me in the neck. 'There's just something about hotel rooms.'

'Room service?' I murmured.

He lifted his head. 'Yeah, that's it.'

Lightning Source UK Ltd.
Milton Keynes UK
UKHW01f0945051018
330010UK00001B/7/P